Sensing Passion

Travels Of A Fifty-Five Year Old Divorcee

Christy Cumberlander Walker

ISBN: 1-4392-5049-9

ISBN-13: 9781439250495

Visit www.booksurge.com to order additional copies

To Emelia
Here's part II
Christy

For Ella, Bill, April, Tessie, Christy, Willie,
Christopher, Christian, Christina, Emmanuel,
but most importantly, for me.

BY THE SAME AUTHOR:

Fiction

Finding Passion: Confessions of a Fifty-Year-Old Runaway

Poetry/Prose

Unleashing Passion: A Heart's Desire (with Tessie May Johnson)

Manuals:

Working with High Conflict People (with Zena Zumeta)

Articles:

The Myth of a Colorblind Society

The Art of Passionate Listening

ACKNOWLEDGEMENTS

This book would not have been possible without the encouragement of family Ella, Bill, April, Tessie, Two, Willie, Leon, Shaun, Bean, and Emmanuel. Thank you to friends Marya, Crevon, Paula and Zena.

A special thanks to Karla Brady and Susan Etheridge, Gae Polisner and other fellow writers at the Next Big Writer and Amazon who read, reviewed, and helped me make it better. Karla, I have my copy of The Bum Magnet and Susan I can't wait to get Secrets.

A special thanks to those that know me and offered words of encouragement and to the women at IWWG Columbus for letting me read and belong.

I thank God for the opportunity to do it again—expose myself and share myself on paper. My chance to put it all out there and be naked to readers. What do you do when you are naked? David danced, with all his might. I'm naked again, giving you the opportunity to sit back, slip between the pages, and dance with me.

WHAT'S A LITTLE CUT BETWEEN US?

SUNDAY NIGHT GAMES

Twenty-three, twenty-four, twenty-five.

If this is over by forty-three, I'm going to treat myself to a dough-nut in the morning before I go to work.

Twenty-nine, thirty, thirty-one.

"Uhh."

Looks like I'll be having my doughnut. It's usually five strokes past "uhh" to completion.

Thirty-seven, thirty-eight, thirty-nine.

Damn, I may miss my doughnut. This could be a close call.

Forty-one, forty-two,

"Oh." That sound is Robert's only verbal concession to an orgasm.

Yippee. I'm going to get glazed.

My husband gets up to wash. I get up to do the same, but I have a lighter step than he does because I get a treat in the morning. He already got his.

Once clean, we get back in bed. Robert thinks it is important to stay with a routine, so we have to be asleep by eleven every night. We will then have what Robert considers the appropriate amount of rest.

Climbing back in bed, I make sure to keep to my side. Robert does not like us to touch during the night. He can't sleep if I intrude on his space. Last night he had to wake me up around three because I had gone over to his side. That hadn't happened in quite some time.

Robert and I have been married for thirty-two years. We are empty nesters with three adult children. We are not so much madly in love as we are sensibly in like. Truly, we are roommates, sharing space but not much else. We've grown older, and we don't talk much now. After all this time, I guess we have said everything we have to say to each other. We coexist. After all, it can't always be the emotional high we had when...Wait a minute. We never had an emotional high. Robert does not like high, emotional or otherwise.

Somewhere in those thirty-two years, I started counting the strokes from start to finish when we made love. It was an unintentional habit; I was bored. However, it should be noted the strokes never vary by more than eight strokes over or under forty-one, at which point he completes his task. Then he is done. If I didn't get mine, tough. I should work harder or focus more.

I tried twice (in the past five years) to add some zest to our marital activities. The first time, I squeezed his ass at around stroke twenty-six. He stopped and withdrew. That in itself was a change. He told me my thoughtlessness made him lose his concentration; he was not pleased. Then he entered me again for fifteen more strokes.

The second and last time I tried, he was performing his strokes. I took his hand in mine, put his finger to my mouth and licked it, before sucking on the tip. This was about stroke number nine.

"What are you doing? Did you just lick my finger?" he almost screamed. Robert never screams. He did stop and withdraw. You would have thought I had stuck a finger up his nose.

I hurriedly tried to explain. "I saw this on a show. They said it would put spice back in our relationship."

"What? We don't need any spice. I like things just the way they are. You are getting a little wild. I think it is from you traveling all over." Robert continues to rant.

"Traveling all over" is definitely a misstatement. I have only had one experience of "traveling all over" in my entire life, but there was no point in dragging out the inevitable. I knew what I had to say, and it's best to get it over quickly. "I'm sorry, Robert, you're right. That was stupid."

"Well, you can't do anything new. We don't like *new*. You have been coming up with some strange ideas in the past few years. I don't like it one bit," he grumbles.

"Robert, it won't happen again," I soothed him. "I don't know what I was thinking."

Finger licking was such a complete and utter failure, I decided I didn't like spice either. It's overrated. Security is what matters. I can always count the strokes until we are done. Sometimes I'll get an orgasm, and sometimes I'll get a doughnut. After all, marriage is about sacrifice and security.

MONDAY EVENING STEW

The next morning, I left early for work. I stopped at the doughnut shop and ended up purchasing two—one stick and one glazed. They taste like an orgasm. I might as well have two.

I go into the public relations firm where I've worked for the past twenty years, since the children went to school. I started out as the office manager and worked my way up to my current position: the executive assistant to the vice president, Harold, who also happens to be the cofounder of the firm. This is my first and only job in my entire life; I never saw any reason to leave. It is a secure position, and I value security.

I perform my normal duties. Mail and e-mail is what I do from the time I arrive until midmorning. From midmorning 'til lunch, I am on the telephone returning or placing calls. I have lunch from noon until one. Then I come back and prepare status reports on projects until my break at three-thirty. After my break, I come back to input information until my final potty break at four forty-five. I go home at five. Unless Harold wants to meet with me, my day is always the same.

I take my regular route back home because Robert likes to know the route I take. If my car breaks down, he'll know the path I'm on, and he can rescue me. I get home at my normal time and head to the kitchen to get dinner ready.

"Lynn, we need to talk," Robert announces. His voice is unnaturally loud as he enters the kitchen. Robert's voice is usually a low, slow monotone. No peaks and valleys of pitch or cadence.

I am cutting beef to make the stew for our supper. It's Monday, and Robert likes to have stew on Monday. Personally, I don't like stew. It's too crowded. I want my meats and my vegetables to be separate not swimming in sauce. Nevertheless, Robert wants stew on Monday. Therefore, we are having the stew I am making.

Ever the dutiful wife, I stop cutting the beef, so we can talk. Our talks are not so much talks as they are listens—with me listening to what he has to say and then following his direction. Robert doesn't like a lot of conversation. He says it's a waste of time. I look up into his face. His mouth is turned down at the corners, and his eyes look cold and distant. His hands are folded on his chest, and his posture is rigid. Something must be incredibly wrong.

"Have a seat. You can finish dinner in a few minutes."

"What is it Robert? You look serious. What happened?" The beef is forgotten for the time being. I do a quick mental inventory to figure out my transgression. I can't think of anything I did to make him unhappy. I take a seat and try not to look anxious about Robert's news.

Robert sits down at the head of the table. The wait for the revelation is not long, but the news is the absolute last thing I would have expected. "I want a divorce. We haven't been close for a long time, and I met someone." His words come out in a rush as he talks down at the table and then he looks over my head as he finishes.

My husband met someone. This can't be happening. We've been together forever. He couldn't have *met someone*. He's married.

Robert goes back to his normal monotone as he continues, "I have decided we should get a divorce. I'll take care of everything. You can keep the house. The kids are adults, so they will not be an issue. It's time for me to move on now. This is really for the best. You like staying home and taking care of things, so you will stay here where you belong. Our sex life hasn't been anything to write home about, no excitement. You don't really like having sex, so that is not an issue. Anyway, this is for the best. You'll see."

That isn't true. I like sex. I like good sex with both parties involved. And *this* is definitely not for the best, as far as I'm concerned. I am thinking these thoughts because my mouth will not work. My tongue won't move, and my jawbone is stuck on closed.

"Now I've already told the kids. You'll be fine. I'll see to everything."

This doesn't sound like Robert. It sounds rushed. He is always a well-spoken, controlled person. I look over at him. I must have heard him incorrectly. "What?" is the only sound to squeak past my lips on air that I have to force from my lungs.

"We will be getting a divorce," He reiterates. He bites off each word as though he is impatient with having to repeat and clarify himself.

"Oh."

Pain, such as I have never felt, clogs my throat and makes it difficult for my nose to inhale air, and my lungs to expel the air trapped there. Pain dims my vision and robs me of the ability to think clearly. *Divorce* sticks in my mind and flashes in capital letters. All my brain cells freeze and consider the wonder of the word. The mental anguish is worse than any physical pain I could imagine.

What can I say to Robert's pronouncement? He wants to end our marriage. This security means the world to me. Once, during our entire relationship, I strayed, but Robert never knew. While I don't quite regret the experience, I knew it could never happen again. I chose to remain here with someone I could grow old with, someone I am used to being around. We are supposed to be together forever—not getting a divorce.

In an effort to alleviate the pain, I get up to continue cutting the beef. The knife feels comforting. Robert is still sitting at the table. I can't think of a thing to say or do, so I go back to what is normal, making dinner. Safe, routine, and not requiring any thought. Maybe the pain will subside if I keep to my routine. Finishing dinner will not require me to think. I could do this in my sleep. The way I'm feeling, I can't imagine when I'll have another thought that will take the place of the shock Robert has dealt me.

"I'm going to get a shower," Robert says as he stands and prepares to leave the room. "When will dinner be ready?" He throws this over his shoulder on his way to the door.

I lift my head to see his back as he passes through the door. I don't think you should ask your spouse of thirty-two years when dinner will be ready after you have told her you are leaving her, and she will be fine. And you shouldn't ask when said spouse has a knife in her hand.

The knife slips from my hand. It sails across the room into the back of his right arm, up by his shoulder. It wiggles a little and stays there. Blood, which I will have to clean up, starts dripping from the hole in his arm. Robert stops walking. He turns around and allows himself to show an emotion—surprise.

My pain eases, just a bit and is replaced by a sense of accomplishment. My brain thaws a little, enough for me to repeat what he had the nerve to ask.

"Dinner? When will dinner be ready?" My brain unfreezes as the heat of betrayal warms me.

"You just tilted my whole world, and you want to know when I'll have your dinner ready? I should cut your throat. You just broke my heart, and you want dinner. I should just cut your throat, you son of a bitch."

Maybe it's my strong language that gets his attention. I'm not a potty mouth under usual circumstances. He stopped me from cursing out loud before we got married.

It could be the fact there is a knife sticking out of Robert's arm, one I placed there by a mere slip of my wrist that causes him to stop in his tracks. I do not make a habit of throwing knives at my husband, under usual circumstances. These are unusual times for me, the damn near perfect wife and mother.

Thoughts come. Thoughts about our life are going through my mind as Robert stands slack jawed and bleeding. I stayed with him through thick and thin, come hell or high water. I have stayed where I have always been—by his side. I spent my entire adult life turning myself into what he wanted me to be for nothing. What am I going to do? How will I live? He met someone else. Shit. I met someone else, too, once. And I didn't leave him…exactly.

These thoughts are going through my mind as Robert stands in the door and continues to bleed. I stand watching and thinking. He still cuts a great image in a T-shirt and jeans. The red of his blood doesn't quite go with the orange of his top, the blue of his jeans, or the interesting gray shade his face is becoming.

Robert is attractive—six foot one and one hundred and ninety pounds without an ounce of excess fat. He works out, and it shows in a six-pack twenty-year-olds envy. His coal-black hair has no gray and looks great with his apple-butter brown skin. My husband, the good-looking bastard.

"What the heck? Lynn, you just threw a knife at me. There's a knife in my arm," he interrupts my thoughts to state the obvious. Originality was never his strong suit.

"Your point, you cheating bastard? It's not as though you are going to clean up the blood. I get to do that. I've been cleaning up your shit, this house, and everything else for thirty-two years, and now you want a divorce?" I am screaming by the time I finish talking. Again, not one of my habits.

He takes the time to point out what he is unhappy with me about before stating his needs. "Lynn, your language. You stabbed me. Have you lost your mind? I need to go to the emergency room. I could die. I can't believe what you just said, what you just did." He isn't yelling because he never yells, but he's talking pretty strongly, for Robert.

"We've all got to die sometime," is my unfazed response. Right now, my thoughts center on how I am supposed to adjust to being a divorced woman. I won't have a husband anymore. He will have left me, and I'll be alone for the first time in my entire life. I lived with my parents, then in a college dorm, and then with Robert. It's difficult for me to get my mind around the idea. I'd rather put my hands around his neck.

"This is so unlike you. You are not a violent person." The knife in his arm would lead one to believe, he is wrong. "I said I need to go to the hospital," Robert reminds me.

There must be something about seeing your own blood trickling down your arm, dripping between your fingers, and dripping on the floor that makes a person nervous and whiny. Robert definitely sounds nervous and sounds whiny. I never noticed before what a whiner Robert is. He is usually in control of every situation. Hell, he is the backbone of the family, or so he likes to boast. It must be the blood.

"Then stop whining and go." I toss him a towel from the table. "Could you use this so you won't drip all over the fucking house you are so graciously going to give me? Blood is *SO* hard to get out of carpet."

I don't have time to listen to this bullshit. It isn't even something I want to hear. I push past him and enter the dining room to head upstairs. I have never noticed the smell of blood before now. It almost burns my nose with its pungency, and it remains in my nostrils as I try to make my way to a peaceful place. I am not hungry anymore. Robert can eat stew or chicken or dog guts for all I care. I don't feel like cooking. I need to think about my future since it is not as placid as it once was.

"Aren't you going to take me?" he has the nerve to ask.

"Me, me, me? Hell no, I'm not taking you. Why should I? You are leaving me." I ask him this without breaking my stride.

I make it up the stairs and into our bedroom, where I collapse on the edge of the bed. What next? This can't be happening to me. I can't think straight as our past starts to claim my brain.

We met while we were in college. He thought I would make a good wife if I could clean up my language and polish my rough edges. I quit actively cursing and polished my edges as if I was cleaning tarnished silver. I never gave him a reason to regret marrying me. I tried to be everything he wanted me to be, and it is still not enough. He wants a divorce.

What's going to happen to me? I don't know how to do anything but be his wife. I gave up *ME* just to be his wife. What did I do wrong? What could I have done differently? How can I make him stay? I don't deserve this. Maybe I could have tried harder, but how or what could I have done.

I am five feet five and make the needle on a scale go from zero to two hundred and ten in three seconds. I think of myself as luscious rather than overweight. I was about fifty pounds lighter when we met, but weight isn't enough to end all these years together. I would have lost the weight if Robert had told me to take off the pounds.

When Robert and I met, my hair was dark brown and always worn straight like I was fresh from the beautician's chair. Now it is graying brown natural hair, worn in twists that hang to my shoulders. If he had told me he didn't like it, I would have gone back to the perm box and had hair dye routinely applied. Hair is no reason to leave.

I still have the same brown eyes blending with my brown skin to make me blend in with a crowd. I have no distinguishing features aside from a smile, the use of which has caused laugh lines in my face. I would have Botoxed if he said it was an issue.

My lack of bosom could also be a demerit, but it has long been a sore spot with me. My breasts are as substantial as two over-easy eggs. However, I'm too paranoid to have them surgically enhanced. I might get the ones that look like concrete, ooze saline into my system, and make me ill. Robert always said he didn't mind the size, but maybe he decided he wants a big-breasted woman. I can be big breasted. I can be anything he wants me to be.

DOTTIE FOR THE DEFENSE

I feel vibrations, pounding. What now? Maybe I'm having a heart attack. A glance at my watch shows two hours have passed by. The vibrations continue throughout my body. I must be dying. As I become alert, I notice the pounding is coming from outside my body. Then I see lights flashing through the window. Red and blue lights.

My brain continues to come back to the present and I start to sweat. Fucking snitch. I bet Robert told the hospital I'm the one responsible for the hole in his arm. He could have just said he fell, but no, he has to bring me into his shit, as if it's my fault. I'm sure he didn't tell them he is leaving me after thirty-two years of marriage. Tossing me aside like used toilet paper.

Damn. What to do? If I turn the lights out, the coppers will know for sure I'm here. I'm definitely not going to open the door. They can't be sure anyone is at home. I hope Five-O doesn't decide to break the door down and charge in to get me. They might shoot me, thinking I am armed and dangerous. I am neither. I wouldn't hurt anybody. I never have before. I'm a nice lady.

I don't know if Wichita law enforcement will see this accident the same way I do. They may not look kindly on accidents that result in people having holes in their body. I grab my cell phone and call my attorney, Dottie. She is not really my attorney. I never needed one before. However, she is an attorney and more importantly, she is a friend.

"Hello, Lynn. What's up?" Dottie answers on the second ring.

"Hi, Dottie. Hmmm…let's say for instance that a man, let's just use Robert for example, got a knife stuck in his arm and went to the hospital. The police are now knocking on his door, and his wife, kind of like me hypothetically, is in the house on the telephone with her friend who is also an attorney. The wife does not open the door for the police. Would you think the police knew she kind of put the hole in his arm, and so they went to her house and might want to take her to jail for the accident? Could she be in trouble if she doesn't open the door?"

Dottie sounds confused when she asks, "Lynn have you been smoking or something? What are you telling me?"

"If I told you anything, would you have to tell someone?" I don't want to incriminate myself, self-preservation being the first law of nature.

"Probably not. I wouldn't have to tell if it was a past crime committed. However, if you were planning to kill him, I would have to tell. I'm an officer of the court," Dottie explains.

"Well, then I think we may need to talk. I may need an attorney." It is a relief to be able to share.

"I'm on my way over." Dottie hangs up on me.

The pounding continues. My ears block out the sound. I don't hear the ringing of the house phone. The vibrating of my cell phone makes me jump. I answer when I see it is my daughter, Rene.

"Mom, did you stab daddy? He's at the hospital, and I am at the front door with the police. They say you stabbed daddy in the arm. They can't be right."

"Honey, I am on my way to the hospital now. Dottie is taking me. Why would you think I would stab him?" This is a difficult conversation for a mother to have with her daughter. It definitely is not setting a good example. Maybe I shouldn't have answered the phone.

"See, I told you my mom wouldn't do anything like that. She's on her way to the hospital now with her friend Dottie. You'll see. There has to be an explanation," is her conversation with the coppers on my doorstep. "Okay, Mom, I'll see you at the hospital. I know dad is going to be okay because he said I didn't have to go there, but I think I should in case you need me." Rene is a talker.

"Okay, Rene. I'll talk to you about it when I see you." I hope I have thrown them off the scent. If they think I am on my way to the hospital, that will get them away from my house without me going to jail.

"Okay, I'll see you at the hospital. I'm sure this will all be cleared up soon. How could they think you would stab anyone? You don't stab people," she says to me. Rene continues to the police, "I told you this is a mistake. You all are wrong."

"Ma'am, we really need to speak with her," I hear a male voice saying as Rene hangs up the telephone.

After five minutes or so, the flashing goes off, and the cars go down the street. I wait another five minutes before peeking out the window. Not a single patrol car left. I shook them—for now. But, they know where I live. Here, with my nonresident husband.

Robert and I are at the time in our lives where we are past taking each other for granted. We are not taking each other at all. We just live…together while waiting to grow old…together. Slipping into the ignoring-each-other habit as easily we slip into an easy chair. We are routine, used to each other. Now he wants to change everything.

The cell phone rings and vibrates again. It's a good thing I have caller id. Otherwise, I wouldn't know it's safe to answer because it is Dottie.

"Hey, Dottie. Are you alone?" The SWAT team could be with her attempting to lure me to the door so they can get a clear shot.

"Lynn, I am at the back door. Let me in," Dottie whispers.

I go down and open the door for her. She doesn't waste any time. "What the fuck is going on? Please tell me you did not stab Robert. Shit." Dottie is an active curser.

"Okay, I didn't stab Robert," I say angelically. She really wants to hear that, and I don't want to disappoint such a good friend. How many people would drop everything and come over for a friend the way Dottie has done?

"Lynn," Dottie warns me, in her don't-jerk-me-around tone of voice. Being a good friend, she can also spot a lie a mile away.

"Okay. I did stab him, but it wasn't on purpose. The knife just slipped and landed in his arm. He lost some blood, which I'll have to clean up. I had better get the peroxide, so the blood won't stain. I don't know what I can use to get the smell out of the carpet. The smell. Maybe if I light a candle." My voice trails off. I might be babbling as I tell Dottie all this as if she cares.

She takes my arm to give it a squeeze and a shake. "Lynn. I need you to focus. Tell me everything that happened." She collapses into a kitchen chair.

I take a seat across from her. "Robert just told me he wants a divorce. He has met someone else and is leaving me. He is going to give me the house and take care of everything, since I don't like sex. Dottie, what am I going to do?" Getting all the words out leaves nothing but tears. I cannot allow them to fall.

"You've got to be kidding. You two have been together forever. Are you sure this isn't a joke?" Dottie asks.

"That's what I thought, too. Apart from not being funny, I realized it wasn't a joke." As I'm telling her my story, I am again aware of the blood scent. The smell is overpowering. I look around for something to use to clean it up.

"Is that when you threw the knife at him? Did the thought of divorce send you into a rage? What made you throw a knife for Pete's sake?" Dottie wants to know.

I think about her question for a minute "No. I wasn't enraged; I was in pain and in ice. A frozen hurt. It was when he asked me how long it would be for dinner to be ready. You know how he likes stew on Monday. Well I was cutting the beef for the stew when he came in and told me all this. While I was processing all this, he had the nerve to ask when dinner would be ready. I kind of lost it. The knife just slipped out of my hand and into his arm. Imagine that, just stuck in his arm, wiggled a little and hung there, didn't fall or anything."

Dottie has a blank expression on her face that is starting to scare me. Then her brilliance kicks in. "Okay. The first thing we have to do is see if they are going to charge you with assaulting Robert and whether the charge will be a felony or a misdemeanor. Shit. This doesn't look too bad. If it were going to be a felony, they would have had a warrant. Then they can break the door in to arrest you right away. They must not consider it too bad since they didn't come in and get you."

"I'm going to the hospital to see what I can find out. In the meantime, throw some things together and make your way to a hotel for tonight. I don't want you to get into any more trouble while I'm gone. Will you promise me?" Dottie must not realize the stabbing was an accident.

"It was an accident, you know. It's not as if I've ever been in trouble or anything before. Do you think I'll have to do time in the big house?" I say to my always friend and now attorney.

"I know, but as you just demonstrated, you are not thinking straight. I'll call you in the morning. Take the day off work and just lay low until you hear from me. I'm going to get you in to see a doctor I know. She can do some anger-management therapy with you." Dottie shares this as though anger-management therapy is chocolate covered almonds.

"But, I don't have anger-management problems. I'm a very calm person," I staunchly and calmly claim.

"Lynn. You threw a knife and put a hole in your husband's arm. You have a problem. We want to show the judge you are cognizant of the problem and are getting help. It is best to start before going to your first hearing. Okay?" She makes it sound so reasonable.

"Okay. I still don't think I have an anger-management problem though."

"But you will make it to the appointment. You will follow through with her recommendations, right?"

"Okay. It really was an accident," I grudgingly respond.

"Yeah. Well I don't want any more accidents of this kind. After we get finished with the stabbing issues, we need to start thinking about the divorce. You shouldn't be here when Robert comes home tonight. I don't want to know where you are going so I can be truthful if someone asks me. I'll call you when I get some information, but it probably won't be until in the morning." Dottie gives me a hug and heads toward the door.

"Dottie, do you think I'll have to do hard time?" I ask her again. "Thoughts of me in a prison getting teardrop tattoos on my face and a girlfriend named Jeff cross my mind and scare me," I confess to her.

"Don't worry about going to prison yet. Let's get through tonight." She consoles as she heads out the back door.

LIFE ON THE LAM

I put away the beef. I don't want it to go bad. Then I go upstairs to throw some clothes in a plastic grocery bag. It ain't easy being on the lam. I will probably only need two days worth of clothes and something to sleep in. It doesn't take too long to get that together and go back downstairs.

The house telephone is ringing, but there isn't any time to answer it. I need to get out in case the coppers come back. I do take the time to pour peroxide over the bloodstains and get them cleaned up before I leave. If you let blood dry, it never will come out. Besides, it stinks. There is only a faint outline of the drops left when I finish.

I could go to my parents, but they might worry if the police show up. Besides, they don't like unannounced company this late in the evening. My father is probably in bed, and he would have to get up and open the door. He would not be happy.

I make the drive across town to the smallest hotel around in silence. For a measly forty dollars, I can get a room the clerk tells me. With room keys and the information that checkout time is at one o'clock, I head straight to the room.

When I open the door, I glimpse the familiar figure of a man. The same man I had shared a life touching two weeks with five years ago. It's really just the shadow of a man in a brim hat but talk about déjà vu. I must be more tired than I thought or it must be my eyes playing tricks on me. I wish I could see him again. Especially now. Seeing him is not possible. Obviously, I have the jitters because of everything going on, and I am hallucinating.

On the off chance, I'll be able to fall asleep, I turn my cell phone off, and so it won't disturb me. It has been ringing and vibrating constantly since the *incident*. I am doing a great job of ignoring it since I see it is not Dottie. I undress then shower before getting into bed. I don't think I'll be able to sleep at all. This has been a trying day.

The stress must have acted as a downer because the next thing I know, it's damn near nine on Tuesday morning.

I turn on the local news to see if they have an all points bulletin out for me. Nothing on the first channel. I listen to as many channels as I can while trying to get out before I am charged for another day. There is not a word about me on any of the channels. Now I feel a little bit safer. Unless they are circulating my picture all around the area. I hope the desk clerk doesn't remember my face.

I dress and turn on the cell phone to call my boss. Harold answers his private line.

"Hello. Lynn? Are you coming in today?" He sounds strange. I wonder if he knows I am a wanted woman. Maybe the police are with him right now. They could be trying to get a trace on me.

"Is everything going alright, Harold? You sound funny." I wonder if we are close enough for him to tell me the heat is on, and they're trying to squeeze him for information.

"Yeah, yeah. What time will you be here?" he sounds distracted.

"Well, I'm not feeling well. I won't be in for the next few days. I'll make it back in on Monday. I have to go to the doctor." My brain tells my mouth to stop talking, before I tell him where I'm holed up.

"Oh. Okay. I'll see you when you get in Monday."

"Thanks, Harold." After I hang up, I wait for Dottie's call. It comes, just as I am ready to go throw myself on the mercy of the court. Of course, my conversation with Harold ended ten minutes earlier, but they could be out there looking for me.

"I have some news. The police filed misdemeanor assault charges against you after talking to Robert. I'll be able to talk with the prosecutor on Wednesday. I'll tell her the situation and see if we can get a preliminary hearing next week. Thankfully, you have a perfect record."

"Here's the deal I want to propose. If you get in to start the anger-management program, they will probably drop the charges. Because of the situation, you won't be arrested. You'll be getting some paperwork in the mail. You will have to sign to show you were served, and you must show up for the court date."

"Okay. Can I go back home now? Otherwise, I will have to stay here, and they could have bedbugs." I don't like this hotel room. It has a ghost, but I don't tell her about him. He is a tease to make me remember when life was worth living.

"Yes, go back home, and whatever you do, no knives, guns or physical contact with Robert. My argument to the prosecutor will be that you were provoked enough to stab Robert. I don't want you provoked again because Robert could get nasty about this," Dottie warns.

"The son of a bitch. Hell, it's not as though I was walking around on the street stabbing random people. It was an accidental reaction to his demand for a divorce. If I had been thinking of stabbing him, I would have cut his throat." Dottie is familiar with the me that lives in my head and sometimes cusses like a sailor. "Not a word to him. Besides, he is probably moving out soon. Maybe this will speed up his departure," I promise Dottie.

"You probably don't hear how crazy you sound. Thankfully, I do. I'll call you with the name of the doctor and the time of your first appointment. Make sure you go and be cooperative," She sternly reminds me.

"I said I'll go and see the shrink. Damn, you accidentally cut someone, and everyone wants to think the worst of you," I unwillingly concede.

"Lynn." Dottie is using her firm voice.

"Okay, okay, okay. Just get me the information, I'll be there and cooperate." I hang up and then breathe a sigh of relief, gather my belongings, and head to the checkout counter.

In the car, on the way home, it dawns on me that my life is irrevocably changed. A quick review shows I will be a divorced fifty-five-year-old with possible prison time in my near future.

My life is not turning out as I anticipated. Robert may be an asshole, but he was my asshole. What will I do without my asshole?

I head home and enter a house that is, thankfully, empty. It is not much different from any other time. However, other times I had the expectation my husband would be home soon. I thought marriage was working for us. It was working for me. I was committed to it. I was blind.

The remainder of the previous night's dinner preparation and the little cut incident need to be cleaned up. After I set everything to rights and clean up a few stray drops of blood, my thoughts turn to dinner.

I reach for the freezer door. It is Tuesday. Meatloaf with salad, mashed potatoes, and green beans is the menu. I start to take out the ground beef to make meatloaf, but my hand stops halfway around the package. Robert has made monthly menus for the past twenty years. He likes the certainty of eating a specific meal on a specific day of the week—no surprises. I like the certainty of having a husband. I turn to go into the living room. We both may as well be disappointed.

The answering machine light is blinking. My father, my mother, and all three of our children called according to the caller identification. I bet I can guess what they are calling to discuss. A push of the play button lets the answering machine tell me its secrets.

"Lynn. I must say I am very disappointed in you. You behavior is unacceptable. I will expect a full explanation at six o'clock tonight." My father demands. He was in the military for twenty years and ran our house in the same manner he ran recruits in basic training. You could never accuse him of being kind, but his belief in routine and appropriate conduct is legendary.

"Honey, call me if you need to talk." My mother, the kindest woman ever born. Never a harsh word, never an errant thought.

"Mommy, what happened?" My middle child, May. She is a black-and-white, just-the-facts type of person. Her view of fairness has not changed since she was a child.

I hear Rene's voice. "Mom, you have to call me right away. I am so worried. Do you know you could have killed daddy last night? What were you thinking? Do you have a drug problem? We can make it through this. If you need to go to rehab, I have a list of places. I know prescription pills and crystal meth are prevalent among the older generation now. I saw it on *Rehab Clinic.* I won't judge you. We just need to get you some help. If you have a mental condition, we can get you some help. The *Head Doctor* show says some mental health conditions do not show up until your age. I know a great bi-polar specialist that could…" The machine cut my daughter off before she could continue.

"Mom, just call me as soon as you get in, and we can get you some help. I see this as you reaching out for help, a cry for attention. I'll be over there this evening to help set up a plan for you." Rene is persistent. She is also a control freak. She likes all loose ends tied up in the way she thinks they should be tied up.

"Mom, I'm at the front door. You're not answering. I'm worried about you. Call me." That is the message from Lynnette, the youngest at twenty-five. Lynnette is a part-time manipulative narcissist. If there is an event occurring, she will find a way to make it about her. However, when she is ready to be caring, no one could be better.

The best thing to do is to get this over in one fell swoop. To let him know I received his order, I call my father first and confirm he will see me there at six. He does not answer his telephone since he will not speak to me until six tonight as he stated. I am allowed to leave a message.

"Hi, Dad. I know you are disappointed. I can explain. I'll be by this evening with the girls. It was an accident, just so you know."

Then I call my mom on her cell phone. I doubt she will answer. She only has a cell phone because my dad has a cell phone, and she doesn't want him to appear more progressive than she does. Mom surprisingly answers on the first ring. I thought she would be under orders not to converse with me because I had done something unacceptable.

"Hi, Mom." I have nothing further to say.

"Honey, are you okay? Is Robert dead?" mom wants to know.

"Yes and no." I have to smile at her order of questions.

"Good and too bad." A look at the telephone ensures me this is my mother and not someone else's. I always thought she liked Robert. He is so much like dad.

"Mom, I'm fine, and Robert, I'm sure, did not die as a result of the accident. I received a call from dad to come and explain myself at six. Is it okay if the girls meet me there? Then I can go over this one time."

Unlike dad, Mom is not a stickler for unexpected company. "Yes, dear. I'll make sure to fix enough for everyone. Do you want to talk about it?"

"No. Thanks for the offer though." I don't trust myself to talk right now. Emotions are too close to the surface.

"Okay, we'll see you all at six. I'll let your dad know," mom volunteers.

My mother is a saint. I try to emulate her because she has been married to the same man for fifty-six years. She never complains, indeed: she never says much of anything. She is a peacekeeper. Mom doesn't like arguments and has contentment with life. I've always been envious of her. Knowing my dad, it must be said again: my mom is a saint.

I sat on the couch to think back over my life and how perfect it was before yesterday. I hear a key in the front door a moment before Robert walks in the room. He looks well rested and not bad at all for a person who was recently stabbed accidentally. He has changed clothes and looks no worse for the wear.

What do you say to a cheating husband after you've stabbed him? I go with, "Hello, how are you feeling, Robert?"

"Lynn, I do not want to talk with you. You stabbed me, and I'm letting you know right now that I'm definitely pressing charges. Your behavior was unacceptable. How dare you."

The contempt in his voice was caught me off guard. He could have been talking to a dog and he wouldn't have sounded as nasty as he sounded talking to me. His wife. Damn. Accidents happen. He gave me quite a shock. It wasn't deliberate.

He starts up the stairs. Halfway up he turns to say, "I expect the salad, meatloaf, mashed potatoes, and green beans to be ready on time."

If there was knives anywhere close, I would so be breaking my promise to Dottie, and this time it would not be an accident. Instead, I call my daughters and tell them to meet me at their grandparents. Then I get my purse and head out with thoughts of how I could stab him again and avoid a prison sentence.

I need to get something to eat before dinner with the family. I don't think I will be able to eat with them asking questions about yesterdays' activities.

◐◑

A MEAL AND CONVERSATION

I drag myself to a fast food restaurant. My appetite is nonexistent, but at least I am out of the house and away from temptation. I end up ordering a cup of coffee and a fried pie. I have time to waste and take a seat. I can listen to other people's conversation and maybe it will take my mind off my own problems. There is a group of three older men who are arguing about everything from the weather to politics to the traffic. They look about retirement age, and it is easy to see this isn't their first encounter with each other or this eating spot. The employees call them by name and keep their cups filled with coffee, black, black with sugar, and decaf with cream and sugar.

It would be nice to know their stories. Are they or have they ever been married? Do they have children who care about them? Would they stab someone by accident and then have to pay for it the rest of their lives?

They are discussing an absent member of their group. He is in the hospital. They all put their opinion of the missing member of the table.

"You have to be careful with sugar. It can really get you," the man with the gold tooth in the front of his mouth warns the table. I am willing to bet money he is from the Deep South, with his plaid shirt and striped pants, as if the gold tooth wasn't a dead giveaway.

"He wasn't watching what he was eating. What did he expect to happen?" This from a guy with sunglasses and a baseball cap even

23

though it is broad daylight, and he is indoors. I think the sunglasses can go because it is not bright in here.

"At least he can rest up in the hospital, with all those pretty nurses to wait on him hand and foot. I need to go to the hospital, and let them take care of me," is the contribution from a man with a relaxer in his obviously dyed black hair. He has a comb-over that doesn't quite work because it does not reach over and his age-spotted bald patch is still visible.

A very pretty young lady approaches them. She smiles at all three men and speaks, "Hello. I'm Mr. Tony's daughter. He can't be here since he is in the hospital. He wanted me to come and let you know how he is, so you wouldn't worry or get things wrong. Let me tell you so you have the facts straight. You know how people get things confused sometimes." She smiles at each of them, and I know she heard the conversation they had been having.

"He was never diagnosed with diabetes or sugar as you call it. He wasn't feeling well, and he went to the doctor. The doctor tested him and determined his blood sugar was out of control, and then sent him to the hospital." She gives them another smile and continues. "As you can see, he didn't know he had a problem, and he just found out he is diabetic. My brothers and sisters will make sure he takes care of himself from now on. Is there anything you would like me to tell him?" She slightly veils her look of reproach under her smile.

They stare at her as if she asked them to strip naked and perform oral sex on each other. The spell breaks and conversation starts again.

"Thanks for letting us know," says Deep South, as he smiles at her.

"We were wondering about him," states Stevie Wonder.

"Yeah. Are you married?" asks Pimp Daddy of the Process.

"It's nice to know he has friends that care. I'll let him know I told you all what was really going on with his condition." She smiles at each of them again and then leaves.

She certainly answered my question. At least one, albeit the absent one, has children, and they care deeply about him.

After she leaves, they decide to make her the topic of conversation.

"She shouldn't just go around talking to strangers. We could have been anybody," opines Deep South.

"How did she know we were talking about her dad?" asks Stevie Wonder.

"Nice boobs," observes Pimp Daddy.

They then turn their conversation to the question of the viability of using duct tape to stop a leak in a faucet or to repair torn clothing. It is comforting to know someone thinks of solutions to these pressing issues. Five o'clock must be their curfew because they all decide to get up and start leaving around then.

Maybe that will be me in a few years. I'll be in sitting with a group of women in a restaurant every day, searching for the meaning of life. Yep. I want a window seat, so I can feel the sun on my back. It is a far cry from the future I had envisioned. The future where Robert and I are sitting in twin rocking chairs on the porch, waiting for the children and grandchildren to visit.

Of course, sitting in a restaurant all day is preferable to going to prison and spending the rest of my life there with no chance of parole. Then I won't have anything to look forward to except visits from my children, and they might not even come. I would have to take one of the younger women under my wing and give her all the wisdom I have amassed over the years.

The wisdom giving would take a day, and she wouldn't take my advice anyway because we are both in jail. With those thoughts and possibilities, I decide to take my depressed ass on over to my parents home and prepare to face the parental music.

The cars parked in front of their home let me know my children are here. I am transported back to my childhood. My father was always the disciplinarian. He expected—no demanded—perfection. Anything else was met with derision and cold, empty stares. Now, I get to go in and face his displeasure. I am fifty-five-years-old. Damn. Am I ever going to grow up?

Mom answers on the first knock. "Come on in the kitchen. Everyone is here, and you can get some meatloaf for supper." She gives me a hug before leading me by the hand.

I follow her into a large, airy kitchen, where my offspring and my father are waiting for me to explain myself. "Hello, all," I address the room before taking a seat and the plate my mother is offering.

My father, from the head of the table, starts, "Please explain yourself at once young lady."

Fifty-five-years-old and I still get the *young lady* from him. "Well, it happened like this." I unemotionally state the facts of the stabbing. My father does not appreciate any emotion except his own displeasure.

"Really, Mom, this is just terrible. I told daddy he should stay home," puts in Rene. "You can't make it without him. I hope he comes to his senses soon."

"Rene thinks you have a drug problem, and we need to do an intervention." This comes from the baby girl with a smile and an eye roll.

"Ridiculous," my father states unequivocally.

"Mom, don't worry. Dad will come to his senses and come back home. Give him some time," says May.

I stop with my fork midway to my mouth and look at the two of them. "Am I so damn pathetic my children don't think I can make it without a man who doesn't want me?" I ask the table of family. Obviously, I must be.

"Your language is unacceptable," I hear from my dad. He also disapproves of expletives in any form, which is strange considering his military past.

"Excuse me, Dad." I am facing life in prison, and he is worried about my language being unacceptable. The reality is I like to curse, although I don't because Robert told me when we were dating that he would not want to kiss anyone with a dirty mouth. I am soon to be divorced. When my divorce is final, I am going to say a curse word every day. Fuck it. I am tired of only cursing in my head. What did my clean mouth get me? I might as well start now.

"The thing is, that cock-sucking son of a bitch is leaving me, and I'm a little pissed off right now."

My mother drops the glass of juice she was bringing to the table for me. My father starts choking and turning unusual shades of red for a brown-skinned man. Rene and May stop all movement and turn to stare at me with twin expressions of horror. My youngest daughter gets up, goes around her grandfather, and gives him a few good whacks on the back to dislodge his food. She looks up and smiles at me.

"I think that about covers it. Oh, there's one last thing. My attorney has me seeing a fucking psychiatrist to help me with an anger-management problem I don't believe I have." After sharing my information, I get up, pick up my purse, and leave everyone sitting or standing frozen in time. I feel good. I said exactly what I wanted to say and didn't burst into flames.

Once home, I again enter an empty house. Robert is nowhere in sight. I wait up for him, but he doesn't come home.

I stay in bed the next day, only getting up to fix myself food to keep from wasting away. I don't bother answering the telephone at all because I don't feel like explaining anything else. The house telephone continues squealing until I turn off the ringer. My cell phone has been begging me to plug it into the wall, and I have refused. It paid me back by dying.

Thursday morning comes and goes with me in bed. I wander around the house after noon, doing more nothing than I have done in years. I finally remember Dottie is supposed to call me today to let me know what the prosecutor said. I call her.

"Hi, Dottie. What is the news?" I am eager for some good news.

"How are you Lynn? I called you. Are you okay?" She sounds concerned.

"Yeah. I had to meet with the family the other night to explain what is going on, so I have been avoiding the telephone," I tell her on a sigh of remembered disgust.

"Oh. Knowing your family the way I do, I don't blame you. Just wanted to tell you the prosecutor is fine with a preliminary hearing next week. I think we can get this done quickly. I am going to give you the name and address of the doctor I want you to see. I have your first appointment set up for Friday at two," she proffers tentatively.

What is there for me to say? She thinks I have anger-management problems. I remain quiet to show my displeasure.

"Lynn, remember our agreement?" she cajoles.

"Okay, give it to me." Armed with the name and address, I get off the phone. So now, I have to go see a head doctor because Robert is such a fucking snitch. My first appointment is for tomorrow since I've been classified as an emergency. It is amazing the connections Dottie has. Tomorrow, I will be officially crazy, with a head doctor to prove it. I grab a sandwich from the kitchen.

I head up to what is still officially our bedroom even though lately it has been housing only me. Robert has not been around from the looks of things. I don't see any clothes waiting for me to pick them up; no towels on the floor of the bathroom, and all of the drawers are neatly closed. As I get out of the shower, I smell a familiar scent. A perfume that is closely associated with a time in my life I have buried beneath my mantle of security and responsibility.

The scent is unmistakable. Where could it have come from? The only bottle I have is in the basement, in the trunk under so much of my history. The Caesar's Woman cologne could not be leaking. Even if it was, I couldn't smell it all the way up here. I climb into bed and drift off to sleep on the thought of that special perfume and that special time in my life.

Around nine, I wake up and realize the entire day is over. There is still no sign of Robert. I prepare a sandwich to salve my hunger, and then I go back to bed. My eyes are wide open until I smell the familiar scent again. I close my eyes to savor the memory and amazingly, I drift back off to sleep.

The daylight streaming in from open curtains wakes me. Still no sign of Robert. A movement by the closet catches my attention: the man in the brim hat. It cannot be. A blink takes the vision away. My mind must be conjuring him up. It's been five long years. I've barely thought about him this year. I wouldn't mind staying in bed and dreaming about that time, that place, that man, but I have a head doctor to see. Besides, I don't believe in ghosts or dreams anymore.

IN SEARCH OF A BETTER SPACE

DOCTOR FEELBAD

I get up, dress, and then set off to find her office. It is in an upscale section of the city, pristine white walls and leather seats in the office. Entering, I think this is a bunch of crap. I am not a mass murderer or anything of the sort. A mere slip of the arm. It could've happened to anybody. I am given the necessary paperwork to complete. Then I am allowed into the inner sanctum to meet my head doctor. The doctor is a blonde, about thirty-two-years-old, and she looks nervous.

"Hello. I'm Lynn," I share as I extend my hand to show I am not hiding a weapon and to get a handshake.

She looks at me. Maybe she already knew my name. Her eyes are like a winter sky and just as warm. She gives me her hand to shake, but it feels like worms, so I quickly drop it. She doesn't have a couch for me lie down on to talk about my mother/father or cheating husband issues. She offers me a chair instead.

"Tell me what brings you here today."

I could say, "I stabbed my husband, and I want to look good in front of the judge." The statement would be honest although probably not be in my best interest. I can't think of a lie this quickly. I remain mute.

"I understand from Dottie you stabbed your husband?" is her next attempt to draw me into conversation. She doesn't inspire me to tell her anything because she is cold—literally and figuratively.

Dottie expects me to honor my agreement to cooperate, so I go with, "My attorney thought I may have some anger-management problems."

She counters with, "Do you think you have anger-management problems?"

"Well, no, I think it was just something that happened. You know, an accident," I say in my best impersonation of a sane person.

"Tell me about it," she demands. She is relentless.

"Look, it was like this. I was cooking dinner, and then Robert, my husband, said he wanted a divorce. Then he was asking about dinner, and then the knife was in his arm."

After the telling, she drones on and on about something before she lets me know, "Some people find medication helpful in stressful situations. Is medication something you would want to consider?"

"Well no, it isn't." On top of being newly violent and crazy, I would prefer not to become an addict. I had a bad encounter with marijuana some years back and don't want to risk becoming a junkie.

She doesn't seem too enthused with my decision judging by the slight frown she briefly displays. "Our time is up for today. I would like you to come back in two weeks. In that time, I want you to complete some homework. Take time and think about your feelings. Put those feelings about your husband, about your marriage in writing. Be as creative and open as you can. Make sure not to hide your emotions. Express what you really feel. Let's see if writing will relieve some of the stress, get you to a better place where anger is not the ruler of your actions."

"I'm not stressed," I inform her.

She just looks at me as if to say, "and I'm Pocahontas" and then she persists, "Come back in two weeks, and we will discuss whether you have anger-management or stress issues."

Maybe we should discuss the meaning of the word accident, but that isn't given as an option. I take her words as my cue to leave. "Thank-you, doctor. I will do my best." I avoid shaking her cold, wormy hand and leave, glad my insurance will cover this experience. A wasted day if ever there was one. I make my appointment with her receptionist anyway, so I can have this wonderful experience again.

☙❧

I stop to get a bite before going home since I have no plans on cooking. A cheeseburger and fries is never on the dinner menu. Robert doesn't like meat in patties. He doesn't want his meat patted and shaped. It has too much touching, and he doesn't believe my nails would be clean enough to pat his burger. I don't give a damn that there is a stranger patting my burger. I want it to taste good.

Robert's car is in front of the house. Maybe this is all just a bad dream. Maybe he came to his senses. When I enter the house, he is in the living room. I put a big smile on my face. "Hi, Robert."

"Lynn, I have some papers you have to sign." No greeting, no apology, no nothing. The only thing he has to say is about some papers he wants me to sign. This divorce and the assault charge are reality.

It wasn't a dream, and he hasn't come to his senses. I try to come to mine. "Robert, I don't think I should sign anything. I need to get an attorney to advise me." My heart starts to beat faster.

"You don't need an attorney. I told you I would take care of everything. Now just sign here. Once this is signed, I'll drop the assault charges."

He shoves some papers in my face with one hand and holds a pen in the other. This man is a stranger. My real husband would not be treating me this way. Maybe I am the stranger. I always follow Robert's direction. Before, his directions were law. He is the man. My husband. My life partner. Times change.

I can't sign divorce papers. I am scared, sweating, aware of the fact that I'm stalling. The fear is here, overwhelming everything except the anger at the fact he is leaving. I am afraid. As long as I have a husband, I have an anchor. What will happen to me once he is gone? We don't have much of a life together, but we are together. For now.

"Not now, Robert." I move past him and head up the stairs while my legs can still work.

"Lynn, what are you doing? I am talking to you." His voice conveys the shock of having me walk out while he is speaking.

I wordlessly continue to the bedroom. Once there, the shaking starts. I hear Robert slam the door as he exits. Useless tears are forming in my eyes. My dad always said crying does nothing except cloud your vision.

I blink the tears away, and I wish there was someone to call and talk to and at least share some of the weight I am feeling. The questions to myself come quickly. Can I do this and not kill myself? Is my life slipping away? Am I strong enough to bear this?

I hear a familiar and much-missed voice tell me, "Yessss."

More memories from two weeks of my life are in his voice. The voice you can hear has experienced the best and worst life has to offer. A life that has been both hard and soft. Hard by forging a path from Africa to America and soft by loving the music that he was able to coax from his fingers, a voice that has embraced life. The tone, medley, and cadence move the cells in my blood with their intensity. I bend closer to hear and close my eyes to savor the sound. The voice is raspy, deep like the core of the earth, hot, and uncovered. It's a voice that sounds like wanting and satisfaction. The voice has promises of ecstasy in each syllable. It can't be him. He is dead. Still the memories of his "yessss" put me to sleep.

I spend the rest of the weekend in a daze. Robert is missing in action or sleeping in the guest room. I feel humiliated, as though I was in the wrong or the cause of what is happening. I am also afraid. If I talk about what I'm feeling, I will not be able to hold back the tears. I don't want anyone feeling sorry for me or seeing my emotions.

My mother has called and come by repeatedly. I refuse to answer the phone or the door. Her messages only serve to remind me of what I aspired to be. I fill my weekend with questions about the past and fear of the next phase of my life. I avoid calls from my children and somehow survive my first weekend as an almost-divorced fifty-five-year-old.

DOWNSIZING MADE EASY

FORTY HOURS

Monday morning comes with the recognition that having a job is a blessing. I still have my job and will be able to support my almost single self. Not all is lost. The thought gets me up and moving. I arrive late, which is not normal for me. It helps I have been a model employee and seldom take time off.

"Lynn, we need to talk," says my boss as soon as my coat is off.

His words make me sweat. Those words take me back to a bad place in my life. I don't think I will be able to stand what comes next. There are no knives handy and that is a good thing. I quickly gather my notebook and pencils. Maybe Harold needs some quick instructions sent out. Judging from his expression, it must be serious. We are finishing up the year-end activities. This includes completing tasks we have been putting off all year. I rush in to hear what is so important to have completely changed Harold's demeanor.

Harold is at his desk looking uncomfortable. Water is dotting his upper lip and forehead. He is starting to sweat, and that is not normal for him. I take my regular seat on the blue leather loveseat beside the cherry wood end table then put my pad and writing instruments down. I am ready to start writing or listen to what he wants to share.

"Lynn, there is no easy way to say this. We're going to have to let you go. There is a generous severance package. The economy, the lack of strength of the industry mean we have to cut every corner. It's nothing personal. I held out as long as I could. I'll be leaving, and, well there is no easy way to say it. Times are changing."

It takes about a minute for my brain to process this bit of news. On top of everything else, I really don't need more change right now.

"What do you mean let me go? What did I do? I've been here for years. This has been my only job. What happened? What did I do wrong? I'll fix it." My skin goes cold as I talk. I, too, am sweating. My heart is skipping beats like a crack addict on an overdose.

Harold is trying to pacify me, but I don't hear everything he is saying. I watch his lips moving and get snippets. "Downsizing." "Employee buyout." "Three-year lump sum." "Effective date" "Three to six months." "Go home." "Robert."

Go home for what. I don't have a Robert anymore. Now it looks like I don't have a job anymore. It sucks being me right now.

"Take the rest of the next two weeks off and let this sink in. Then we'll talk." Harold stands up.

"Take time off?" I ask. It comes out as barely a whisper. I have nothing to fill the void of time off I have acquired.

"Yes. You have more leave than anyone else does at the company. Comp time, sick time, and a boatload of vacation time. Don't you ever take a vacation?" Harold wonders aloud. He regularly took time off work, but I never did.

"Sure, yes," I answer automatically.

"That's right. You went to Great Britain a few years back," he belatedly remembers.

"What? No. Yes. I don't know, Harold." The trip never actually happened, but no one knows about my experiences during those two weeks. I have never talked about it to anyone because no one would understand. I gather my materials and wobble to a standing position. I manage the trip out of Harold's office before the emotions can erupt. I stand at my desk and stare at the walls. I've been looking forward to retiring from here and staying home with Robert. What will Robert say? Is my life finally as far in the toilet as it can get? Maybe. My life right now is shit.

Harold said talk to Robert because he will know what to do about everything. What if he won't say anything because we are no longer a couple? I have to try. There isn't anyone else to talk to about this.

Harold did say things are only in the initial stages. I take his advice, put on my coat, and head toward the door. "Hey, Harold, I'll take you up on that offer and be out for the next few weeks," I poke my head in the door to say. "I need to think." I drive around aimlessly before going back home. It isn't even noon.

Robert's car is in the driveway. Mine goes in behind it instead of on the street, which is my designated parking area as dictated by Robert. I don't want him to run out as soon as I enter. I haven't seen him all weekend, but I'll bet as soon as I get in the house he'll leave.

"Robert, you'll never guess." I start talking as soon as I enter the house. I know I am yelling, but this is an exceptional occurrence. He is in the living room on the telephone, which makes me pull myself to a stop midstride. Robert seldom talks on the telephone.

He hangs up the phone and turns toward me with a guilty look on his face. "Hello, Lynn. Shouldn't you be at work?"

"Who were you talking to when I came in?" That sounds like a civil question. I have a sneaking suspicion it was his new love. The thought makes me all too aware of what a big nothing his wife is to him. Bastard. The fear of the unknown court date is the only thing that keeps me from busting his head open. And I am *not* a violent person.

"Why?" He doesn't even bother to get off the couch to pay attention to the excitement in my voice. As I look at him, I contrast us—me wanting to stay *us*, while he is already spending nights and conversations with his new love.

"Lynn, we are divorcing. Who I talk with is really none of your business."

"It's pretty obvious, but shouldn't you wait until you actually leave before you have telephone conversations and overnights with her? How do you think it makes me feel? What if I was seeing someone else and talked to him here in our house?" These rapid-fire questions are legitimate in my opinion.

Our years together have honed my ability to see his thought process. Sometimes, I can pinpoint what he is going to say (with the obvious exception). Robert thinks my question is crazy.

He looks over at me as though I might be losing my mind. "Lynn, get serious. You wouldn't see anyone else. You aren't like that. Besides, who else would want you?" He laughs as he turns and leaves the room. On the way out, he stops and says, "I'll be back. Oh, you came in as if you wanted to tell me something. What was it?"

His callousness is a reminder we are splitting up soon, and my news is really my business, not his. I have to start separating my life from his as effectively as he has separated his life from mine. He is also right—nobody else would want me. I'm so far over the hill the trees I planted on the way up have matured.

"Nothing. Umm, you can't leave, I parked behind you."

"I still have keys to your car. I'll pull it out and park it on the street where it is supposed to be. And please do not park behind me again. You know you are supposed to park on the street." He keeps going toward the door. "You seeing someone else," he laughs as he shakes his head.

I could be as stupid as Robert is being now. I had an affair five years ago, or more aptly, an encounter. I could have kept it going, but my marriage and security were more important to me. Maybe I should have kept it going. No, Robert is right I'm not the seeing-someone type of person. I wish I were, and then there would be someone to turn to and share this calamity. At least Robert didn't ask me about dinner.

MEMORIES OF MR. M.O.P.

Robert's comments set me to thinking about my encounter. I had bought myself a vacation to Great Britain five years ago. On the plane to New York, my seatmate was a percussionist from Africa. About five feet nine, with skin as golden as a french fry and salt and pepper hair, he was a vision of maleness. He had a voice like a bedroom scene on the radio, making you imagine naughty things. He took the word *yes* and stretched it out, putting in promises of satisfaction, and us and loving, making it *yessss.*

He mesmerized me and connected with me on every level. I felt as though I knew him. He assured me we had been together in past lives. Mentally, his conversation was stimulating. He shared stories of his life that were fascinating because they were so foreign to me. Physically, he moved his hand over my arm, my leg, my back until he had me branded and ready to eat out of his hand.

By the end of the flight, I had agreed to spend my two-week vacation traveling across the United States and Mexico with him while he toured. He promised me a tourist activity in each city we visited, as a way for me to experience the world. He played different venues, with me watching and planning our sightseeing adventures.

With each city, I found more and more of myself through the new perspective I had on life. From Cleveland to the Grand Canyon, I had never felt more accepted or wanted. His wife even came to us in Nashville and prepared us for our time together. She shaved us, rubbed us with oil, and dressed us before she went back to Paris.

She explained the concept of an elusive orgasm. According to her, people who connect on spiritual, emotional, and physical levels are the only ones with the ability to experience the ultimate release. She was secure enough in her relationship with him to accept the inclusion of me in his life.

Those were two of the most magical weeks of my life. I always referred to him as Mr. M.O.P. (Man on Plane). If I had used his name, I would have surely spoken it out aloud in my sleep.

Mr. M.O.P. frequently came to the United States and wanted me to continue seeing him. He felt we had been together in a previous lifetime and were merely picking up where we had left off. I always declined. I did not want to risk my marriage for what we shared, although it was mind blowing.

Often, during the first two years after we met, I would wake up, knowing he was on my continent, feeling his allure, and burning to see him again. He would leave messages with his tour dates and locations on my cell phone. He would always let me know there was a ticket with my name at the door.

Once when he was playing close to me in Wichita, I gave in to temptation and went to see him perform. I did not tell him I was coming. When I saw him on stage, I realized the instant connection between us at our first meeting was still there. His head toss and smile acknowledged me from the stage. I did not speak to him because I left before the end of the performance, afraid of being weak again, afraid of going back to the magic of him. Still, he told me he had felt my presence and relished the reconnection in the voice mail message he left on my cell phone. I never spoke with or saw him again except in my dreams.

In my basement are mementos of the places and the time I had spent with him. His music CDs, Caesar's Woman cologne, the clothing his wife dressed us in when we were in Nashville, corsets and push-up bras from Vegas, and other items. These items have remained unseen and untouched for years. I try not to think about the time with him, but now it all comes rushing back.

It started with the shadow in the hotel room I somehow thought was him. Then smelling the perfume and finally hearing him say *yessss,* stretching the letters out to get maximum enjoyment. I guess I am under too much stress, and it all must be getting to me. I decide to forgo supper and head to bed.

As I undress, I continue to think about Mr. M.O.P. Again, the unmistakable scent of Caesar's Woman cologne he gifted me with in Vegas creeps into my nostrils. My face unconsciously bends into a smile. I try not to think about him anymore. Then, thankfully, sleep comes.

The next day I get up to go to work before remembering there is not a job to go to anymore and get back in bed. I need to get more information about my almost unemployed status, but it can wait. I stay in bed. Hunger pains don't hit, listlessness captures me. The day turns to night, and I remain in bed.

The next morning finds me still lying in bed long after my regular getting up time. Robert did not come in last night. I remember making it all the way to the other side of the bed during the night, and he was not there to stop me. This brought me wide-awake, heart racing, sweating, and looking for him. Then it was if my eyes would not stay open. I felt remembered fingers closing them to get me back to sleep. When I awoke again, it is time to shower and dress, preparing to face the world.

Still at home, I am facing the aloneness Robert's decision has caused. I have not felt quite right since he told me of our divorce. It's only been a little over a week, but damn I feel lonely. I don't have anyone to call and tell about the change in my life. I could call my children, but I don't feel like talking to them. They don't think I can make it without their father, as they showed at the family dinner. Besides, I wouldn't feel comfortable talking to them about my relationship with their father. Our situation should not include them or make them feel they should take sides.

This will be the hardest part of being single, the solitary existence, the knowing I am not wanted. Robert never was one for company and did not like me to have friends. He thought they were a distraction from my attention to our family. I don't really have any friends except for Dottie, who is more like family, and Kadijah, who I have known since elementary school. She refuses to let Robert's rudeness deter her. However, she moved to Georgia to get away from Kansas cold and to be with the latest love of her life.

In the front room, I think about what can be done to occupy my day. I decide daytime television is as good a time waster as anything is. Jerry Springer is on with people who want to stop weddings. I'm in agreement with them. Marriages can only end in divorce or death. The cake throwing and name-calling have me cheering for the toothless, braless mother of the groom to kick the toothless, braless almost bride's ass.

Robert comes in a short time later. "What are you doing home?" he asks. He stands there as though he still has the right to question me.

I look up to respond, "I am losing my husband, so I am in mourning," I turn my attention back to Jerry. Mother Trailer Trash is winning.

"Lynn, this is no big deal. I will continue to take care of everything. I just won't be living here," he explains as if makes a rat's ass worth of sense.

He can't be leaving and still be in control here. "That doesn't sound fair to me." I hate to sound pleading, but I want my life back. "Robert, why are you doing this?"

"Don't worry about it. Just sign these papers, and everything will be fine." He is unaffected by anything, save his selfish desire to be divorced. He goes into the kitchen. I resist temptation to follow him.

The break gives me the opportunity to cement my decision. I tell him when he returns a short time later. "Robert, I am not signing anything until I see an attorney."

The delivery and the tone make him quiet, thinking up another strategy since the usual commands are not working.

"Have you forgotten you have a court date tomorrow for stabbing me?" He asks innocently.

"No. I haven't forgotten." I do forget all about Jerry. Sweat starts to come out from under my arms. My heart rate increases. Robert knows where my weakness is and is willing to exploit the weakness.

"I just might drop this if you cooperate," he tempts.

I wouldn't have to go to court for stabbing him, but I would be summarily single. What he doesn't acknowledge is there are so many sacrifices I made because we were *we*, such as bowing to his every wish. Taking a stand against him is hard but empowering. The papers may be fine, but I will not sign them. "I'll take my chances."

"What has gotten into you?" Robert is starting to get angry. I can tell because the veins in his neck are noticeable.

"I guess it's the effect of being dumped." It takes a lot for me to say it aloud. If one of us doesn't leave soon, I am going to be doing something I will definitely regret.

Robert looks at me as if I just pulled a puppy out of my nose. "You'll regret this." He heads toward the door, slamming it on his way out. For some reason I feel victorious.

I feel the voice before I hear it. *Yessss.*

I look around expecting, hoping to see him. Nothing. Logically, I know he has been dead for the past three years. I learned he had died from the radio and his wife, Alita, when she returned a poem to me.

When Mr. M.O.P. and I were together in Cleveland, he had asked me what my passion was. After getting me to admit it was writing, he asked me to write something for him. He inspired the poem "In Your Passion" my first foray into writing in over thirty years. I gave it to him as a gift. Alita sent it back to me via mail after his transition to the next life on stage in Vancouver. She and I have kept in touch every year around the anniversary of his passing.

I stop and smile for our time together, and the power he put in one word. After a few minutes of remembering the past, I come back to now. Maybe I should sign the papers. I pick up the phone and call Dottie. "You won't believe this. Robert is trying to pressure me into signing divorce papers. He said if I signed them, he would not go forward with the prosecution. What should I do?" I tell her all this without taking a breath.

"Lynn, don't sign anything. This is going to be okay. I'm on my way over, and we are going out to dinner."

True to her word, she comes and takes me to my favorite Japanese restaurant. The food is tasteless or maybe it is just my mood. She doesn't threaten to put me out by the side of the road when I can't keep up my end of the conversation. After trying repeatedly to engage me, she throws in the towel.

"Lynn, I can't pretend to understand how you feel. Just know I am here if you ever want or need to talk."

"Dottie, I appreciate you more than words can say. Your friendship means so much, but I feel lost. I don't know what to say except thank you for understanding." We have the remainder of the meal in silence.

When she takes me back to the house, she encourages me, "You have got to know this is going to be okay. I'll pick you up tomorrow, so we can ride to the courthouse together. Be ready at eight." She hugs me tight.

I get out of the car and into my empty-feeling house, where I go straight to bed. Sleep is as elusive as my unfaithful husband is even though all the lights are out, the television is off, and it is eleven forty-five at night, which is past my bedtime. Pain, my almost constant companion, is still here along with his cousin Despair. Their friend Confused is also in attendance, and they show no sign of leaving. I am off my routine and may be up quite late judging by the way I am feeling—afraid.

Robert stealthily comes in around one and goes to the next largest bedroom. He doesn't even check on me to see how I am doing. I debate going into the room and climbing into bed with him before I turn over and avoid sleep. I hold my breath. If I allow myself to breathe normally, the tears would start to flow, and I don't know if I would be able to stop them.

The tears start falling and wet my face and the pillow. As hard as I try to keep them in, to show I am strong, they keep coming. As I drift off, finally feeling the need to sleep, I feel someone holding my face and kissing my tears away. I open my eyes and look around. No one is here. I am alone with the scent of Cacsar's Woman and the sound of *yessss.* Comfort and sleep come.

COURTROOM NUMBER ONE

WILL THE DEFENDANT PLEASE RISE?

The next morning, my lack of sleep is evident in the red color of my eyes. Drops clear them up, so the judge won't think I'm a drug addict. I need all the help I can get. I select the most conservative of my six conservative black business suits and pair it with one of my nine white shirts and black pumps from my selection of five pair. I look at myself in the mirror and consider what a judge would think about me. I hope that the judge won't think me militant because of the twists in my hair. I always wear them pulled back in a low ponytail. It makes them less threatening. I want the judge to give me the benefit of the doubt so I cover them with a muted floral scarf. Better safe than sorry.

The telephone rings, and Dottie asks, "Are you ready or should I come in for coffee, since I'm here a few minutes early?"

"I'll be right out." I head out to the car with my head bowed to hide the scared look on my face.

"Are you okay? You look like shit. You look as if they are going to take you to jail now. That won't happen. Cheer up," Dottie says by way of a greeting. The downside of a good friend is she is honest enough to tell you when you are not on your A game.

"But they could, couldn't they, Dottie?" I ask.

She doesn't answer.

As we drive to the courthouse, I'm wondering how to keep them from taking me away in chains screaming, as Dottie tries to allay my fears. Entering the building, Dottie tells me to wait in the hallway while she checks in with the court officer.

Looking at all the criminals and crazies in the hall, I almost overlook some familiar faces. All three of the children are here, along with my mother who waves. The most surprising face of all is my father. He stands erect as always and deigns to give a head nod in my general direction. I go toward them.

"What are you doing here?" I wonder aloud, the disbelief making my voice screech softly. I am not alone after all. Even though I had been avoiding them, they are here for me. My throat starts to clog as my nose and eyes prepare to leak.

"Well, we couldn't very well let you come down here by yourself," comes from May.

"You know we love you both, but we're here for you," says Lynnette.

"We have to tell the judge we are ready with the intervention if need be," shares Rene.

My mother hugs me and elbows dad. "Walter, don't you have something to say?"

"You are my daughter," my father tells me as if those words say it all. I guess it does.

Having everyone here comforts me. I do not have to go through this with only Dottie to lean on. Family is wonderful.

Dottie comes out of the courtroom and over to us. After greeting my family, she turns to me. "Lynn, we'll have to go in. This is a preliminary hearing. The charges will be read, and you will enter a plea. You don't say anything else. The judge will decide if bail is necessary to ensure you will show up for your next court date. From there, we will get the next court date. Try not to be nervous."

As we enter the courtroom, I am buoyed by the support of my family. Even if I do have to do time in the big house, my family would come to see me. I see no sign of Robert and ask Dottie about him. According to her, he is not required to be at the preliminary hearing, since this visit is for me to enter a plea.

The courtroom is crowded with more shady characters than were in the hallway. The judge is a middle-aged unsmiling black man sitting in a black robe at an elevated seat where he can look down on everyone else. He is going through people, passing judgments, and asking few questions. He is the only calm in this room of madness. The court officer is calling a man charged with disorderly conduct.

The prosecutor, a short, balding, white guy who appears to lack any personality reads the complaint. He shares the man was on probation when he had his latest encounter with the police. He ends on a request for the judge to put the individual back in jail.

The disorderly's attorney speaks. "Your honor, on behalf of my client, I beg for leniency. Please allow my client to remain free until his court date. He is not a flight risk. He is a member of this community and has lived here all his life. He will appear at his next court date. You have my word." He looks trustworthy. His client is another matter.

"Sir, how do you plead?" The judge doesn't look up from writing.

The miscreant answers, "Not guilty." He looks guilty to me. Both ears have multiple earrings, and he is wearing a T-shirt that hits him at mid thigh. His jeans are sagging low enough for him to have to stand wide legged to keep his pants up. His boots are untied, and he has on sunglasses even though we are indoors.

The judge looks up directly at the man. "When I saw you last week, didn't I tell you that if you came back into my courtroom, I would lock you up?"

"Your honor, it was an accident," the man starts to answer before his attorney motions for him to be quiet.

The judge smiles. It is not a pretty smile. "Well, this is on purpose. Bailiff, take this young man into custody. I hope that being in jail will encourage him to stop being disorderly in his conduct. Set the court date at thirty days from now. No bail."

"Your honor, please. It was an accident," the criminal says.

Your honor smiles.

"Thank-you, your honor" the attorney says, obviously relieved to be leaving.

Your honor continues to smile. "Next."

A very big, very scary bailiff moves forward and handcuffs the prisoner. He starts to struggle and the bailiff makes his arms go so far up his back before cuffing him. The disorderly is on tiptoe as he is led from the courtroom. His pants fall, but he continues forward, propelled by the very large bailiff.

Another bailiff, equally large, then calls my name. Damn. I sure as hell am not going to go with the accident defense. Lesson learned.

The prosecutor reads the complaint, which says I stabbed my husband in a fit of rage. She is telling a bare-face lie. I was not in a fit of rage, but accidents aren't working real well as a defense from what I can see.

"Ma'am, how do you plead?" Judge Lockemup asks me, as if I'm going to answer.

"Not guilty, your honor," Dottie tells him. "My client was shocked and had a moment of clouded judgment. She is deeply remorseful and is seeking help for her anger-management problem. She is currently under the care of a therapist and is following the therapist's recommendations. There is not any risk of flight from my client. She pleads for the court to allow her to remain free pending resolution of this matter."

The judge looks over at me. "Ma'am, did you mean to stab your husband in the arm?"

"No, sir." I could honestly say with a straight face. I wish I had gone for his throat, but I don't want to share this tidbit with the man who could make people go away and give me a worse day than I've had lately. Especially since my days lately have been sucking grapes through straws.

"Will you continue to attend whatever treatment you are currently undergoing if I allow you to remain free?"

"Yes sir, I will." I will go see the cold fish that is my therapist even more often if he doesn't put me in jail.

My judge turns to the prosecutor, "Any objections?"

"No, your honor. We do not believe her to be a flight risk. She has not had any prior contact with the court."

"Write it up. We will set the court date for two weeks," the judge commands.

I am relieved and grateful, and I want to tell the judge so. "Oh, thank you so much. I promise I'll be good. You know it really was…"

Dottie tells me in an undertone, "Shut up." My mouth snaps shut.

My judgeship looks up from his writing to say, "If I see you back in here, I will not be so lenient." I saw what he did to the last guy. I believe him.

When we turn, I see Robert in the back of the courtroom. He is not happy and starts to storm out without acknowledging our children by so much as a glance. He stops to speak with my dad or rather my dad stops him by performing a body check like a basketball player. I do not want to hear what they are saying. There is too much testosterone flowing. Robert listens, nods curtly, and leaves.

I am on top of the world! I'm free—as long as I don't do anything stupid within the next two weeks. I ease out of the courtroom behind Dottie, ever so thankful that I am free. The family follows me. Once in the hallway, everyone starts to talk, with the exception of my father. He holds himself above the fray and allows my mother to give me a hug by pushing her toward me after whispering in her ear.

Mom and dad start to leave, and she lets me know, "I will be over Saturday morning. We'll have breakfast together."

I hug them both. "Thank-you so much for coming to be with me. Girls, thanks for being here."

"We are family," is the pronouncement from my dad. He should be called Colonel Obvious. He gathers my mother's hand, and they leave.

"We may need to have a family meeting," May tells me.

"I still think we need an intervention." Rene demands. She is an intervention pit bull. She can intervene her own self since she likes the idea so much.

"I'll be by on Friday, and we can go to dinner," Lynnette hugs me and whispers in my ear.

"Sure. Make it next Friday at six. I'll be ready," I tell her in an undertone. We don't need the other two in our business. We can do both she whispers to me.

Dottie and I stop for a bite to eat before she takes me home. I am ecstatic about not being in jail, and my appetite reflects the fact I am free. I don't even give a hoot about the calories in belgium waffles. Who the hell cares if bacon is pork, and pork raises your blood pressure? I'm free. After we eat, Dottie drops me off.

Robert has been home and taken some of his things. This is evident because he did not even bother to close drawers or tidy up after himself. Clothes are hanging out of open drawers, things he dropped are lying on the floor, and a bottle of cologne he spilled is on the floor. He left it for me to clean. I sit on the edge of the bed and stare. Everything is so wrong.

I want to cry. Tears for my past spent sacrificing dreams, ideas, and hopes to be his wife forever. Tears for the future I will face alone.

Tears for now and my current state of being—empty. I have no useful purpose in life. But neither do tears.

I think about doing something but do not feel energetic enough to make any effort at activity. I take a shower and climb into bed to enjoy the quiet instead. The next morning, I decide to stay in bed all day and sleep.

Evening comes, and I have to prepare for my dinner with Lynnette. She picks me up, and we go to an Italian restaurant with a great Merlot. I enjoy my dinner with her. There are no questions, no pity party, just dinner.

When she drops me off, she tells me, "I love you no matter what."

I go in and go to bed.

I see mom Saturday, when she shows up with breakfast and greetings from dad. There is no sign of Robert. She doesn't press me for conversation. I appreciate that and her cooking.

Sunday I stay in bed and ignore everything and everyone

On Monday, I am ready to go back to work. Unfortunately, I am off for the next week. Harold calls me in the late afternoon. Well, what else could possibly go wrong?

"Lynn, I wanted you to know I, for one, really appreciate all you have done for the company. You, as much as me, have helped it to grow. I wanted you to know I appreciate your efforts," Harold sincerely states.

"Thanks, Harold. It means a lot to hear you say those words out loud." Harold is not one for much praise, so this is good for me to hear.

"I also want to tell you the company will be giving you a lump sum of fifty thousand, and then you will still have your retirement when you reach sixty-two." He sounds more relaxed than he did the last time we talked. "How do you really feel about not working?"

"It's the shock of it all, the feelings of being worthless, useless, and unwanted. The opportunity to sleep late is enticing but then what?" I ask him.

"What if you found another job?" Harold wants to know.

"No one will hire me. There aren't a lot of opportunities for fifty-five-year-old women is my view of the situation."

"I know some places that would love someone like you. Honesty, loyalty and dependability are qualities most employers value above education and experience. Do you want me to make some calls?" he offers.

"Sure, let's see what happens." Miracles do happen, so why not see if one will happen for me?

"What does Robert think of all this?" Harold wants to know.

"Harold, Robert and I are getting a divorce," is my surprise revelation.

"Oh. I had no idea. This must be doubly hard on you," he commiserates.

"Yes, it is," I agree.

"Lynn, I'm glad you're taking some time off. Get used to relaxing and get your life together. You deserve a rest with everything going on. There won't be anything definite completed regarding the downsizing for about four months. Take some time and do you," Harold encourages me.

"Thanks, Harold. I'll be in touch." I hurry off the telephone and into the bathroom barely in time to hold my head back to prevent the tears.

It takes some time to stop them from wanting to fall. I have had quite a bit of experience so I know to lean the head back and close my eyes tight. The tears will go to my nose and throat to exit. It's not crying if the moisture comes from your nose and mouth instead of your eyes.

I wander around the quiet house, walking from room to room. There is no one here but me. No one to talk to and share the latest calamity to befall me. This is hard. I go back into our bedroom and look around. It is empty, and I hate being here by myself. There isn't anything I feel like doing right now. I decide to go to bed.

I almost choke myself from the emotion coursing through my body. My nose is completely stuffed, making it difficult to breathe. I have to open my mouth to let air in and sound emerges. A loud, keening wail captures all the sorrow that is in me.

The crying does not stop although the sound eventually fades. Around midnight, I feel comforting arms and tender fingers stroking my face. I look around and see nothing. It must be my imagination because I am still alone. My eyes drift closed, and I wait to ease into sleep. It does not come until after I feel arms, as familiar as my name, enfold me.

I stay in bed for the next few days. Then remember my appointment with the head doctor is coming up soon. This starts me thinking about my assignment. I have to write some stupid something about my marriage. The cherry on top is I have another shrink session to ruin my day.

I turn my thoughts to my marriage and my feelings. What would I like Robert to know? I sit at the dining room table to write. The words just seem to flow, and it doesn't take long to capture the essence of my feelings.

I go to bed for another bout of sleep and broken sleep.

A POEM FOR YOU

Thursday I go to my head doctor appointment. I don't have to wait. I am on time, and so is she. I enter, and she greets me before I have the opportunity to introduce myself again.

"Hello, Dr. Khorsley. How are you?" I ask first.

"The most important question is how are you, Lynn" she counters.

"I lost my job. I had my first court date for stabbing Robert. I think it went pretty well, considering it was my first time in court," I share with her.

"Have you been calm?"

"Yes." I haven't stabbed anyone. Since stabbing is what I use as my measure of calm, I am calm.

"Are you coming to terms with the divorce?" she wants to know.

"Yes." I tell her this to show I do not need to keep coming.

"Did you say you lost your job?" she finally hears through her false concern.

"Yes, they are downsizing and letting me go. Once you reach a certain age nobody wants you, not your husband, not your job."

"Lynn, I wish you would consider the medication. Zoloft is good for depression," she shares with me.

"No," I reiterate to her. I know this is trick of doctors to develop an income from patients. Look at Elvis and where medication got him.

She changes the subject. "How are you sleeping?"

"I've been doing fine. Things are going smoothly. I have not had any altercations with Robert. I'm good." If I tell her I haven't been sleeping well, she will keep pushing the medication.

We chitchat a bit longer before she asks, "Did you work on the writing assignment I gave you? I think your writing will help me see where you are in relationship to the ending of your marriage."

"Yes, doctor. I did work on it. I tried to show my emotions and my thoughts. Would you like me to read it to you?" I'm glad I completed my assignment.

"Yes, you reading it would be a good idea. Then I can see where you place emphasis. I will get a clear idea of your feelings in your own voice."

I pull out my work and begin to read.

We should always be together
We should always be together because it is right
I thought we are married now and forever
Therefore, we would always be together

I have your name
I can't bear to give it back
Because I thought, we would be together until you die
You worthless piece of shit

If you were on fire,
I wouldn't piss on you to put you out.
I don't care that you are leaving.
Go you bastard. Go

She interrupts me with her coughing. I look up. I put a lot of work into my verse. It doesn't actually rhyme, but it effectively sums up my feelings. Except for the "Go" part.

It isn't the best poetry, but I haven't had much practice. I thought she would be happy with my efforts. I did the work. She knew I wasn't Maya Angelou.

"So, doctor, what do you think? I don't need to come back, do I?"

Her face looks as though someone has sucked all the blood out. She is as white as milk. "Lynn, may-may-maybe be you mi-mi-might wa-wa-want to think about the medi-medi-medication I mentioned," she stammers.

"I'll think about the medication if you want. I don't think I need it. I did my writing, and I think it helped. I know it's not Pulitzer material yet, but it was my first try. It proves I don't have an anger-management problem, right?" I try to prevent my voice from rising and possibly scaring her.

"Let's talk about this some more next week. Our time is almost up for today." She is packing her pencils and papers. She then stands up to let me know it is time for me to get out.

"Okay." I am ready to go anyway.

"Since you do not want the medication, I think we'll have to try another relaxation method. I would like you to try to get into a yoga class and maybe see a play. It may reduce your stress level and get you to a better space. Have you ever considered taking yoga?" Doctor Khorsley asks.

"Well, yes. Once I did think about taking a yoga class." I don't want to tell her I was going to take a yoga class to get limber enough to pleasure myself. Those specifics would be way too personal to share with a stranger. Besides, I never went to the class. Robert says yoga is heresy.

"You're the doctor. I'll give it a try." Obviously, she is not impressed with my writing. Everybody is a critic. She did not appreciate my literary proffering. Yoga and a play it is. I go out and make my appointment for two weeks from now. The judge expects me to be cooperative.

I'M NOT CRAZY

DINNER AND A LYNNETTE

On Friday morning, Lynnette calls me to arrange plans for dinner. I decide to go, so I can get out of the house. We go to a Chinese restaurant, and she starts in after she orders the appetizer.

"Are you doing okay?"

"I don't know. Sometimes I want to wake up and find out I've been dreaming," I admit to her, even though I haven't to anyone else.

"Maybe it's for the best. Now you can do some of the things you want to do, instead of what everyone wants you to do." Lynnette is more insightful than I give her credit for being.

She then starts talking about her day and all things Lynnette. Her ability to be self-absorbed is amazing. Of course, she loves me. She just loves herself above all else. She will be my role model. She wouldn't be crying about the breakup of a marriage. She would be putting on makeup and staring life in the eye through lashes made long by mascara and eyelids thoroughly covered with color.

I am going to try to emulate her in the future. First, I'd have to buy makeup and I don't feel up to taking that task on today. I've seen makeup done wrong and don't want to be the subject of a conversation about the lady with the scary eyes, I get home and in bed for the night. I hear Robert come in around twelve. He continues past our room to go to bed in the next room. When I get up the next morning, he is gone. I tell myself "He is missing out on a fantastic opportunity to be with me."

Over the weekend, I take telephone calls from everyone and give assurance that I am coping well but do not want any visits. The shame of my husband leaving would show on my face and invite pity.

Monday morning, I go back to work. Mail and e-mail are reviewed, the telephone is answered, calls are placed, and information is inputted. I manage all this without thought. Tuesday is a repeat of Monday. Then I remember my homework.

THE YOGA EXPERIENCE

Where do you find a yoga class? None of the people I know has ever said anything about taking yoga. A newspaper tells me there are Saturday morning and Wednesday evening classes close to home for a nominal price. I get yoga supplies—a mat and a water bottle and then feel prepared to find the better space this is supposed to take me to according to Doctor Khorsley.

Wednesday evening finds me at a yoga class. In class, the instructor encourages us into positions that will cause us to "open" ourselves. I don't want to open myself. If I open myself, I might catch something. Other people are doing things and spreading themselves. I just stand there wondering if this will count as following the doctor's orders.

Ms. Please Go Eat a Burger speaks "Put your left foot on your right inner thigh and hold your hands to the heavens. This is the tree stance."

The judge may have a spy in here, so I hold my hands in the air. My left foot makes it to my right ankle. This interaction has me feeling I have mastered the pose.

Then the unnaturally thin chick says, "Let us get in connection with the earth. Touch the earth with your hands and feet." She bends over and puts her palms flat on the floor in front of her without bending her knees.

I watch. Then I put my hands on my knees and bend my body so it would look like I was participating for the spy in the class. The last time I was in this position, there was a fascinating man in back of me making it worthwhile and fun. I keep my hands there, on my knees as long as everyone else has their hands on the floor.

"This is the downward-facing dog position," her voice is monotone and she sounds like she would rather be somewhere else. She does not inspire me to do anything. If she isn't excited about it, why should I be?

"Go to your place of strength. Bend your knees and sit on your heels." She has her knees bent and is sitting on her heels. So does everyone else in the class. Except me.

Getting to my knees takes a minute. There are no handrails or chairs to help me get down there or back up again. Sitting on my heels is impossible. My thighs and my calves meet up and conspire to prevent my ass from touching my heels. I have my knees on the floor as though I had mastered the pose. God knows I have not. God smiled.

"Now we are going into the inverted tree pose," Yoga Queen spouts. "With both hands on the floor in front of you, slowly lift your right leg from the floor. Put your head behind your left leg. Put both arms out to the side. These are your branches. Your toes on your right foot are reaching toward the sky. Stretch it out and touch, touch, touch the sky." She has her front to her back and her upside down. So do the other people in class. Except me.

I bend over farther and with both hands on the floor, my knees can't help but bend. I try to get up enough security to put my right leg up and touch, touch, touch the sky. Not only are my toes not going toward the sky, but both my hands are remaining on the floor in front of me. My branches are nonexistent. The law of gravity says if I take my foot any farther up or my hands anywhere close to out, my whole body will meet the floor. God laughed.

"Let's get on all fours now and connect with the tiger spirit in us," Yoga Lady instructs us.

I figure I can do all fours. I make it down there since I am there anyway.

"Now arch your back like a cat."

No problem. I can do a cat.

"Take your left leg and bring it up to your abdomen as you bring your chest up to meet your spine."

This is still working.

"Take your left leg and bring it in back of you while you balance on your left hand and right leg. Stretch your right hand upward."

This may not work

"Put your left leg on the floor in front of you. Take your right hand and reach back to grasp your right foot and bring it to your left ear."

Are you serious? She has no fat. I do.

I stand up, get my newly purchased yoga mat, pick up my water bottle, and head toward the door.

I think I hear her command her pack of twistables, "Look at the sole of your right foot and stick your big toe up your nose. Wrap your left leg around your neck."

I walk out. I'd rather do time.

WHO TOOK THE PLAY OUT OF PLAY?

I call off work for the rest of week. I have time; I may as well use it. I remain in bed for the next three days until my body recovers from my attempt to stretch it into odd shapes.

On the fourth day, I look on the Internet for a play I can go see, so the doctor will know I am cooperating. There is one called

Bluebird. They have a cheap matinee and open seating. The cheap meets my requirements.

I arrive at the theater in time to get a good seat, close to the front. The theater is three-quarters full, so this must be a winner. I am ready for that better space now and prepare myself to be entertained.

The woman sitting beside me whispers how great the story is and what good acting there is in this play. I hope she's right, and I am happy to waste an afternoon here getting to a better space.

The first act of the first scene takes place in a dirty efficiency apartment, which looks as depressed as I feel. There are only two people in the entire play, a girl and a guy. He has on shorts and a khaki shirt. She has on a black and brown dress. They have matching brown hair in their brown efficiency.

The girl is talking to the guy about how his mother died. The mother died in her sleep. He talks about how she could not feel her feet. How sad. The girl lifts her right leg showing off her foot, which is in a black stiletto heel. She rotates her ankle. I guess to make sure she is not dying.

The woman beside me is either the author of this drivel or the parent of one of the performers. She claps at every pause. At intermission, she is on her feet applauding while I am trying to wipe the sleep from my eyes. I wish I could take them out and clean the lens. It would also help if I could move the time clock back to the moment before I thought coming to see this shit was a good idea.

Our hapless couple returns to the stage. I watch as—for her own good—he puts a chain around her waist and locks her to the heating register before he leaves. She has a drug problem and this way, he doesn't have to worry about her going out to get high. She allows him to chain her, without protest. They do not appear to like each other very much. They have no pleasant conversation. It is mostly her antagonizing him and vice versa. They really need to let each other go.

They have enough problems to make mine look insignificant. They both have drug problems, and they have birds in their apartment flying around randomly. Bluebirds, hence the title.

From one depressing event such as not having food to another such as having the audience watching them, our hero and heroine have each other. I don't think the togetherness is doing them much good. Their bizarre relationship thoroughly depresses me.

I get to the ending and wish someone had spoiled it for me. Then I could have left at intermission. There is a sick beauty in the finale. They both die—him from an overdose of heroin and her from an under dose of acting ability.

I paid to come here. Thankfully, it was a matinee. Otherwise, I would have had to dress for this bullshit. The author/mother is on her feet, cheering and clapping enthusiastically. I want to slap her, but that may not play well in front of the judge. He might think I have an anger management problem. He would understand if he saw the play, but I can't risk it.

She asks me, "Have you ever seen anything so moving?"

I could go with the laxative answer, but she is serious. There are tears in her eyes. There are tears in my eyes. I made them watch this all the way through. "I must say I have never seen anything to compare with this performance," I respond. This is true. I have never seen a boil on the ass of a rhinoceros, oozing pus. The boil would be preferable to sitting through *Bluebird*.

"Thank-you. The heroine was my daughter. This is her first starring role. I am so proud of her I could burst," she shares. Then she smiles at me as if we are now best friends.

"Oh, my." I have to stop talking or I will ask her why she did not dissuade her daughter from pursuing a career for which she obviously does not have enough talent to play a coma victim. As a mother, she should have called for the curtain to be closed, went on the stage, grabbed her daughter by the hand, and taken her to the head doctor, maybe the one I'm seeing, and gotten her some help to get over her delusions of possessing any acting ability. I'm in a good mood I guess, because I just smile, nod my head, and leave.

As for cheering me up and relieving stress, this rates right up there with getting a herpes outbreak. I do not ever want to see another play in my entire life. As a matter of fact, I do not want to see anything or anyone. I wonder if I can go through the rest of my life with my eyes closed. Seeing has not gotten me anywhere. I'm tired of what I have seen, and I'm definitely not in a better place.

I head home. If I could chain Robert to a heating register, I could keep him there until he came to his senses. I might have to beat him occasionally, but I'm up to the task. If he would snap out of this and say we will stay together, then I would not be afraid. Instead, I take a shower and get ready for bed, and what I hope will be a good night's sleep. I go to the space between sleep and awake. I catch the scent of an elusive perfume, feel familiar arms comforting me, and drift off to sleep.

◌⃝◌

BACK AT THE DOCTOR

Monday I get up and go to work, and it continues to be routine. Nothing new or unusual. It is winding down. Harold is encouraging in his own way. The reality is closing in—I am losing my job and my husband. The week is passing slowly.

Robert is in and out of the house. With each coming and going, he never wants anything other than for me to sign the papers, if he deigns to speak to me at all. He thinks he can wear me down.

My next doctor visit is on my mind when I get up on Thursday. I know she is going to ask me stupid questions. I dress and head to see this woman I am not sure is really qualified to talk to me about the sun about shining. I go anyway. I wonder what she would do if her husband of many years left her high and dry the way Robert is doing to me. I'll bet that would change her better-space attitude.

"Hello, doctor," I state. I don't care how she is, and it is a pleasure to prevent myself from asking.

"Hello, Lynn. I am wondering if you took the opportunity to try a yoga class or see a play. Were you able to find a better space, somewhere less stressful?"

"I did try the yoga class for relaxation. I don't think it is going to work for me though," I share with her.

"Why not, Lynn?"

"Well, I had some positional problems. My body does not like to pose. I did not relax. I was very afraid I was going to pull something or break my damn neck. Do you really think I need yoga in order to get to this better space you are so quick to mention?" It could be my tone or maybe it is what I'm saying. In any event, she stops faking attention and looks at me.

"Positional problems?" she asks.

"Yes, my head does not want to go up my ass. I found it very challenging. In addition, I get dizzy when I bend at the waist. I cannot lift both legs off the floor and balance on my finger, and I don't want to be a tiger crotch."

"Lynn, I think maybe yoga was not the way."

My look says thank-you Doctor Brilliant.

"Did you try a play?" That was her other "get to a better place" suggestion.

"Yes."

"How was the play?" is her determined question. "Did you enjoy it?"

"No. I went to the play to relax. I didn't. I hated the play. It was bad—bad acting, bad premise, bad everything. It was about two junkies, who were both crazy as hell. He chained her to the register whenever he left home. In the end, they both died. I don't feel any more relaxed, although, it did give me some ideas. If only they were legal. I was pissed I paid money to see it even though it was half price. My husband is still leaving me, and then there is my soon-to-be-unemployed status."

"Tell me what you are doing during the day," she wants to know. Probably so she can figure out a way to order more torture.

"I'm not doing anything. I am home or working." When I say it aloud, it sounds pathetic. I probably should not tell her about the visions of Mr. M.O.P., the auditory hallucinations, smelling the perfume or him holding me at night. She might think I am crazy, and I know I'm not.

"Umm, Lynn, I think we really need to try the medication." She is dedicated to medicine.

"I do not need medication," I remind her.

"In the past ten years, tell me about the best you have ever felt," she queries.

I have to think about this for a few seconds, not because I am thinking of an answer. I don't know if I want to say it aloud and to a stranger.

"Once, for two weeks, I almost found myself, and then I ran back to the safety and security of home. I started writing a book and almost completed it. I put it in my memory trunk because Robert said he didn't think I had anything to write that people would find interesting. I loved writing, and he didn't even bother to read it. I have been keeping the peace for thirty-two years, changing my opinion to fit his, saying what he wanted to hear instead of what I believe." I pause for a second and then continue.

"Not cursing because he doesn't want to kiss anyone with a dirty mouth. I've lived thirty-two years of speaking in soothing dulcet tones, because real ladies don't yell. Doing everything, I could think of to keep my family intact, instead of allowing myself to be me. Now he is leaving me. This bastard, this cock-sucking son of a bitch is still leaving me."

"Are you angry?" she wants to know.

"No, I'm not angry at all." I never thought I was angry.

"When was the last time you looked in your memory trunk?" she probes.

"I don't know." I don't want to tell her. It is too personal.

"Why not look it over, see what is there? I am also strongly recommending you to try medication for two weeks. Try it, please, and see if it improves your mood." She is starting to sound firm about the medication.

"Do you honestly think I need medication to get to the better space?" Maybe I am angry or depressed and don't know it.

"Yes." She answers unequivocally.

"Why not, nothing else seems to work." This is turning out even worse than I expected.

"Lynn, I would like to see you back in two weeks to see how the medication is working. I'll have your prescription at the receptionist area for you to pick up when you make your next appointment." She gathers up her belongings signaling the end of our time together.

I dutifully make my appointment, pick up my prescription, and leave her office in the same space I arrived.

MEDICATION, SCHMEDICATION

I stop at the pharmacy and get the prescription for my better space—my happy pills. People are moving in and out of the store because it's rush hour. I don't hear the sounds of the people or the cars I barely dodge because I don't see them. Actually, my world is coming increasingly quiet. I pop two pills and head home, ignoring the caution to not take them and drive.

I go in and decide to put something on to eat. I don't know what to have. I do not want to use the menu for the week. It is the last menu anyway since Robert has not made anymore. I decide on baking some chicken and vegetables. I am not hungry, but I can't remember the last time I ate. I put everything in the oven then head to the living room, pop two more happy pills, and take a seat to think.

"Mom, we need to talk." Rene appears in front of me.

"Hello and how are you? What do we need to talk about?" I do not feel like company.

"There is food burning in the kitchen. I just turned it off. You didn't hear me knocking at the door. You didn't answer your telephone. I'm concerned you're not talking with us about how you are feeling. I saw on a show that when people who have been married for a long time are getting a divorce, they should stay in close contact with their family."

"Do I look like I want to talk?" I ask her without heat. My brain isn't working quite right. How did the food burn when I just put it on?

"No, Mom it's not just that. It's just, well; you seem to be getting strange. You aren't taking this so well. You didn't smell the food burning, and it looks like you're losing weight."

"Well, that's what happens when you don't eat." I state the fact she should already know.

"See. If daddy were here, you would have to cook for him. You wouldn't be losing weight." She shares this as if it is not obvious.

"I think I lost all the weight I need to or rather it lost me. I'm one hundred and ninety pounds lighter since your father left me. That's what I am like it or not. I don't want to talk about this anymore. When I feel like eating, when I can appreciate my food again, I'll eat."

"Mom, we need to stay close." Her voice is close to breaking. I do not want to have to comfort her when I can't comfort myself.

"You're right dear. I've got to get somewhere now. Let yourself out. I'll talk to you later." I try to appease her.

"Really, we need to talk about an intervention." She doggedly states without moving an inch.

"Not now, Rene." The fruit of my loins is rotten.

"Promise me we will get together over the next week then," she wheedles.

"I can't. I don't know what I will be doing," is my response.

"Promise me or I'm not leaving." She folds her arms and puts a determined expression on her face.

"Okay, I promise. We will get together over the coming week," I tell her so she will find her way to the door.

She believes me and heads out. After she leaves, I go to the kitchen and survey the damage. I shouldn't cook and take happy pills. I clean up the mess and admit I have no appetite.

I decide I need another week off work and leave a message on Harold's line informing him I'll be using more of my vacation time. Then I head to the basement to see my memories.

In the basement, in the family room in a large metal trunk four feet by three feet is all the history. The trunk has two shelves inside on top of a large storage area. The first shelf holds photographs of the children from birth through now. Under that in the second shelf are their school report cards, plates, handprints, cards, and other keepsakes. In the largest storage area, is the out-of-season clothing.

At the bottom of the trunk in a black cloth shoulder bag are the memories of him. The last addition was made after his death three years ago. I pull out my attempt to commemorate our time together. My book has over one hundred pages, and it's a travelogue intended to show the world what I had experienced in cities from Cleveland to Tijuana.

Robert caught me writing one day and decided to show an interest in my activity. Probably because it was giving me so much pleasure and had nothing to do with him. When I told him I was writing a book, he laughed until tears were streaming from his eyes. He told me not to be silly. I didn't have anything to put into a book. I packed up what I had written and put it with my other memories.

I look at the whiskey we got at the distillery in Tennessee. I take out the push-up bras and corset from Las Vegas. I hold gold chains that had bound us together to experience each other on a physical, mental, and spiritual level—the elusive orgasm. This was my time-out-of-time experience. Since I live almost alone, I take these things up to my room. They give me comfort and sorrow in equal parts. Comfort for what was and sorrow for what might have been. The intense desire to cry lets me know it is time for more happy pills.

I get into bed, happy pills by my side. They do not seem to be working. I sleep for a while, think about getting up, and continue to sleep. For a time, I stay in bed with my eyes wide open. I get up and start to leave my room before I realize I don't have anywhere to go. It must be happy pill time.

I watch the window. Light follows dark. Dark follows light. Light follows dark. I have to get rid of the light. It is hurting my eyes. I close the curtains, and there is only dark. I just want the dark. I will not turn on the light.

I slide to the floor and continue to sit. I don't know what is going on in the world. I feel nothing. I sit. I don't feel cold even though I'm naked. I don't feel anything. I don't feel the tears falling onto my thighs, until my hand slips in the moisture, as I try to get up off the floor to sit on the bed.

I don't see the light and dark, day and night. I have not eaten for some time. Taste eludes me. I can't distinguish steak from custard, so I'm not hungry. I want to keep sitting and taking happy pills.

I have not bathed for I don't know how many dark to light day to night times. It doesn't seem important to me. I can't smell myself. Maybe I stink; maybe I don't. I don't care. There is probably bad food in the kitchen. I don't care. I am going to keep sitting here. I still won't care. I'm going to sit here and keep taking my lying happy pills. If I wake up dead, I still will not care.

Then the random thoughts come. If you put a pickle in a banana peel, you can grow it on a bush. Quarters could fly if they are dipped in chocolate. I could fry a pillow if I could find a pot big enough. Sam Walton was abducted by aliens and travels between Mars and Communist China. They plan to join forces and merge Indiana, Illinois, and Ohio to form one super state that will crown Sam Walton king and sell Chicago to Communist China. Gout and the bird flu were created by Wal-Mart to destroy poor people.

I stagger up and go to the bathroom. As I wash my hands, I look into the mirror. I do not recognize the woman there. I see her outline, but I don't see her. The history in her face, the knowledge she can succeed and move past the chasm of self-pity she seems unable to climb out of right now. I do not see me. I don't see me in the present and I can't even contemplate a me in the future. I don't know where I have gone, and I don't care if I come back. Life is too hard for me to bear.

I try to tell myself to snap out of this bad, soulless place, but I don't hear me. My mouth is moving, but I don't get the message. It falls on deaf ears. I go back into the bedroom. At first, I don't feel the tears falling down my face and onto my breasts. My hands brush them away as I wrap my arms around myself. My arms are covered by the replacement tears coming from the never-ending faucet with the unstoppable drip that my eyes have become.

The cold of the room does not penetrate the frigid, rigid screen I have built to freeze myself. I guess I will stay this way until some unknown point in the future, when I will thaw enough to truly feel again.

SERENDIPITY

After some period of time, I take more happy pills. They seem to be working. I don't feel stressed at all. I go to bed and stay there. My bed is becoming my lover; it comforts me. My bed accepts me as I am. My bed lets me cry and holds me close. My bed keeps me warm. My bed, I love you. I don't want to leave you. Ever. I pull the blankets over my head.

"Lynn."

How did anybody get in here? From my place under the blankets, I consider answering. I reject the thought as too much work. I remain under the blankets. Unmoving and uncaring of the fact my killer knows my name.

"It's time to get up," the accented voice whispers to me.

I remember the voice. It has haunted my days and my dreams. It is from a time when I ran away and was not missed by anyone. My one foray into adultery.

"Lynn."

Yes, it sounds familiar.

"Come," the voice beckons me.

I have heard that word from that voice before. In two weeks of reality and five years of dreams. How could it be him? He died onstage in Vancouver about three years ago.

"Come," he demands of me, stronger this time.

The blankets are sliding down and off my body. They continue to slide determinedly toward the end of the bed. I make a grab to keep them from falling, and to keep me from facing my past. They fall silently to the floor. I close my eyes. With the way I've been seeing lately, I must be blind. I might as well leave them open.

Standing at the foot of the bed is Mr. M.O.P., my one indiscretion.

"Am I dead?" I ask him in awe. Death doesn't feel like I thought it would. This ain't so bad.

"No, sweetheart. I came for you," he gently speaks.

I have a fear of ghosts, but he is special. "That is nice of you. I'm ready to die. Everything is gone. My life doesn't mean anything. Will I die lying in the bed like this? Where are we going anyway? I can't go to Abraham's bosom. I'm not Jewish. Mohammed doesn't need to give me twelve virgins because I wouldn't know what to do with them. Is this going to be painful? I was hoping for a quick, painless death." I think I may be rambling.

He starts laughing. "You are not going to die. You are going to live."

"For what? Everything is gone. You even left me. I am a terrible wife and an even worse girlfriend. No one really wants me for me. They only want me for what I can do for them. I think I would much rather stay here in bed." I make a grab for the blankets. They move further across the room away from me. I get up to face him.

"What are you doing, lying there?"

"I seem to have lost myself. I have this shell that remains, and it wants to remain in bed."

"You are no longer sensing passion," he observantly states.

In a mumble I explain, "I am no longer sensing anything. The passion I brought back from my time with you is long gone. I have even hidden away what I wanted to share of you through my passion. Now there is nothing. I don't feel anything. All my senses are on hold, and my husband is divorcing me. The doctor put me on happy pills, and this is me happy." I turn to climb back in bed and hug the pillow close to my chest.

"You must allow yourself experiences to sense passion again," he urges me, as if I could be any different.

"How dare you come back here? You left me. You died. Now you show up. For what? So you can leave again? So I can miss you again? What the hell do you want from me? I've got nothing left to give. Nothing. Damn it all to hell, what do you want?" I force the words through an emotion-clogged throat, but my voice breaks at the end of my tirade.

"I want you to live not merely exist, waiting to die. To relish your existence instead of wallowing in what you believe to be loss. I want you to recognize that you have the ability and the capacity to start, no, to *continue* to live. Without the job you didn't really love. Without a husband who was more a roommate. I want you to sense from within your own strengths. Utilize all your senses and step forward. To remember when you, when we, did find passion. To become the woman you were meant to be." He tells me this as he removes the pillow and attempts to gather my body into his arms.

"I'd rather stay in my bed. It is unchanging," I tell him, as I turn away and reach for my happy pills.

"Come, everything has the opportunity to get better. What's really holding you back?"

Hearing those words trigger memories of how and when we met. He sat beside me, mesmerized me, and offered me the opportunity to find passion with him by asking the same question years ago. I did run away for two outstanding weeks before I came back home to the bastard I married. I made the choice to keep intact a marriage my husband is now dashing in my face without much thought or consideration for me.

"Where are we going, if I was going?" I inquire as if I am really going anywhere with him.

He responds, "This is your journey to reclaim yourself, to sense passion."

"Are you coming with me?" Maybe I will consider going somewhere with him, otherwise I can be here by myself.

He smiles before reminding me, "We are connected through lives and past lives. However, this is your journey. You have to sense the passion in each city for yourself."

"I don't know if I can do this. I do have a life here." I don't want to leave what little security I have left, my home.

"I know you're not really living now. All your senses have dulled. Come." He has not changed at all. He still makes me want more of him.

I start to tell him why I can't come with him, as I did on the plane. The reasons I gave then had to do with a husband. That reasoning doesn't apply. Besides, I could no more deny him now than I could deny him five years ago.

"Okay. I'll go." I crawl out of bed to stumble toward the bathroom. As the water is running into the tub, I think about what I'm leaving behind. Nothing. The children are firmly settled in their own lives. Robert has certainly moved on with his life. I'm the only one who's stuck.

I get into the tub and feel the aftereffects of the happy pills. If I just slip into the water and stay there, everything could be over. I'm tired of living anyway. I start a downward slide, like his hands used to do on my ass.

"What are you thinking about," is the question from his perch on the sink.

How did he get in here? Oh. He is a ghost. He can do stuff like that. "Nothing," I mumble and begin to clean myself.

Back in my room, I start to get ready. My overnight case had not seen the light of day since my fate touched my Great Britain trip. It comes out to get some action now. "What should I pack? How long will I be gone? Where am I going? What day is it?"

"You worry too much. You are going to Indiana. Pack enough for three days. The weather is cool so pack warm. You only need casual clothes. Today is Wednesday."

I respond with, "Wednesday, huh. No one wants me, and no one will miss me. I'm not worried. I'm asking because I don't want to be naked. I want to be prepared."

"Sweetheart, you are so much more than you allow yourself to be. Take this journey. It will be wonderful."

"How am I going to get there? I don't have a ticket." Driving is not an option, and I can't fly without a ticket.

"You will fly, as you were meant to do in life. Go to the airport. All arrangements have been made. You will need to be there by three this afternoon," he instructs me.

"Are you going with me?" There is no response. I look around for him, but I am alone. Maybe it was just my happy pills in high gear. I must have lost my mind. I reach for the beautiful bottle of forgetfulness. I need to get back in bed.

"GO!" resounds through the room, accompanied by the unmistakable scent of Caesar's Woman.

I complete my packing and think about how I will get to the airport. I do not want to tell anybody I am leaving. It would be difficult to explain why or anything else about this trip.

What could I say? The man I had an experience with five years ago when I was supposed to be going to the United Kingdom came and told me to go to Indiana? Of course, he has been dead for a few years now, but we were uncommonly close. I decide to catch a cab.

TASTING BLOOMINGTON

HOW CAN YOU MAKE WICHITA LOOK BUSY

On the ride to the airport I wonder what will happen if the plane goes down. Nobody will know to look for me on the list of casualties. I should call and tell someone where I'll be. Even if the plane doesn't go down, what if the plane's hijacked?

I inhale the scent of Caesar's Woman, and it calms me. I remember hearing the olfactory sense has a straight line to the brain and triggers memories. It's true because the scent, which reminds me of hot sex, has me thinking about the past instead of worrying about the flight to come. If the plane goes down, someone will inform my family I was onboard. Besides, it's not as if anyone would miss me.

At the airport, a glance at the clock tells me it is one forty-five. I have no idea which airline will fly me. How the hell am I supposed to get on a plane that goes to Indiana at three when I don't know which plane to get on? I certainly do not want to look suspicious and have the security guards notice me wandering aimlessly. They might think I am trying to escape prosecution. The security guards are whispering to each other and pointing my way. Am I allowed to leave the state?

There is a screen with departing flight information in my line of vision. It indicates what airline is going to Indiana. In bright blinking neon pink, I see an arrow along the back wall. It is pointing toward Delta, and I head in the Delta direction. At the counter, I step up when it is my turn.

"I need to check in for Indiana."

"We need to see your identification." The airline attendant informs me.

I pull out my driver's license. I could be turned away at this point and realize I am truly devoid of sense. I haven't purchased any tickets anywhere. As the desk attendant inspects my identification, I think about how easy it would be to get a cab back home.

"Do you have a seating preference?" she wants to know.

"Who me? Uhm, no."

"Your seat is nine B, a window seat. Please go directly to gate B seven, as your plane is almost ready for boarding. Enjoy Indianapolis."

I make it toward B seven, through security, to the gate. In the line, I can't believe I am actually leaving Wichita for Indiana by myself. Once on the airplane, I start to doubt my decision again. What the hell am I doing here? I don't know anybody in Indiana. Where will I sleep—on the street or will I be staying in the airport like the people on the news?

When I get in my seat, the aisle seat is empty. I will be able to spread out. As we prepare for takeoff, the flight attendant starts the safety instructions. She goes over what to do in the event of an emergency over water. Damn. Are we going over water? This is not welcome news. I pay close attention because this information may come in handy.

I haven't been on a plane in five years. I have gotten over the abject terror of takeoff and landing, but this water stuff, I don't know about that. It doesn't sound safe at all. I don't want to fly over more water than I can swallow.

I look out of the window as the earth gets farther and farther away from me. My heart starts to beat faster and sweat starts to form under my arms. My head is getting light, and I may pass out because my breathing is quick and shallow. I don't have a parachute in case of a true emergency. I should call the flight attendant.

"Hello."

I turn to my seatmate who has deigned to arrive. "Hello. You're here," is the only semi rational thought I have to tell Mr. M.O.P. His smile still has the power to make my vagina moist. "You're here," I smile and repeat myself. "You're here."

"Through life and lifetimes." He takes my hand as he did on numerous flights years earlier.

My heart rate slows. My breathing slows and becomes deeper. My head remains light because I am in such close proximity to this special man. We continue to Indiana.

I feel my eyes get teary. This should not feel so right. I start to think about us, as if we belong together. Surprisingly, I go to sleep with his hand in mine. The feeling of safety and contentment make sleep easy and untroubled, and permeated with visions of us.

When I wake up, the plane is preparing to land in Indianapolis. I am alone and come alive, feeling the afterglow of dreaming about him. Of course, if I were at home, I would be sitting in my room feeling sorry for myself. I would be losing time taking happy pills. A plane to Indiana is better than having a pity party at home.

Once off the plane, I don't know where I am going. The scent of familiar cologne gets me heading toward the car rental area. I see my name on the board in the back of the attendant and walk up to confidently state, "I believe I have a reservation here." A glance at the place where I saw my name shows it has been replaced with the company name and logo. I hand over my driver license.

'Yes, you do. We have a luxury car ready for you to pick up."

"A luxury car? A compact will be fine. A luxury car is unnecessary." Robert always said luxury cars were a waste of money.

"The reservation is for a luxury car. We just need your signature. There is no need for you to return it on full. The gas for the reservation has been purchased. You can bring it back empty. Have a nice trip."

"Trip?" I thought this was my trip.

"Our records indicate you are driving to Bloomington," the attendant informs me.

"Yes, yes, I am." Where the heck is Bloomington, and why am I going there?

Ms. Helpful lets me know, "We have included a map to your hotel in the glove compartment. Go straight out of the door and turn right to the pickup area."

"Thank-you." I go toward the car and give my paperwork to the car pickup person. He gives me a Chrysler 300 for my driving pleasure.

I look at the map to see I am in for an hour-long ride. Bloomington is fifty-two miles southwest of Indianapolis and is about as familiar to me as a pair of mink panties. I never heard of it before. I've lived fifty-five years blissfully unaware of Bloomington's existence. As I pull out of the airport, I wonder what there is to experience in Bloomington. I find the freeway and head out 70 West to find out.

My driving adventure consists of: trees, trees, and trees. Scary barren, empty spaces where trees used to be. More trees, trees, trees.

This car better not break down or my body will never be found.

Then, still more trees, trees, trees.

Finally, I encounter signs of civilization. They give me hope.

I drive until I hear, "Turn here."

I look over at the voice. "Well, fancy meeting you here. Where am I going?"

"To your hotel," he informs me.

"I know that much. I have been driving out here by myself, and now you show up. I could have been attacked." Now that civilization is at hand, I am angry he left me alone.

He has the nerve to ask, "By whom?"

"By crazed lunatics who live in this forest. I have been driving through some rough territory." I am surprised he didn't know this being a ghost, coming, and going as he has been.

"You didn't need me."

"What? Of course I did." Then I think about what I just said.

He wants to know, "For what?"

"For, for, for…. Well I just did." I didn't want to tell him it hadn't occurred to me I actually could do this by myself. At the same time, I acknowledge to myself, I didn't need him.

"I am here through life and lifetimes," he comforts me.

I give a loud sniff to show my displeasure. My mother, the queen of sniffs, would have been proud. "Where is the hotel?" Inside I am proud of my accomplishment. Who would have thought I could drive somewhere by myself.

"We're going just ahead, on your left."

I pull into a hotel right off of the freeway. It looks safe enough. In the lobby, I look around to see if there are loiterers or undesirables. The lobby is empty except for the desk clerk. So far, so good.

She looks up. "Hello. Do you have a reservation?"

Aside from the fact there does not appear to be a crowd waiting to get into this place, it looks clean and decent. I have no idea if I have a reservation, so I wordlessly give her my driver's license.

"We have you down for a three-night stay, leaving Saturday. Check-out is at noon. Enjoy your stay." She gives me the keycard, my license, and a smile. I wonder if she can tell this will be the first time I have spent a night in a hotel room alone by the way my hand is shaking as I take my key.

Heading to the room my only thought is to sleep and continue my plane dreams. I'm no longer angry with Mr. M.O.P. The room is basic—two queen-size beds, a spacious bathroom, television, and refrigerator. I make sure to lock the door, so no one can come in and kill me.

Turning from the task, I wonder what I will do tomorrow. I should probably eat, but I am not hungry. I also don't want to go back out since it is getting dark. I contemplate calling the children and discard the idea. The call would generate too many questions.

Instead, I go to bed and immediately fall asleep. During the night, I wake up once because I feel myself drifting to Robert's side of the bed. Through my sleep haze, I remember Robert is not here, and I stay in the middle of the bed.

In the morning, I head out in search of nourishment. A restaurant next door makes me decide to sample the local fare. The small eatery is practically empty, and a sign at the front directs diners to Seat Yourself.

In a booth with a view of the freeway instead of the kitchen, I sit contemplating my life. What the hell am I doing here? Mr. M.O.P. has yet to put in an appearance yet today. I could turn tail and run home, except there is no one there either. Why bother? I order the mega breakfast: pancakes, sausage, bacon, hash browns, and eggs. It also comes with coffee.

The breakfast is terrible. The pancakes are crunchy, and the bacon is soft. The sausage has an extra helping of salt, and the hash browns are not brown. The eggs are chirping, and the coffee tastes the way I would imagine industrial strength cleaner would taste. Next time I'll order a vomit sandwich with sludge on top as the condiment. It couldn't taste any worse than this.

After breakfast, instead of heading back to the hotel, I drive around and see what there is to see in Bloomington. I drive twenty miles to the right of the hotel. Nothing to see there. I backtrack, turn left at the hotel, and drive twenty miles. More nothing. I go back to the hotel and go forward from the hotel in search of signs of life. Nothing. The largest facility I see is the stadium where the local college plays football or basketball or jai lai. I return to the hotel intersection and head in the opposition direction for twenty miles. There is nothing in that direction either.

How in the world can you drive for twenty miles in each and every direction and not find a thing worth looking at? NOTHING. Why did I let Mr. M.O.P. convince me to come to this barren, unfriendly, uninhabited godforsaken slice of hell?

Now it is time for dinner. I go to another local restaurant; not many people are there. I wait for the hostess to seat me, as the sign says she will. She does not appear. Other employees are wandering around. They do not offer to assist me.

I stop one and ask, "Could you get the hostess?"

I stay in what is not a line since I am the only one there for another ten minutes. There is still no sign of a hostess. When she finally does come, I look at her before I decline the invitation to follow her.

Her dress has stains, and she has an open, three-inch sore on her uncovered forearm. Her blond and green hair is worn in a Mohawk. The style allows a view of the decoration of ears rings, studs, and chains as they go around her ear from top to bottom and connect with the chain in her nose. Something is crawling up the middle of her chest.

She effectively ruins my appetite. In addition, I am convinced someone in this restaurant would spit in my food, and I wouldn't know if the blood was from undercooked meat or the PMSing cook. I leave for whatever other place there is to eat. Thankfully, there is a steakhouse a few doors up. It may be promising.

I am seated, and my order is taken immediately. I get my steak and baked potato back pretty quickly after ordering. Unfortunately, dinner is a continuation of breakfast only in a more elegant surrounding. More sludge topped vomit. The steak refuses to be cut by anything as tame as a steak knife. They should have served it with a chainsaw. I chew the fat, literally, to get a little nourishment.

Unintentionally I begin counting down the hours until I can put this place out of my conscious thought and head back to Wichita. Is there anyone in Bloomington with the ability to cook a decent meal? Bloomington has no redeeming social value except to keep this area of Indiana from being a barren wasteland. Moreover, it is not doing a very good job of that.

Once back in the room, I watch the walls for any sign of Mr. M. O. P. Nothing. I should have brought along my happy pills. They might improve my mood. Television holds no appeal, and I don't have a good book. I go to bed instead. Sleep does not come easily. It has to fight through my questions regarding my own sanity to claim my attention.

Friday, after getting up and dressed, I go to the front desk to do what I should have done yesterday. I ask the clerk what there is to see. The clerk looks at me with a blank expression before asking, "In Bloomington?"

No, in Atlanta. "Yes, I wanted to see the city. What do you recommend?" I reiterate.

"I can't think of anything," is her honest answer.

I go back to my room and try to sleep to sleep off the lingering effects of the happy pills and heartache. In late afternoon, I test fate once again and go to a fast food restaurant. There is a quality of sameness that permeates fast food worldwide, and I am ready for anything edible at this point. They do not disappoint. It may not be haute cuisine, but it is the best thing to enter my mouth since I arrived in this city. I spend the remainder of the day endlessly walking around seeing more nothing.

The next morning, I am up by ten. Lying in bed, I wonder what will become of me. Those thoughts are guaranteed to depress, so I try to focus on brighter thoughts and a better space. This trip has not been productive, aside from getting me out of the house. Now it is time to checkout, a thought guaranteed to bring a smile to my face.

∞

JUST A SIP

Driving back to Indianapolis, I see billboards for a winery alongside the highway. It has guided tours on Saturdays. I definitely have time to stop. This is the first thing of interest I have found in the entire state.

I pull into the parking lot of the Clee Winery. The building entrance is the country store. Stone renderings of faces greet everyone inclined to enter. There is more artwork from Indiana artists, paintings, and limestone sculptures scattered on the walls. Dips, cheese, and sweets complement the wide variety of wines. The center of the store boasts a large area off to the left where you can taste the wines.

The tour of the winery will start in ten minutes. I should broaden my horizons. Todd the tour guide calls out to interested visitors five minutes before the tour will begin. I get in the group that follows him out of the back door. There are over one hundred acres to the winery. It started in the seventies by a woman who saw Indiana as the California of the Midwest. In the 1980s, her son Brian took over.

"Clee is Indiana's oldest and largest winery. The vineyards were replanted in 2000, and we buy grapes from all over the country. We use oak barrels to make dry reds, which take six months to two years to make. Wine barrels are not placed on the ground when they are filled because the flavor would run out," Todd shares as if we are the first people he ever told this joke.

We head out to a dome shaped area to see the lined stainless steel tanks constructed to hold up to a thousand gallons. "Clee uses a cold stabilization process in their enology, the fancy term for wine making. This removes potassium from the wine. They bottle thirty-five thousand bottles per day. The wine has to remain in cooling jackets to keep the temperature even." The fountain of information, Todd, continues.

"There is a valve at the bottom of each tank. This valve is opened periodically to remove the sediment that settles at the bottom of the wine tank. A centrifuge spinner removes other particles to make the wine clear. It is also important that oxygen be kept out of the wine process. Otherwise the wine would look cloudy, and the taste would be ruined," Todd informs.

The entire tour takes about twenty minutes. I go back into the general store and take part in the wine tasting. Tasters may select six wines for five dollars. I try the Pinot Grigio, Chardonnay Merlot, Shiraz, and the peach and blackberry flavored wines. Surprisingly, as they flow over my tongue, I can taste the robust and subtle flavors of each. I decide to purchase what will be a case and have it shipped to Wichita. I also get a bottle of Merlot to slip in my luggage and take home with me.

I go out and sit at the pond with its sculptures and waterfall. There are picnic tables set up for those who would like to bring lunch and enjoy the grounds. The peace here lulls me into a desire to remain. However, this is just an interlude. I have to go back. Overall, it has been informative and given me a greater appreciation for wine, in addition to sharpening my sense of taste.

I get into the car, back onto I-37, and head to the airport. I check in for my flight without incident. The flight back to Wichita is uneventful, and there is a waiting taxicab to take me home.

On my porch, I do a happy dance with myself before going into the house. I did it. Damn, I did it. I went somewhere I knew no one at all, and I made it back. So what if the trip sucked except for the wine? I did it. Alone and on my own, mostly, I did it.

I head to the kitchen to fix myself something to eat. I settle on a steak and a sweet potato, even though steak is a Wednesday-night food. The wine guide suggested pairing the merlot with red meats. The coupling takes my mouth to a pleasurable place. My taste buds are singing new songs and craving for the excitement. I wish the rest of me were as energetic as my mouth.

I am worn out. I decide not to check the blinking light on the answering machine. It can wait until tomorrow. I go to bed and to sleep with the smell of Caesar's Woman in my nose and a smile on my face.

"Lynn."

The sun streaming in the cracks of the curtained window proclaims morning has arrived. "What do you want? Why did you have me go to such a hellhole by myself?" I ask Mr. M.O.P.

"Tell me what you found," he coaxes.

"Nothing," I respond flatly. He wasn't there so I refuse to share my experiences with him.

My answer is turned into a question. "Nothing?"

"It was a complete waste of time. I hated the city, and there was not a thing to do the whole time. The food sucked, the people were not friendly, and I was miserable." I end with a sniff.

"What about the winery? Did you see it on your way there," he wants to know.

"No, I didn't see on the way there. It winery was nice, but it was on the way back. Besides, I don't want to count it because it was good, and the confession would ruin my complaining.

He starts laughing that deep sound that is contagious. "Well, they didn't just build it for you. You were not ready to experience it until you were on your way back."

"Okay, so the winery was nice. In fact, it was peaceful sitting outside enjoying the view. In addition, I have some great wine coming. It wasn't too bad," is my grudging admission.

"Enjoy," is his parting comment as he disappears as quietly as a cotton ball falling.

GETTING BACK INTO THE MOLD

I dress and prepare to do nothing. In the front room, the answering machine is clamoring for my attention. There are three calls from Lynnette, seven from May, and twelve from Rene. Mom called every day, dad called yesterday to tell me my mom was getting worried about me, and I should be ashamed for making her worry.

Robert left a note on the table that I missed seeing last night. It demands I call him as soon as I arrive home. It also tells me we are out of bread. I plan to call everyone this evening except mom. I call her right away.

"Hi, Mom. I was out of town." I start with an explanation for not calling.

"Out of town? What were you doing out of town? You don't know anyone out of town. I am worried about you."

"I just went away for the weekend." I don't travel at all. For me to go anywhere is cause for attention.

"Away where?" Mom sounds anxious.

"Bloomington, Indiana." I share with her.

There is complete silence on the other end of the line. "Why? There is nothing in Bloomington." It sounds like she has been there before.

"Just to get away."

"Honey, please make sure you check in. I was very worried. I went over and saw your car. I was afraid something had happened to you." Mom sounds relieved and pissed off at the same time.

"I'm sorry, Mom. I'll keep in closer contact," I promise.

"I want you to be safe. I love you," is her concerned response.

"I am, Mom. I'm fine. I love you, too." I hang up knowing before the hour is up, everyone will know I am safe, and I went somewhere, anywhere. Even Indiana.

♋

MY TRAVEL TIP FOR BLOOMINGTON

Don't go all the way there if you can avoid it. Go to the winery and savor the reds.

THE EX FACTOR

MURDER IS STILL ILLEGAL

In the kitchen, I think about what I have to do today. Not much. The telephone demands my attention.

Dottie is on the other end. "Lynn, I want to let you know there will be a court date coming up for the divorce. This will be the preliminary hearing for the judge to possibly issue some temporary orders."

"What does that mean?" I whisper. I don't know why I am whispering. It could be fear.

"Well, Robert wants to get this over as quickly as possible. He wants the divorce to be final yesterday. The only way it can be over quickly is if you cooperate and agree to everything."

"What should I do?" I am confused and need some guidance. I have never done this before. I start deep breathing to help myself focus.

"Just think about how you want this marriage to end," she pushes gently. "We can talk about it after you have had some time to think."

"I don't want it to end." I tell her for the first time. I am speaking loudly now, almost screaming.

"I'm sorry. It has to be hard on you. Think about it okay. We go to court on Wednesday. Do you need me to come over now?" Her voice is calm and soft, almost as if she is speaking to a child. I can hear the concern in her voice.

"No. I'm okay." I lower my voice to show I'm getting myself under control. I'm not okay because my knees and hands are shaking. But, if she comes over, she will be company, and I will feel it is my duty to entertain.

The rest of the day passes in a blur. I go out to be a part of something. There is nothing to lure me and capture my interest. I head to the fast food restaurant and listen to the old guys chew the fat. At least they have a purpose.

When I leave, I remember Robert's note about bread, so I include the grocery store in my travel route. I head to the bread aisle to get the hazelnut, flaxseed, oatmeal, and wheat concoction Robert says we need to eat to stay healthy. It tastes like the underside of a car, but since Robert won't allow any other type of bread in the house, it is what I always buy. I personally hate nutty goodness in every bite. I want soft, carbohydrate-filled badness. I pick up a loaf of potato bread and head to the checkout.

I go home to find Robert there. Good manners dictate I greet him. "Hello," I say in my professional voice. Distant while still bowing to basic manners.

"Where have you been? I've been here several times over the weekend. You weren't here. What do you think you're doing?" Robert has his hands on his hips and obviously expects an answer.

"I went out of town, I'm sorry I didn't tell you," Is my automatic response. I want to bite my tongue at the slip of an apology. I go to the kitchen to get away from him.

"You don't go out of town. How could you go out of town without telling anyone? That's irresponsible of you," He upbraids me

"You're right." I have to stop apologizing. He isn't apologizing for leaving me.

"Why haven't you been at work?" Robert walks closer until he stands in front of me to ask, hands firmly remaining on his hips.

"Umm." I got nothing. I give a shoulder shrug and head roll. My heart starts to beat a little faster.

"I hope you aren't trying to get more money from me in the divorce by getting fired from your job. I'm making you a decent offer. You should take it and be happy. The only thing that will change is we won't be sleeping together, and you are getting too old to be having sex all the time anyway. I still will take care of everything." He removes his hands from his hips to reach out and shake me on my shoulder.

I look closely at him, someone who has shared more than half of my life. I never knew he could be so callous. He takes my silence for consent, as always. Amazing. Did I ever go against him, ever have any backbone?

I jerk away and pull out the loaf of potato bread like it was a flag, and I am in the middle of a patriotic rally. I take my time and open it to pull out two slices and put them on a napkin. Defiantly I ask my soon to be ex, "Would you like a sandwich?"

"Try to be more considerate in the future. I'll expect to hear from you before Friday. In addition, no more going out of town without notifying me. You're supposed to be here in case the children need you." Robert takes a closer look at the loaf of bread still in my hand. "What kind of bread is that? We don't eat bread like that. Throw that stuff away. It's not what we eat here." He turns to leave, secure in my compliance.

I follow him into the hallway. The red heat that started at my ears as I listened to Robert works its way to my brain. The warmth covers my arms and face, forcing my mouth to open. "How dare you. You think I don't enjoy making love? Nevertheless, here is the question. When was the last time you made love to me? When was the last time you touched me, held me, and stroked me? Do you think I don't want to be desired? You arrogant ass, you are completely wrong. Things will not stay the same. I plan to be more active in my own life, without you telling me what to do or what to think or what and how to cook. Those days are over since you're leaving me. And I happen to like potato bread."

Robert looks as if I had stabbed him again. "Clearly you're overwrought. I will talk to you when you are more coherent and less emotional." He leaves and takes his bad karma with him.

I turn and flounce back toward the kitchen, the heat fading as it is replaced by satisfaction. I expressed myself. I go in the kitchen and make myself a grilled cheese sandwich with potato bread. It tastes delicious. If the husband I have wants to eat bread here anymore, he had better develop a taste for potato bread or shopping. I go to bed and sleep like a baby.

THE THREE FURIES AND MOM

Monday, bright and early, the door opens on all three of my off-spring and my mother. They are not here for a regular family visit. This must be the intervention Rene has been threatening.

"Mom, we called your job and found out you weren't at work. We understand you left town," Rene starts the conversation.

"Without telling anyone," May continues.

"And went to Bloomington." Lynnette smiles.

"I had to tell them. They were worried about you," Mom says in an attempt to pacify me.

"I wanted to get away. To get some perspective," I tell them all to prevent the rest of the intervention.

"We were supposed to all get together," Rene forges onward.

"Over the weekend," May forges with her sister.

"And talk about this," Lynnette sounds bored.

"We're worried, and Rene says we need to intervene," Mom holds up her end of the intervention.

I bow to the inevitable. "Let's talk."

The children proceed to tell me how I should behave from now forward. (Stay close to home because Robert may come back.) What to think. (How will I be able to make it up to him since Robert leaving me for Brenda is a midlife crisis.) How to feel. (I will graciously forgive him and happily be the wife he wants.) They sound like Robert.

"I'm sure you all mean well. What I really want is some time for me. It means so much to know you're here if I need you. It's hard, and I don't have all the answers, but give me some space," I plead.

"Are you sure you don't need some more intervention?" Rene asks. I am going to find her television cable and cut it.

"Please don't shut us out," May earnestly pleads. Her concern is touching.

"We love you." Lynnette has a way of baldly stating a fact. She gets it from her grandfather.

"Do you want to move back home?" asks Mom. Bless her heart. She is serious. And delusional if she thinks I want to leave my low-security prison, where Robert pops in and out for the maximum security prison her and Dad represent.

I feel my head to see if I have developed a cocaine habit and am so glad I don't feel addicted. I love the fact they care, but wish they didn't care so much. Since I do not intend to leave town again, it won't hurt to make some concessions to my loved ones. "Thank-you so much. I promise I'll stay in touch. I won't leave town again without letting someone know." It makes me happy to make the promise because I don't have to agree—I choose to agree.

"You girls go on out. I'm right behind you," mom tells her grands. Then she turns to me. "Lynn, you will probably need some money. I have this little something for you. This is just to tide you over the hard times, especially with you going out of town all the time." She reaches into her purse and pulls out a folded check.

"Thanks, Mom, but I'm okay." Money is not a major concern of mine right now.

"Keep it just in case. I know your daddy wants to give you something from us, but this is from me. It may come in handy. If not, put it aside for a rainy day." She presses the folded check into my hand.

I open the check and see that it is for five thousand dollars. "Mom, where did you get this money? You have never worked. Where did you get money?" The name on the check is hers alone. I hope she isn't into selling drugs. Where else do you get a large sum of money without working?

"I have always believed a woman should have a little something just in case. I never needed it, but there is nothing like a plan B. Now take it and use it wisely. If you need more, let me know. I love you." She hugs me and heads out the door. "Lynn, you can make it through this. You are probably better off without him."

"Mom, you can't be serious." I thought she would be disappointed. It cheers me greatly to know she doesn't blame me.

She gives a royal sniff as only she can give and says, "I never liked his pretty ass anyway."

This is a shock. "Mom, I thought you liked Robert."

"I tolerated him because he was what you wanted. He was too bossy. You're better off without him." She hugs me, and it feels like when I was six and came home crying from a bad day at school. Mother comfort still works fifty years later.

Thoughts of tomorrow cloud my mind once peace is restored after the family invasion. I have plans to go to work. I get a shower and exfoliate myself to recover from everything. I don't answer the telephone. I will return calls when I feel like talking. I bask in the glow of absolution before being doused with the reality I am going to bed by myself. It won't be so bad now that I can have the middle of the bed.

In the evening, when I am well rested, I check my answering machine. There is a message from Robert. "Lynn, I want you to get my things packed up. I will pick them up when I get a chance." He doesn't bother with a greeting, only a demand. The bastard.

I think about calling Dottie and imagine the conversation. "Dottie, what do you think would happen if I put everything of Robert's in a large garbage bag with raw fish and limburger cheese?"

Dottie would be silent for a moment then answer, "Remember those stabbing charges that got you into therapy and working on the anger-management issues you say you do not have?"

"Yes," I would hesitantly answer.

"Well, I don't think the court would look too kindly on seeing you again." She would inform me.

"Do you think the judge would know I did it? I don't want any repercussions." I would try to feel her out and keep hope alive.

"Yes," she would state with finality and disabuse any notion I had of escaping detection.

"So, I'm hearing just pack his stuff and leave out the fish," I need to be clear about this.

"Pretty much," she would agree without hesitancy.

"All righty then, gotcha." I would breathe a disgusted breath before hanging up. Curses, foiled again, even in my own mind.

I am going to make myself something good to eat before making the attempt to pack. After eating, I don't feel like packing anything tonight. I call the job to let them know I will be in tomorrow. Once in bed, the cold seeps to the bone. It is not the temperature as much as it is the emptiness. I head to the middle of the bed where the warmth is centered.

I get up and head to work on Tuesday. The day is totally uneventful—mail, e-mails, and telephone calls. I am working by rote, but this is taking away from the time I have to feel sorry for myself.

Unsurprisingly, the end of the day arrives as quietly as the beginning. I head home and do more nothing to while away the hours.

◕◔

REVOLVING COURTROOMS

Dottie calls me in the morning to tell me she will pick me up for court. "How about having some coffee ready? I'll bring doughnuts."

When she arrives, the rich smell of my good coffee that I only brew on special occasions fills the kitchen. It's french vanilla, and costs more per pound than good chocolate with pecans. If this doesn't qualify as a special occasion, I don't know what does.

"Dottie, I'm afraid," I admit. I am tearing up the doughnut instead of eating it. My coffee is being swirled around more than clothes in a washing machine, and I haven't taken a sip yet

"Of what?" Dottie asks around a mouthful of glazed and french vanilla.

"Of the future, of being alone, of everything," I tell her as I watch my spoon doing three sixties around my cup in the grip of fingers that move without me thinking about moving them.

"I can understand, Lynn. It makes sense to be afraid, but it will be fine. How is the therapy going? Is talking about it to her helping?" Dottie asks as she reaches out to still the spinning and hold my hand.

"No. It sucks. She has me taking some kind of happy pills. They do not make me happy." I say with disgust and pick up a piece of a cream-filled doughnut.

"Well, let me see if I can get your court date for the stabbing set and get it resolved. Then you won't have to keep going to criminal court. I think you should find someone you're comfortable with and try to process this through with more therapy. The important part of therapy is finding the right therapist." Dottie looks concerned. She comes around the table and hugs me as if she means it. Hard and long. Then we get down to the good coffee, remaining doughnuts, and conversation.

I appreciate the body contact. "Okay, I'll let you know what I decide to do when I decide. What will happen in court today?"

"Robert will try to have the court adopt his proposal to end the marriage without further delay," Dottie explains as she sips the good stuff and eats a stick doughnut.

"If I sign the papers he keeps bringing for me to sign, what then? Could it be over today? Could my marriage be ended so quickly? It was over thirty years in the making; it should take a long time for it to end. Is there anything I can do?"

"Yes," she flatly responds. "Lynn, sometimes divorces can get messy. Accusations and allegations can be made about each other and people can use time and resources to stretch out a divorce for years. The people tend to get bitter and want to hurt each other instead of getting on with their lives."

"I don't want to end it like that, but I'm not ready to roll over and play dead. I may not be able to stop him from getting a divorce, but I don't want to make it easy for him. I feel like I have made everything easy for him all through our marriage. I want this to take all the time possible. I don't want to agree to anything." I am feeling militant. It should not be this easy to dump me.

"Why, Lynn?" Dottie is looking at me with concern. "I don't want to see you hurt any more than you already have been by this marriage. Why do you want to prolong the inevitable?"

"Because prolonging the divorce is the only thing I can do. The only voice I have that he will hear. The only stand I can make." I try to get Dottie to understand. "I am tired of him running over me, with me taking it like the woman from the play who allowed her boyfriend to chain her to the heating register when he left. For her own good. I know he will get his divorce. I want more time to get used to the idea. Can you feel me on this?"

"Yes, I think I do understand. If that's the way you want it, then that is what I will do." Dottie smiles and hugs me again.

We are ready to leave after four more doughnuts, the remainder of the pot of coffee, and some emotional conversation. We are in agreement regarding how we will proceed, and I am walking straighter than I have in some time.

Finding a place to park is a nightmare, and I am getting anxious about being late even though we could drive around another half hour and still be on time. Finally, Dottie seizes a space in the parking lot two blocks up when someone drives out. We park and head inside.

We enter the courthouse and find our courtroom. It is a cold building with tiled floors and metal seats. Large bolts secure the seats to the floor. I guess it's to discourage people from stealing or throwing them. No one went over the budget on decorating the place. The walls are a stark gray, and the florescent lights serve to illuminate the depression. This is a fitting place for ending marriages.

Dottie goes to sign in with the court officer while I have a seat in one of the secured black metal seats. I look around and see smiling couples, glaring couples, and everything in between. I use the time to try to match up the husbands with the wives and guess who wanted the divorce. I have no way to know if I'm right or wrong, but it serves to pass the time.

Robert enters with a man I guess is his attorney. The attorney is about two heads shorter than Robert is and has a briefcase. His briefcase is larger than his torso, and he is struggling to keep up with Robert's easy stride. The attorney is talking loudly, and he is talking about me. He has to look up at Robert and try to keep pace. He is having a hard time,

"Man, don't worry about anything. I'll have you divorced by this time next week. I know the judge on this, and it will be a piece of cake. I do this all day, every day. This is nothing. Do you hear me? Nothing." Where in the hell did Robert find the littlest lawyer in Kansas with the biggest mouth?

As they pass, Robert barely acknowledges me with a head nod. How can he do that? Not speak after we have shared so many years together? How can he let this shrimp of a lawyer call our marriage nothing? I turn my head to the door of the courtroom and keep it there. The blood is boiling in my veins, and if I were a few shades lighter, my face, ears, and neck would be red. I'm sure the breath coming from my body could melt plastic. It takes all my concentration to not go over and hit the little short cock-sucking son of a bitch on the top of his head. Then kick his client in the space where his balls used to be. I start to rock slowly then gradually faster.

Robert is sitting rigidly in his seat, not allowing his back to touch, so he won't get other people's germs on his suit. He doesn't look over at me. Instead, he pulls out his telephone and dials. He keeps the conversation low. I know he's talking to the tramp he is seeing. He has the nerve to give her a play-by-play of what is going on.

I see Robert's attorney enter the courtroom as Dottie is coming out. He stops her, and they both go into the court. After an hour, they both come back out. Robert's attorney is wearing a frown. My attorney is wearing a smile.

Dottie rushes over to me and says, "Let's get out of here." She grabs me by the arm, and I have no choice but to follow her down the hallway and out the door. "Did you mean it when you said you want to make this difficult for him?"

"Yes."

"Well, here's what we are going to do."

I look back to see Robert's attorney bending down and talking to him. His face starts to form the same frown that his attorney is wearing. He is going to call my name, very sternly, in about eight seconds. I don't want to be around when he erupts. I increase my pace.

Dottie starts to explain our strategy to me as we head home. We stop for nourishment since doughnuts don't give much strength on a stressful day. Over lunch, she tells me she has requested affidavits from Robert.

"I said it's because we believe Robert has been hiding assets. Further, we're asking for spousal support of thirty-five hundred dollars per month. In addition, we want Robert to continue to pay the mortgage on the home and all the utilities. We want him to trade cars with you since your car is older, and you need reliable transportation to travel to and from work. How's that?"

"Damn. That's cold. I don't need spousal support because I have a job. I can also meet the mortgage payments since the house will be paid for in another year. I wouldn't mind having Robert's car, but I would rather get a new one of my own. Was Robert's attorney pissed?"

"As a two-dollar whore missing a fifty-dollar trick. You should have seen him. He started sputtering about how upright his client is and everything. The little guy almost stomped his foot. I would have felt bad if it wasn't so damn funny. Yes, I'd say he was pissed," Dottie laughs. "We are also asking for a restraining order to keep him from removing assets from the checking account or selling anything. We want him to surrender his keys to the residence because his behavior is erratic."

"What. Robert will kill me. When will all this happen?" I am laughing and feeling better about this divorce since I have done something to piss Robert off.

"The judge will review it once I submit it in writing and issue temporary orders within forty-five days. The request for the restraining orders on the assets is a done deal."

Food never tasted so good. Dottie and I laugh over everything. I feel better and more in control than I have since all this started. It feels good to let him know he can't push me around anymore. I can push back damn it. Dottie and I laugh and talk until early evening. When she drops me off, I am happy. I am in the better space the therapist said I needed to attain. In addition, the wine I ordered is on the porch.

After I sit a bit, I get up and gather trash bags. I take Robert's things out of the drawers. While pulling clothes out of the closet, I do not cut all the buttons off his shirts, but the temptation is strong. I do not succumb to the urge to blow my nose on Robert's favorite silk shirt. I load bag after bag of my life and feel the high of success leaving me as I feel more of a failure.

By the time I finish, there are six large trash bags. I tried not to pack them too full so I would not have a problem getting them downstairs. I need a crate or box to put his shoes in for him to pickup. They'll have to wait because I'm out of energy.

Wait a minute. Why should I worry about taking his belongings downstairs? They are his not mine. Let him come up the stairs and get it. In an act of defiance, I move his things to the hallway so I can move around in my bedroom. He is not the boss of me anymore. I go downstairs and open a bottle of Chardonnay.

Thursday morning I go to work and am able to make it through all the mail and e-mail. The amount is decreasing, but still the backup takes all morning. I let Harold know I will be out on Wednesday. I know he understands because he has been divorced twice. There is no reason to tell him the court date is for stabbing Robert.

Over the weekend, I make calls to the children and the parents. I have a meal with each child, and Sunday I have supper with my parents. This meal was a lot smoother than the previous family meal. Overall, it was a good weekend. I felt the love from those I love. I didn't miss Robert and kept to the middle of the bed at night.

Monday and Tuesday are workdays. They follow the same routine except for a visit from Robert. He is in the house when I got home on Tuesday and ready to pounce.

"Lynn, you know this is foolishness. We can work this out between us." This is the Robert I met years ago. He is the smooth talker, able to charm me with words as false as breasts in Hollywood. He is smiling and trying to go for the reasonable sympathetic angle.

"Robert, I won't sign anything. Have your attorney talk to mine about any issues you may have. I don't want you to talk to me." I move past him and go to my bedroom I take a shower and get in the middle of my bed.

My dreams are of my marriage and how content I was with my life. There are flashes of our wedding, the birth of the children, and then graduations. They go right up until the final scene with me standing beside him, and him telling me he wants a divorce. The next morning, I wake up far from refreshed but glad I resisted his attempts to take me back down a well-traveled road last night.

COURTROOM NUMBER ONE, AGAIN

Today I am facing a dilemma. My eyes look like a vision in red. The question is what do you wear to court to convince the judge you are not a violent maniac? That it was a slip of the wrist, a mere accident that your cheating bastard of a husband was cut. Well, maybe I did that shit on purpose, but I will not admit it. I have to try to beat this rap. He was asking for it. Dottie calls me before I can get too deep into paranoid thoughts.

"Lynn, I'll see you at court this morning. I want you to dress conservatively, nothing flashy. Most of all, you have to be remorseful. I have talked to the prosecutor about this. She knows you are genuinely sorry, you have been cooperating with me, and that you're seeing a therapist for your anger-management issues."

She continues, "Even though Robert has admitted it was situational violence because of the surprise of the pending divorce, she is not convinced. He does not want the charges dismissed. You have to fit the image of a remorseful defendant for the court today. Don't forget."

I attempt levity. "So does that mean my salmon-colored suit is out?"

"Lynn!" Dottie warns.

"Okay, okay, I was just joking. I don't even own a salmon-colored suit. I will be there in the 'I'm sorry' colors. I will scream abject remorse. I can do this," I try to convince her.

"Lynn, let's not overdo, okay?" Dottie says with a smile in her voice.

"Okay." If she can smile, it can't be all bad.

I get dressed in a standard blue business suit. I resist the urge to pair it with a canary yellow blouse and opt for an unassuming cream top that buttons to the neck. My one-inch pumps with coffee-colored pantyhose complete my ensemble.

I see Robert coming out of the guest bedroom where he slept in last night. Since the accident, he has not shared our bed. He probably stayed here to make sure I didn't break and run. He has on a turtleneck and Dockers. He doesn't look remorseful. He looks well rested. If I had a knife now, he would look quite different.

"Good morning, Lynn. We'll ride to the courthouse together. And you left my clothes in the hallway."

"Um. You wanted them packed. You can take it from there."

"Come along. You should sign the papers, so I can move out completely."

"Robert, even if I, the mother of your children, have to do time in the big house, I won't sign. I thought I made myself clear last night. What is your hurry?"

"Come along. We can't be late."

He turns and goes down the steps then toward the kitchen. I guess his mind wanders to our last kitchen encounter. He changes directions and goes into the living room.

"Robert, I'm not trying to be difficult. I just need a little time. Is that too much to ask?" I follow him, trying to sound firm.

"That is enough conversation on this topic," he decrees.

"Okay," I say out loud. I can deal with this. He's trying to goad me into stabbing him again. It is not going to work. I have my head on straight. I can handle this.

"Go to the car. I am on my way." Robert tells me.

I get in his car and wait, and then start to feel like a kid. He is probably in there talking to his girlfriend. I could have driven myself. He is not the boss of me anymore. Robert comes out and gets in the driver seat. I promise myself this is the last time I will allow him to drive me anywhere.

We choose not to talk to each other during the twenty-minute drive. To me it seems strange a defendant and a plaintiff would enter the court together, after having ridden in the same car, but it's about to happen.

As we enter, I try to talk to my husband again. "Robert. I really don't mean you any harm."

"I want this divorce over, and if I have to use this incident to make that happen, I will." He tells me this in a low, vicious voice I have never heard from him before. Of course, I've never crossed him before.

"I would not have thought you were so low that you would want me to go to jail." I am trying to remain calm, but it is difficult. How can I convince him we need more time to think this through more thoroughly?

Thankfully, the family shows up. The flurries descend on their father.

"Dad, aren't you going to drop the charges?" Rene questions.

"Mom could not make it in prison," May states.

"Do the right thing, Dad," Lynnette appeals to the better self she thinks he has.

"Robert." Mom and dad acknowledge Robert's presence.

I see Dottie coming out of the courtroom and tell them all, "I need to talk to Dottie to see what is going on." Let them continue their conversation without me. Let Robert explain to them that he wants to have me in jail, so he can have a divorce.

"Go ahead," Robert, allows.

"I wasn't asking permission. I was stating a fact." If I had a knife, I would gladly do the time and put the world out of the misery of having this selfish bastard take air and space. No. Doing time scares the hell out of me, but, if I had more nerve... I head over to Dottie.

"Hi, Lynn, I think we will be able to work the deal. The charges are going to be dismissed. It's a good thing you don't even have a parking ticket, or this couldn't have happened."

I see a smartly dressed brunette talking to Robert. He seems agitated. She is obviously telling him what Dottie just told me. He doesn't seem too happy. His face is red, and a frown shows the wrinkles in his forehead. He starts talking to her like he normally talks to me when he is displeased, getting close and taking her personal space. I bet that if she had a knife, she would put a hole in him too. Unlike me, however, she rises to her full height and says something before walking away with a head toss.

He looks across the lobby at me. I resist the urge to smirk at him. Instead, I turn back to Dottie. "Do I have to go in and testify? Are they going to grill me and try to break me on the stand?"

"Lynn. You need to get out more. This is not Boston Legal. In the whole scheme of things, you are not Bonnie of Bonnie and Clyde fame. I need you to pull back a bit. Sit there," she indicates a row of uncomfortable-looking chairs. "Look innocent and remorseful at the same time. Do you think you can manage innocent and re-morseful?" Dottie smiles and gives me a wink.

"I will give it my best, especially if it keeps me out of the big house." I take my *maybe-I'm-crazy* ass over to the chairs. I sit there looking like the mother from *Psycho* thinking, Butter wouldn't melt in my mouth. Of course, I had not done as much damage with my knife as that psycho had, but still, "the man" is probably watching me. I turn to talk to my daughters and parents. They give encouraging words and hugs. I feel the love, and love the feeling.

Robert soon gets close. "What did you do to get the charges dropped? I really need this divorce."

I do not shout at him. I demurely say, "Robert, I don't know what you are talking about. I am ready to accept any punishment the court metes out to me. I am genuinely sorry I stabbed you in the arm." A little voice says, in the neck, in your neck. I should have gone for the throat. I continue aloud, "I regret you are so eager to get a divorce that you would hold this over my head in an effort to make me sign the paperwork."

Robert looks at me and shakes his head. The children glare at their father, and my mother rolls her eyes before giving her fa-mous disdainful sniff. Dad stands apart, hands fisted at his sides watching Robert.

From the door of the courtroom, Dottie motions for me to come in. Robert pushes past both of us to be the first one in the court. I go with her to stand before the judge. The prosecutor is on the other side and starts the conversation.

"Your honor, the State of Kansas would like the charges against Ms. Westner dismissed."

The judge doesn't even look up. "What do you say, Ms. Westner?"

Dottie jumps in before I can say Hell yes, your honor. "My client is currently undergoing therapy. This unfortunate incident occurred because she had been deeply traumatized. She has a perfect record, not having even a traffic ticket in her history. We respectfully beg the court to grant the dismissal the prosecution has requested."

The judge looks up at me. "Are you sorry?"

"Yes, your honor. More than I can say. Words could not express my sincere regret for this incident."

"I better not ever see you again or else," he threatens.

"You won't, your honor." I would do a better job of escaping the dragnet and fleeing to a neutral, third world country before I get caught by five-o, but I don't say *that* out loud.

The judge proclaims, "The charges are hereby dismissed."

"Thank-you so much, your honor. You won't see me again. I'll never come back."

He stops writing and looks up at me closely for the first time. It appears he is not the friendly sort and does not want to talk.

Dottie grabs my arm and starts backing me out. The judge still does not say a word. He has his pen suspended in midair and continues to look. He would never win a personality contest.

He deigns to speak. "Get out," he growls.

Dottie quickly obeys the court order with me in tow. The children and my parents start to hug me once we are out of the courtroom and away from Judge Grumpy. Robert is nowhere to be found. I look for him because he is my ride. I am as embarrassed my husband would leave me here without a word, as I am that he would leave our marriage.

The family gets ready to leave and offers words of support. Mom and May ask if I want to go shopping with them. I decline. Dad remains. He stands like a post, erect and unmoving. I hug Dottie and thank her for everything.

ꚙ

LUNCH AND A DAD

My dad comes closer to us. "Dorothy, I greatly appreciate your efforts on my daughter's behalf. I am satisfied with the outcome of this unfortunate incident. I will be responsible for her legal expenses. I will expect the statement within the week." He is the only person I know who calls her Dorothy. Another downside of knowing someone since childhood is they know your real name, and they may use it.

"Ye, ye, yes, sir," Dottie stammers. My dad has the ability to make the world uncomfortable because he is so staid.

Her payment is one less thing I will have to worry about in the near future. Dad has always been a stickler for making sure people accept their responsibilities. For him to offer to pay my legal fees must mean even though he is disappointed, I am forgiven.

He turns to me to ask, "How about a bite to eat?" It was not an order but a request. I go along for the ride. Sometimes even a nicely worded request is an order. Besides, I never actually apologized for my outburst. This would be a great opportunity.

Dad drives us to a soul food restaurant. It is a hole in the wall place with great bad-for-you food. They have a heart-smart menu, but I have never seen anyone eating anything from it. I order the greens made with ham hocks, potato salad, and chicken, fried, of course.

Dad has the green beans cooked with smoked neck bones, meatloaf, and a side of mashed potatoes loaded with butter. The food comes quickly, and then he gets down to conversation.

"Your mother is worried about you," dad starts.

"I'm sorry, Dad. I don't mean to worry her." Dad must know I would not deliberately hurt either of them.

He lets me know, "She thinks you should move back home."

"Why?" Am I on drugs? I must have heard wrong. I haven't lived with them for over thirty years. We would get on each other's nerves the first night. Patricide will definitely get me jail time.

"So she can take care of you, make sure you get enough to eat, mother stuff."

"That is sweet of her, but I'll be okay at my house. Robert will be moving out soon," I let him know.

"What about you, Lynn? You'll be there all alone. What if something happens to you? Your mother loves you. She wants you to be safe," he tries to convince me.

In my entire life, I cannot recall my father owning affection. He shifts affection to my mother, making sure his hands stay clear and clean of the emotional stuff. If I weren't so used to it, I might think he didn't care. I know it's just his way. I don't know why kinder words refuse to come from his mouth, but they don't. I can't remember him ever saying, "I love you." Instead, he gifts. He buys things to show what he cannot put into words. I know this lunch says I am here for you.

"Dad, tell mom I'll be fine. I don't want her to worry about me. I am scared, but maybe this is for the best." I reach out and cover his hand to still it from drumming on the table.

"Lynn, who will take care of you? What if your car breaks down? Who will take out the trash and clear the snow? Your mother just wants you to be taken care of." He is looking all around the restaurant, anywhere but at me as he asks these questions. He takes my hand and holds on to it for a moment. His mouth becomes a tight line and his throat contracts several times. Moisture comes to his eyes, but I know he will not allow a tear to fall.

"Your mother wants what is best for you."

"I know, and I love her for that. I love you, too. Dad, maybe I'm going to have to learn how to take care of myself," I tell him gently, squeezing his hand.

"Well." He finally releases his equally tight hold on my hand and hurriedly rises to get away from emotion and affection. "It's time to get you home." He signals for the check, pays, and leads me to the car without another word.

In front of the house, he parks. "Look in the glove compartment and get the envelope. Your mother wanted you to have it, so you can get an attorney for this divorce. She really cares about you," he tells the windshield.

I take out an envelope with my name on it written in my father's handwriting. Inside is a cashier's check for ten thousand dollars. This will certainly cover the cost of attorney fees.

"Dad, I have some money set aside. I can pay attorney fees." Why do my parents think I am destitute?

"Your mother knows you can. She wants to do this for you," he says reaching for my face and giving it a comforting stroke along my jaw.

"Tell mom thank-you for me." If I say anything more, I will start leaking, and dad hates tears.

"I will. She will expect to hear from you on a regular basis, so she knows you are doing okay."

"She will." I squeeze his upper arm, then get out of the car and head inside the house. Once he sees me inside the door, dad honks and drives off.

SEEING SEDONA

PACK UP YOUR TROUBLES

Robert is here. He does not ask how I got home. He looks at me with contempt and snarls, "You won this round."

"It isn't a fight. Sorry you feel that way," I want to bite my tongue for the apology, but it is already out there.

"I'll be back." He takes a suitcase I had not noticed from the corner of the room and heads to the door.

"When?"

"When I want. This is still my house. I'll be by to get my mail. Just leave it on the table." He heads out of the room.

After the front door shuts, I sit and stare at the walls. I try to freeze the blood in my veins, so I won't feel. I will not cry about this. He was not an ideal husband, but he was mine. Now I am truly alone, and I don't like being alone. I head to bed. He didn't bother to move the bags out of the hallway. I drag them into the spare bedroom and don't care when they block the door. The events of the day have me sitting and staring. I don't want the happy pills. They didn't help much before.

Mr. M.O.P. says, "Pack your bags. It is time to go."

"Not you again. I can't go anywhere now. I need to be in misery, alone."

"Why not?" he wants to know.

Can't he see? I answer him, "Because I am busy."

"Busy with what—feeling sorry for yourself?" he counters.

"Looking at my life realistically," I share.

"Come. Phoenix and Sedona are waiting for you," he tempts.

"No," I tell him, but he has piqued my curiosity. "What's in Phoenix and Sedona that would interest me?"

"You'll see. Come. What is really holding you back?"

My choices are to stay here and wait for something to happen or go to Phoenix and Sedona. Arizona wins.

My overnight case comes back out. "How long will I be gone?"

"'Til Monday. Your flight leaves tomorrow morning at ten. You'll need to get a hotel in downtown Phoenix and be at the airport a couple of hours early," he tells me. "Your car is already reserved."

"How am I going to pick out a hotel in Phoenix? I don't know anything about the city."

"If you look online and find something you want to see, get a hotel close by."

"Is it cold? What should I pack?" I am now committed to going.

"No. The weather is mild. You will be spending some time outside in Sedona. You may want to take some jeans and tennis shoes. There will be a concert in Phoenix for you to enjoy." He is smiling and his eyes are full of caring.

"What clothes will work best for Arizona? My closet is a long way from a boutique. Will you be there?" I look around when there is no response. I see only air.

I sit on the edge of the bed after getting packed. With everything that has happened today, sleep may not come. I go to grab a shower. I get out and dry off, taking the time to examine my assets. Looking in the mirror, I wonder what a man would see looking at me now.

My reflection shows the imagined man would be in for a handful. A closer perusal shows I have towel threads in my pubic hair. I start removing them only to find they are attached and are not threads from the towel. They are shining white hairs. I try to smooth them. They do not lie down. They stick straight out and feel like straw. If too many of them get together, they could form a weapon. Maybe I should condition them. Anything so they are not so noticeable. They are evidence to the fact I am graying all over. What do you do about that?

I run to my makeup bag and get out the mascara. As delicately, as if I were putting it on my eyes, I stroke the brush over my pubic grays. They still stick straight out, but they are now brown. It slowly dawns on me there is no one to see my pubic hair, gray or otherwise. I go in the bathroom and wash the mascara off my private parts. Why bother? I will probably never have sex again. Nevertheless, the next time I wash my hair, I'm going to rub some conditioner down there. Hair doesn't have to be hard as long as Bonner Brothers makes hair products.

On that realistic thought, I go to bed. Sleep must have come because the next thing I know, it is seven in the morning. I remember my promise to the children and my parents before leaving town. The first call is to my mother. "Mom, can you let everyone know I'm going to Arizona?"

"For what? Lynn, are you feeling quite the thing?" Mom's voice is rising at the end of the question.

"Well, I want to get away for the weekend," I let her know.

"Honey, are you sure you should leave? I mean you were just somewhere already. It was Bloomington, and maybe it shouldn't count, but you went somewhere." My mother is not a traveler. She likes to stay put and wants everyone else to stay put too.

"Mom, I need to get away, so I can think a bit. The doctor thinks it will be good for me." I haven't been back to Doctor Flaky, so the statement is not actually true, but she will have less opposition if she thinks the doctor wants me to go.

"Where will you be staying? How can we get in touch with you?"

"I'll have my cell phone with me. I promise to call when I get there and every morning and every night. Will you tell the children for me?"

"If you are sure you need to do this," she concedes with a sigh.

"I'm sure, Mom."

"Okay, honey. Have a nice time. Do you need some money? I've got a few hundred in cash if you need to come by and pick it up," she asks before we hang up.

"No, Mom, but thanks for the offer." Where is she getting these large sums of money?

My final call is to my head doctor. I cancel my appointment because I am leaving town. I do not offer to reschedule. I might look for someone new, someone I feel comfortable talking to, later.

It wouldn't be nice to leave without a note or call to Robert. Because what I honestly want is revenge without having to do time, I decide to write a letter to him. I go to the computer and do some serious cutting, pasting, and writing from a place of revenge. I use the services available on the Internet. Once I am satisfied with my efforts, I print my work on the high quality paper and slip it in a high quality envelope I bought in case I need to send résumés.

After that, I search the Internet to find a hotel in Phoenix close to the arena where there's a jazz concert tomorrow. I reserve a room and get a ticket to the concert. Now, it's time to go.

I take a taxi to the airport so I don't have to drive myself or find a place to park. On the way, I ask the driver to take me by the post office, so I can mail Robert's letter. We go to the one close to downtown. I get out and deposit the fruits of my labor. As I drop the letter into the mailbox, I smile. Sometimes being a bitch feels damn good.

Once at the airport, I look around wondering which airline goes to Phoenix. The scent of Caesar's Woman has me heading toward the correct one. I find this will be a two and a half hour flight and with the time change, it will be close to noon when I get there.

Boarding pass in hand, I get past security and on to the plane in seat seven A. Unsurprisingly, seven B is empty. I pay attention to the safety instructions. It sounds the same as the last set of instructions. I know damn well we are not going over water, so I zone out wondering what Arizona will be like.

After takeoff, my seatmate arrives. He takes my hand and smiles.

"Can anyone see you besides me?" I have not had any previous experience with spirits before him.

"Of course," answers Mr. M.O.P.

"Well, doesn't the flight attendant think it strange you appear after takeoff and are not here for landing?" Planes shouldn't have people coming and going during a flight.

"She doesn't think anything is strange at all. She and others see what they need to see." He assures me.

"So, I don't look like I am sitting here talking to myself? It may be best not to call attention to the strangeness of you. Are you real?"

"I am as real as I need to be. Physically, we do not connect. Mentally, spiritually, we are connected over life and lifetimes."

"If we can't be together physically, how come I can feel your hand in mine? How could I feel you kiss away my tears and hold me at night?"

"Those are limited bursts of energy, when you need me most." He informs me.

"What if I want more? Remember I told you when we were together I know I'm greedy." I haven't had a wide variety to compare him with, but he was the most thorough, exciting, wonderful lover of my life. He listened to me talk, encouraged me in my passion, and made me feel complete.

"Next lifetime, look for me."

"What?" I ask the air as the plane touches down. I wish he would stick around long enough to make it plain what we can and cannot do.

I head to the car rental area with my luggage rolling behind me. My name on the signboard lets me know I'm in the right place. I admire the city on the drive to the hotel. After checking in, I notice a stack of activities for Phoenix. I grab a magazine with an awe-inspiring picture of orange mountains on the cover and plan on having a good time in Phoenix and Sedona. There are enough things to escape the boredom I faced in Indiana.

I go to the room, deposit my belongings, and then grab a shower to freshen up. The place across the street looks busy enough to investigate. They are setting up for the concert tomorrow. I watch for a time before going out to drive around Phoenix.

Thankfully, the clerk knows where the closest mall is, so that is the direction I point the car in. The mall has me window-shopping before purchasing a pink dress to wear to the concert. It is a vibrant pink and loud enough to stand out in a crowd; totally unlike any dress I currently own. Cut low in the back, it looks demure from the front, and stops just above the knees. It makes me look like I have a shape. Just what I need for the new person I am now.

I feel sexy. Thinking about sex brings the thought to the forefront. It's been a long time. However, sex may be over for me. I am fifty-five-years-old and likely to never have sex again. I'll have to find a sex substitute. Chocolate with brazil nuts or chocolate with toffee and raisins should do fine. Doughnuts are substitutes for bad sex. I need a substitute for no sex.

A local bar-b-cue restaurant is close to the hotel, and it looks perfect for dinner. The food is good, the people are friendly, and I share my concert plans with the waitress. She tells me the history of the arena. They have free concerts during the summer to give youth an activity. Her voice exudes the pride she has for her city.

I leave, happy to have had conversation, and return to the hotel to shower before going to bed.

There is not any reason to get up early the next morning. Even after I wake up, I stay in bed, stretching in all different directions. When I do get up, it is to leave the hotel and drive around. An antique mall with armor, Tiffany lamps, and stone eggs in the window catches my attention. It keeps my attention enough to spend a couple hours looking at someone else's history in the form of glassware, old toys, train sets, and other items. My appetite is returning slowly. Before heading back to the hotel, I stop at a locally owned restaurant to have something to eat. I love making my own decisions.

∞

THE DICKS YOU MEET ON A DANCE FLOOR

Back to the hotel and my body needs another shower to clean away the sweat. I put on a dab of Caesar's Woman at my pulse points. I even put some in my pubic area, to make myself feel better. I wonder if there will be a man intrigued enough to try to pick me up.

I slip into my pink dress and look in the mirror. Not bad, I think to my reflection.

"You're looking well tonight," Mr. M.O.P. admires from his position on the bed, his eyes glued to my ass.

"Thank-you. I am going to expand my horizons." I love the look in his eyes, as if he would sop me up with a biscuit. I wish he could.

"You will attract attention in your pink dress," he observes.

"Attention can't be all bad. Who knows, I just might get lucky." I wish I could get lucky with him. He is familiar and wonderful.

"Remember, physical longing is easily appeased. Enjoy." He encourages me with those words before leaving.

I continue dressing. What if I do meet someone tonight? What will he say? What would my response be? It's been a long time. I think these thoughts to myself as I put on strappy flat sandals. I'll figure it out *if* it happens.

I head to the arena. I hear the music before I get there, a mix of salsa and soul that makes me move. The concert will be held outside, and this will be a new experience for me. The sounds are intense. There is dancing. The music is vibrating.

I watch the people in the front as they dance and enjoy life. They are jamming and seem without a care. If I go down there, could I shed my cares and inhibitions as freely as they seem to be doing? Might as well go down front and try. Maybe the freedom can be contagious.

I move to the center of a mass of people, and my inhibitions fall like leaves in autumn. I rock and weave, letting the music guide my body, not using measured steps, but trying to internalize the music and move with feeling. My soul wants to feel again. Something. Anything. Strangers are better to be with than being by myself tonight. I close my eyes and continue to sway, swirl, and twirl. I bump into a body I didn't know was so close to me and open my eyes to administer my apology.

My eyes travel up and up and up the body I had bumped into. It looks like a penis on legs—long legs. Forty to forty-five-years-old, about six feet six inches, too light brown for my taste, being somewhere between cream and bone in color. I like a color more chocolately like Hersheys. With his shaved dome, he makes me instantly think of a penis—a big one. The thought is erotic enough to make me stop breathing. He has enough bass in his voice to command attention when he opens his mouth to speak.

"Oh, I'm sorry," he apologizes.

I stare before finally managing to squeak out a "my bad." Even though his color is not what I like, his body brings the memory of how good sex feels to the forefront of my mind. I would love to have him between my legs. It has been such a long time. He has brought my memory of an orgasm to the forefront. I wish I had a doughnut because he couldn't possibly be interested in me. I need a dozen doughnuts. Stick doughnuts.

He takes ownership of the collision and shouts over the music, "No, it's my fault. Sorry, I'm Donald."

Looking like a dick and sounding like sex is a wonderful combination. This man is physical perfection. How often do you meet a dick on a dance floor? The excitement continues to build. He dwarfs me as he stands in front of me. I get a kind of scary feeling because he is tall and attention getting. I am so horny and want to get laid in the worse kind of way.

"Are you okay, I didn't hurt you did I?" he asks. He puts his hands on my shoulders and starts us moving in an impromptu loose dance

"No. I'm fine. It was probably my fault. I wasn't looking where I was dancing." I smile up at him.

"You can dance over me anytime. I like the contact." He gives me a smile and a wink then removes his hands.

What the hell am I supposed to say to that? "Yeah, me too," That sounds stupid. Is it too forward? I hope he doesn't think I am a tramp. If I were a tramp, I would want to tramp with him. I am out of the dating, flirting, and getting laid loop. My shoulder is still feeling the warmth of his hands.

He smiles and takes my hands to turn me as we continue to dance. We come together, way close together, enough for me to know I fit perfectly at his nipple and for him to feel my pubic hair. The gray ones.

The sane hemisphere of my brain speaks to me, "Lynn, watch yourself. Don't do anything stupid."

My private parts respond to my brain. "Shut up, we're taking him home to make sure everything still works."

It's very distracting to be constantly on the edge of an orgasm. The more I tell myself not to think about sex, the more I think about sex. The best I ever had, the worst I ever had. Will I ever get some more? Right about now nothing is as important as getting laid. What if he is not interested in me like that?

He dips me gently. The closeness lets me know he is interested in me like that. I don't know if I can do this. I am married, mostly. He will see me naked. I have gray pubic hair and titties that resemble weenie dogs.

My pubic area yells, "You can do this. Please do this. For us. Please don't fuck up this chance."

He bends over and captures my mouth. He kisses me. He is a very good kisser. He gently sucks my bottom lip then licks my lips to end the mouth contact.

"People are looking," I say as I pull back.

"Then why don't we go to some place more private?" he suggests as he pulls me close. I can tell from the feel of him that he is ready and able.

My pubic parts are doing the anticipation dance. They tell me, "Girl don't mess this up. He looks like he is going to be good." My titties perk up at the possibility they may get sucked. My nipples are hard as jawbreakers.

I may never have this opportunity again. Men are not breaking my door down. Mr. M.O.P. is unavailable, him being a spirit and all. I'm horny. Donald's here. I'm here. He might think I am a slut. I will never see him again. If I give him a fake name, he will think my fake name is a slut. Could I live with myself? Yes.

My brain wants me to stop and think, which isn't a bad idea. "We can go to my hotel room." I wouldn't want to go to his house. He may have bodies in the basement. At the hotel room, I can be seen with him. "I am staying across the street." This is my concession to my brain.

"Okay. What's your name?"

Damn, think fast. "I'm Elizabeth from Jackson. Are you from Phoenix?" Small talk is hard. I don't give a damn where he is from, only where he's going—between my legs. If I can make it to getting my clothes off, I'll be getting laid. He could be from east hell, and it wouldn't make a bit of difference.

"Yes, I am. We could go to my house. My car is in the parking garage on the corner," Donald offers.

'No, but thank-you very much." I sound too damn prissy.

"Lead the way. I'm yours," he laughs,

Well at least for tonight, I think. I hope I haven't forgotten what to do with him. This is going to be an encounter with a man who is not my husband. Act cool. Act natural.

"Do you come here often?" Donald asks

"No." My mind goes blank. I have forgotten how to make small talk before sex.

"What brings you to Phoenix?" Donald perseveres.

My brain is being a bitch and stays blank. My pubic area takes over. "Sedona. I wanted to see Sedona. I have to go there tomorrow. On business." I sound disjointed because I'm making it up as I go.

"Huh?"

"This is a business trip." I hope he doesn't delve any further.

"I'm glad I met you tonight." Donald takes my hand. The physical attraction is undeniable.

We enter the hotel. My brain gets jealous of the workout my pubic area is in for and goes back to work. It tells me to take precautions, have someone see him just in case he is a rapist. I lead him to the desk. "Are there any messages for me, room 1514?" I ask the clerk. I turn back to him. "So, Donald," I say his name extra loud so the clerk can hear me, "you're from the Phoenix area, right?" If he tries anything funny, there is a witness.

"Yes, east of here" he lets me know. "Are you sure you don't want to go there instead?"

The clerk heard him. Just in case. She will be able to identify him judging by the way that she is staring at him, as if she would slip him her number. Tramp

"There are no messages for you," the clerk says to tall and fine standing beside me.

Good, take a close look. He could be a pervert, and I will need you to tell the police what he looks like.

"Thank-you for checking," I tell her so she can focus back on me.

We go toward the elevator.

"Would you like a drink? We can stop in the bar if you like," he offers.

"A glass of Chardonnay would be nice. Dancing made me thirsty." It will also get his fingerprints on a glass.

We stop in and get wine for me, and whiskey, neat, for him. The bartender has a hard time tearing his eyes off my partner for the night. He pours Donald a triple and gives me enough wine to wet the bottom of the glass. My dress is wasted on the bartender. If I had boobs like Dolly Parton and a face like Nefertiti, the bartender wouldn't care, he is only interested in Donald. Drinks in hand, we go to my room.

Inside the room, he looks at me as if I am supposed to know what to do. I look at him because I don't have much of a clue on how to start, and he is so damn fine. He kisses me again.

I turn off the lights except for the one in the bathroom. We can see our outlines, good enough. I wouldn't want to send him running screaming from the room if he saw me in the bright light. We continue kissing and start shedding our clothes. Once naked, we climb onto the bed and under the sheet.

His size is impressive my hand tells my brain. He must be packing ten inches. He has an equally impressive girth. I am not sure this is going to fit without tearing something. Namely me. I have stretched to accommodate the birth of children, but the doctors had to damn near knock me out with painkillers for the experience. I don't know if I can do this without an epidural.

He does some good touching, and then he covers me. One. The first stroke gets him a ways into me. It feels like this might not work. Two. The second stroke has him still a long way from me. No, it's not fitting. He withdraws. Three. This third stroke has him embedded about halfway in, and me thinking, Okay, this might be worth the trip. I settle more comfortably in the mattress and prepare for pleasure.

I hear an "aaah," and then feel nothing except his body collapsing on top of mine. What just happened? Is he finished? *Already?* That's all? That can't be all. We're not finished yet, are we? I took my clothes off for *that?* Hell, I didn't even get a chance to move. Ain't this a bitch?

I am processing the speed of his completion. Then this bastard has the nerve to go wash his balls. Does he think he had performed on stage and worked up a sweat? Why is he washing his balls? We can't be done yet. I should cut his dick off and give it to him. Then he won't think about having another woman end up being disappointed with his lack of stamina

Mr. Speedy comes back with a smile on his face bright enough to shine through the darkness. "That was intense."

He lies down and closes his eyes. Maybe it was good for him. I was not impressed. I am still stunned that he is finished. I brought this man here because I was horny. I started taking my clothes off because I was horny. I allowed him into my body because I was horny. As tall as he is, as well hung as he is, I should not still be horny, and he should not be asleep. What to do?

I really have no choice. This is bigger than I am. I get up and put on my nightgown. Then, for all the women who have taken off their clothes only to be doomed to disappointment, I reach over. I roughly and firmly shake him awake.

"You know what? It's time for you to go. I really don't sleep well with someone in bed with me. I have restless leg syndrome, and I snore. I like to sleep alone. Could you please dress and leave?"

He opens his eyes and appears surprised. He can't be. I'm sure he doesn't get a call back from women after their first sexual encounter. The guy is as inept at fucking as a monkey is in a kitchen fixing Sunday dinner.

He starts dressing, talking all the time. "What is going on? That was fantastic. Do you have somewhere to go? When can we get together again?" He puts legs in the pants I am shaking in front of him.

"I'll look you up the next time I'm in Phoenix." I say this with a straight face since I'll never be in Arizona again.

"We were great together. We both like to dance."

I am buckling his belt and throw out another sop, "Donald, if you ever get to Kansas City, give me a call," This is said as I help his arms into the sleeves of his shirt.

"I thought you were from Jackson?" He stops to ask.

I move to the front to help him button his shirt. "That's where I grew up. I live in Kansas City now." He wants to make plans, but I'm using all my available energy to propel, tug, and drag him toward the door.

"What's your number? I would love to call you sometime" He asks this as I continue fastening his shirt and putting his shoes in front of him for him to step into. I'm ready to tie his shoes except they are loafers.

"Seven-eight-three-two-five-eight-six-five-one-five -four," I tell him as I open the door.

"That sounds like too many numbers. I can't remember them."

"I'll write it down for you." I run to the desk and scribble down some numbers. There are fourteen digits. I'll have to erase the first number because it's a zero. He would know it was a fake number. I take another number out of the middle. It looks right. I fold the paper and stick it in his pocket as I push him out the door.

I could thank him for his two minutes of service. That would give him a whole minute and a half more than he deserves. I'm an ego booster, but why lie any more than I already have? "Bye, now."

I have him on the other side of the door and shut it on the question he is forming his mouth to ask. I lean against the door and turn every lock in sight before returning to bed. All that tall. All that bass. For what? For thirty seconds of shame. Not having sex at all is really better than bad sex. I would rather sleep alone than with someone so inept.

Besides, now I can lie sideways in the bed. Robert never allowed sideways sleeping. Sleeping alone has benefits. I'll get a doughnut in the morning. On my glazed thought, I go to sleep.

The next morning I wake up to laughter. "Bravo. Bravo," from Mr. M.O.P., who is laughing his ass off.

"I suppose you saw the performance last night?" I ask, hoping he will say no.

"All three strokes," he confirms. "He was not much of a lover," says an excellent lover.

"Are you a voyeur? How could you watch?" I want to curl up and disappear. "There was certainly not much to see. I had an inept partner."

"I remember you, dear heart, I remember. I wanted to see how it went. Are you satisfied now you are a desirable woman?" he probes.

"I remember you, too, and I was hoping to recapture the excitement. It was a confidence booster for the thirty seconds it lasted," I admit longingly.

"And then?" he laughingly questions.

"And then I wished I hadn't bothered. I'm still horny as hell and still unsatisfied. In addition, I don't know when I will have another opportunity," I confess.

"It doesn't seem to have been worth the effort," he observes.

"That is an understatement," I agree with him.

Mr. M.O.P. doesn't let it go; making me ask questions of myself I don't know how to answer. "Does this mean you will no longer look for physical release?"

I want to be honest, so I take time to ponder the question before speaking. "There was something satisfying about being wanted, even by a stranger. If he weren't such a terrible lover, maybe I would want see him again. He was a good kisser. If he could get some blue pills, I might want to get to know him better. No, he wasn't very interesting to talk with and physically, I've had more pleasure from chocolate with cashews. I can live without ever seeing him again."

Mr. M.O.P. laughs, "Better luck next time. Now it is time to arise. The day awaits you. Are you ready to see the sights?"

"If I must. Where am I going, and how will I get there?"

"Zena, your Sedona guide and an old friend of mine, will pick you up in about an hour. She will drive you to Sedona," he shares.

"What will I see there?"

"You will tell me," he answers before leaving.

I get up and dress in a T-shirt, jeans, and tennis shoes. I grab an egg biscuit sandwich and a cup of coffee to go from the hotel restaurant. I find a comfy chair in the lobby to eat and await the arrival of Zena.

಄಄

KISS OF THE SUN AND MOON

As I finish my food, Mr. M.O.P. says, "Time to go."

A short silver-haired, white lady enters the lobby and says, "Hello, old friend. I heard of your transition. Was it everything you wanted it to be?"

"Yes. I love Vancouver. There was no better place to transition."

"To what do I owe this honor?"

"Lynn is in search of peace and the ability to see the beauty of life. Sedona has to be the perfect place to see the beauty of life."

Zena turns to me and allows me to share her smile. "Hello." She is wearing a blue T-shirt and blue jeans. She also has a blue and white kerchief around her neck causing her to resemble a train conductor. She looks like a cherub when she smiles.

"Hello," I respond.

She looks me over and walks around me. "What an interesting person you are," she observes, coming back to face me. She walks closer and hugs me very tightly. She must be real, or I could not feel her hug, right?

"I'll go and get the van. Meet me out front," she throws over her shoulder. Mr. M.O.P. has gone again.

I wait a few minutes wondering if this is a good idea. I don't know her. I make my decision to go based on the fact I didn't know the guy I slept with last night either. Besides, someone special recommended her. I head out and get in the car with a stranger.

On the drive, she talks about the place we are going. I don't pay much attention to the scenery at first. But it is becoming so incredible; it gradually starts to command my attention. I have the opportunity to see mountains the size of city blocks and the color of cinnamon mixed with paprika, and other shades of orange. Like pumpkin and salmon, the mountains cross several tints of colors so wonderful that they practically scream at me and dare me to ignore them. Mountains so big and scraggly they make humans look insignificant greet me in Sedona.

When we park, I wonder why we're stopping. We could continue our drive, and I could see everything from the car. I think this is so beautiful that I don't need to see it up close. I can feel the power of the mountains from a distance. We've seen the rocks and the mountains. I see the beauty of nature. I get it. "Where do we go now?" I ask my guide.

"There's a vortex. We're going to get close to it." She imparts this information as though it will make me happy.

This sounds dangerous. A vortex is nothing to play with. There aren't any danger signs, but I know this is a bad idea. "Zena, maybe we should stay in the car." I saw a vortex on Star Trek and it almost sucked the Enterprise in before Captain Kirk got them out. A vortex is nothing to casually view. It could take me out of this world.

Zena doesn't act worried about the vortex. She gets a long walking stick and starts off down a dirt path. I follow her through the woods and through more woods. After fifteen minutes of hard walking, we come to a clearing. There is a stream running beside a huge span of flat red rock. Zena continues to walk.

The flatness of the plateau is inviting, and I go over to sit on the red stone. My body feels tired and energized at the same time. The energy seeps into my system as though I am connecting to the ground. I imagine my troubles are flowing downward through my feet to the red dirt under my shoes and through my hands to my stone seat. The sound of the water in the near distance lulls me.

Zena continues to the end of the pathway and comes back around. I see her through half-opened lids.

"Do you feel the vortex?" She is standing in front of me. I see her as though she is in slow motion.

My body feels heavy, and my mind feels rested. "No, I feel really peaceful right here, like I am connected to the earth." It sounds to me as if my voice is coming through an echo chamber.

Zena smiles, "You are experiencing the vortex."

"Oh. I'd like to sit here for a few minutes." As I sit, I feel strengthened. I am getting a shot of confidence. I hope it lasts. I'll need it for the times ahead. I wish I could stay here where it's peaceful. To stay here, I would need to be able to live off the land, and I don't see any steak and potatoes growing on this land. The lack of ice cream would also be a drawback, and there isn't a doughnut shop for miles.

"Look, over your shoulder, Zena says, pointing to my left. What do you think of Cathedral Rock?"

I had missed the most fascinating sight while sitting on my vortex. Cathedral Rock rises proudly among the red and demands homage. It is framed by the trees that dwarf us with their height. Looking through the trees we were watching, it makes me realize how insignificant I am in the scheme of the world. The various points and arches of the mountains put me in mind of pictures of ancient churches—welcoming and majestic. They represent strength gained through weathering storms.

"Come, we have farther to go." Zena turns and retraces our steps. My lethargy leaves, and I bounce up to follow her. We head back and pass where we entered. We continue to move out of the forest and up to the water's edge. "The only way to get where we are going is to cross the creek," Zena tells me, as she stops to roll up her pants legs and remove her shoes.

I copy her movements. "And why do we need to get there? We saw the rocks already." Nobody told me anything about a creek crossing. She better not fall in because I can't swim.

Zena smiles, "You will see it from a different point of view. It helps to look at things from various angles. Then you see what you have missed. What was hidden in plain sight."

How many ways can you view mountains? I'm here, so I guess I'll be seeing at least one more angle. I have to move fast to keep up with Zena.

She takes off and makes her way to some stepping-stones that are the only way to cross the creek. She is halfway to the other side without incident when my mouth closes.

I have never crossed a creek using stepping-stones. Some of the stepping-stones are actually stepping-*pebbles*. I go much more slowly than Zena because I don't want to fall in the creek. I can see the bottom, so I am not worried about drowning. I just don't want to have to walk around with wet clothes.

It takes twenty-three steps and much prayer to make it to the other side. Zena has her shoes back on and her pants legs back down. I feel victorious and follow Zena into the woods again. I made it through the challenge. When I tell my story about Sedona, I will describe my journey as navigating miles of white-water rapids.

Half an hour later, we come out on the other side of Cathedral Rock. This view does not have the interference of the trees. We are much closer. With the unobstructed view, it seems even more majestic. Looking up, I am content to stand, look, and reflect.

The grandeur leaves me standing dumbfounded. How did this mountain come into being? This piece of perfection doesn't care that my husband is leaving me. It has weathered storms through decades and is still standing and still commanding respect. How many people have come to this spot and had this experience? Did it change their lives? If it's possible to inhale peace, that's what I'm doing right now.

It comes as a surprise when Zena touches my arm to tell me it is time to leave. It seems as though we just got here. I look at my watch and find we have been here four hours. I feel energized and exhausted—energized by the views and the sense of purpose in the place, and exhausted because of the heat and the walking.

This time I make it back across the creek in half the time it took me to get here. Zena is inexhaustible and leads the way as a mother duck would. When we are back in the car, I fasten my seat belt and wonder what will come next.

"Lynn, how about dinner. I know a place that you will love and is close to our last stop for the day."

"Well Zena, you know the area better than I do and you're driving so I'll go wherever you take me."

Our restaurant is located a short ride into the mountains. It has a perfect view of Bell Rock, which looks like it would sound an alarm through the state if you could push it. We eat in silence. I think about the sights and the connection to earth now in my possession.

"Now come, we are going to the moon," Zena says, and we hurry to complete our meal. She drives a short distance and parks. We get out on the side of the mountain to mingle with a crowd that is standing around. On the right side of us, there is the sun, a true red ball. Suddenly, the moon appears on the left, and begins its ascent to meet the stars.

It looks close enough to touch. I discern the different shades of blue, black, and gray that is mixed with the white to make up the fluff of the moon. The crowd quiets as we see the greeting between the sun and the moon, as they pass each other and exchange a kiss on our mountain. This is true beauty, the earth in its splendor, a glimpse of perfection. That's what I experience.

"Lynn, it is time to go." Zena brings my head down from the clouds.

Words fail me, and I follow Zena back to the car in silence.

"What will you do with yourself?" Zena starts our return drive conversation.

"What do you mean?" I've done everything. My kids are grown.

"With your life. How will you leave your mark on the world?"

"If you count the kids, I already have three marks. I hope I don't have any more marks to leave."

"Sure you do." She wants me to believe.

"I am in the middle of a divorce, and I'm rather hesitant to make any grand plans. They have a way of falling through at the most inopportune times."

"This is the perfect time to make plans. You get to rewrite your future," Zena says excitedly at the prospect.

"I'm not particularly skilled at anything," I admit.

"You need a bigger stage. An opportunity to grow. Now that you have it, make use of it." She proclaims.

"I'll think about it." I have to—life is going forward not backward.

"Find your passion, accept it, and release it to the universe," Zena advises.

My life has changed, and I need to do the same. We spend the rest of the drive in silence, while I turn her words over repeatedly in my mind.

Back at the hotel, I get out. "Thank-you, Zena, for a wonderful day."

'Don't thank me. Return the favor," Zena barters.

"What? I don't have anything to offer. I can't."

"You can anything. Remember that. Now you have seen Sedona, show someone else." Zena says with a smile.

"I'll try." I reach over to hug her ad then get out of the van. I stay outside for a few minutes longer to watch Zena leave and look at the moon, so recently mine for the touching. I will sleep like a baby tonight because I feel at peace.

I head back to my room. There is a message on my telephone. It's from Donald. He wants to know if we can possibly get together to-night. He also deduces I must have been sleepy last night because the number I gave him has too many numbers.

I want to sleep alone without further frustration from him. I would pull the phone out of the wall if I didn't know the hotel would charge me for it. Instead, I call the front desk and ask them not to put any calls through to my room for the remainder of the night. There is no way am I calling him back or speaking to him if I can help it. I dutifully call my parents and children before going to sleep.

Sunday I decide to walk around the Phoenix area. The air is soft, and I barely feel it going into my nose. The weather is great here, however, there is no grass. I miss seeing green. Everything here is red. There is red dirt on the street and the sidewalks. Red air.

Everything has a red tint. I have certainly seen a different side of the country here.

I go back to the hotel and get something to eat. There is no visit from Mr. M.O.P., and I make my children calls before going to sleep.

Monday morning, I prepare myself mentally and physically for home. On the plane, he comes to me. "What did you find?" he asks as he takes my hand.

"It was more than I could have anticipated. The beauty, the spiritual awareness, the ability to think and see clearly was wonderful. Thank-you," I tell him.

"I didn't do anything, you did. You opened yourself." He smiles and squeezes my hand. We hold hands and fly in silence before sleep claims me. He again leaves before we land.

NAG, NAG, NAG

I head home, where I find Robert's car in the driveway. I need to talk to Dottie about changing the locks on the doors. I go in and find Robert standing in the living room.

"Lynn, I need to talk to you."

"What is it, Robert? I told you I won't sign anything without my attorney." I wonder if I look different. I have been with someone else. It wasn't any good, but it was a confidence builder. Someone else wanted me at least once. No twice, I correct myself.

"Where have you been? You haven't been here since Thursday. Today is Monday. You haven't been to work. Where have you been?" he asks as if he has the right.

"I'm sorry, Robert. I was in Phoenix and Sedona." Old habits die hard, and the need to assuage Robert with an apology is something I have to work on.

"For what? I demand to know what's going on with you." Robert likes to demand.

"Why? As you tell me, we are getting a divorce." I sniff. It's time to put new habits into practice.

"You are really changing. I don't like your tone," he tells me as if it matters.

"I'm sor... so glad you stopped in to visit," I tell him sarcastically. "What do you want from me? You can't keep control over me like I'm your wife and then not be here to be my husband," I confront him.

"You have never had to deal with anything before. You aren't used to making decisions for yourself. I'm just looking out for your best interest. You should thank me," is Robert's point of view, secure in his domination of me.

That may have been true in the past, but I have to change his perception. "I have to start looking out for my own best interest," I state. The peace found at the vortex seeps from my brain to all parts of my body.

Robert looks at me as if I am an idiot. "You don't know how. I've taught you how to cook and what to cook. Now you aren't even cooking the way you're supposed to anymore. I am most displeased. I can't believe I was going to sleep with you tonight."

I look at him and cannot believe I was so lost to myself. "Robert, can we talk later? I am tired. I don't need or want pity sex." I let him know without apology. I take my suitcase and head upstairs.

"Lynn, I am talking to you. Come back here," Robert calls in his firm voice from the bottom of the stairs. I keep walking.

"Leave the papers on the table, and I will take a look at them," I tell him without looking back.

Wow, how lucky I would have been. Robert was going to sleep with me tonight. I get into bed and lay sideways. I hear Robert leave. Sleep comes quickly after.

Harold calls me late in the morning. "Lynn, I tried to call you on the house phone, but no one answered. Would you look in at the office, please? I'm heading down to Florida to look into relocating. If you can check the mail and everything on Thursday and Tuesday, it would be great. I'll be back by Friday."

"Sure, Harold, I can do that." I could say no and continue to use the time I have accrued, but I don't have anything else to do, so why not?

"Great. When I get back, we can talk. I may have a job lead for you."

"Okay, Harold." Days are long, and I don't have much else to do. I get up and go to the answering machine. Sure enough, there are messages. I didn't hear the telephone ringing. There are five new messages, one from each of the kids, each a replica of the other. Why aren't I answering the telephone?

I stay in bed, mostly staring at the ceiling instead of sleeping. I spend the time contemplating my two journeys and the lessons learned. I have been doing some serious growing.

My Travel Tips for Phoenix and Sedona

Never sleep with a man who looks like a dick and you meet on a dance floor. You will be disappointed. Go out to Sedona and watch the sun go down and the moon come up.

IN MY OWN DAMN HOUSE

MOTHER LOVE

I spend Wednesday walking around the house, drinking wine from Indiana. When hunger pains hit, I have tilapia to fix for dinner. White fish is for a first or third Friday meal, according to Robert. Heavier fish like tuna and salmon are for the second and fourth Friday. We are divorcing, so I can eat whatever I like.

On Thursday, it's time to get up to go to work. Everyone is buzzing about the downsizing. They think I have inside information and want to know where I've been. I field the questions as best as I can. Harold is due back Friday, and from the looks of things, he hasn't been doing much of anything since I left. Being at work does a poor job of keeping my mind off everything else. It gets me out of the house, but it's just busywork with a change of scene. There is little effort expended in catching up on the ignored calls, letters, and e-mails. The welcome interruptions from coworkers break the monotony.

Thoughts about how a new job would feel creep around my subconscious. I would have to get used to a new rhythm, new people, and new office politics. Is a new job doable at my age and with my temperament or is it time to find new interests? I am not ready to sit home all day being bored to tears. A new job may be just what the doctor should have ordered. It would have to be more exciting than my current employment. A new job that involves travel would be a dream job.

At the end of the day, I have returned all the calls and sorted through the mail. Responses to   non-urgent e-mail and snail mail can wait 'til Tuesday. After tidying the office, it's time to head home.

Robert is in my house, the bastard. When I come in, he starts with me. "Lynn, I think you should know I intend to start bringing my friend here."

His comments stop me from walking past him. "You can't be serious. Your friend is a home wrecker. You can't expect me to entertain that woman in my home. You can't bring her here."

"I certainly can. This is my house, too. I intend to act like it. You won't have to cook for me anymore because she will see to my meals." He smiles at me as if he were giving me a treat.

"In my kitchen?" I need him to clarify this for me. I want to be wrong.

"In our kitchen. She'll be here tomorrow." Robert gives me a self-satisfied smile. "Or you can sign the paperwork and be done with this sham of a marriage."

"Robert, you are a sanctimonious bastard. I'm not signing."

"You should clean up that trashy mouth you're getting and give me what I want," Robert says as he heads toward the door and parts unknown.

The curve ball Robert threw makes me recognize the need for the assistance of a higher power. I call my mother. "Mom, Robert is going to start bringing his girlfriend here. He says it's his house too. She is going to cook for him. In my kitchen." I do not take a breath as I share this latest news about my husband the jerk.

"Hmm. What do you think about that?" Mom asks politely.

"I hate it. It's so disrespectful, but I don't know what to do to stop him. He gets to do whatever he wants, and I have to take it." My voice is steadily rising until I am speaking louder to my mother than I ever have in my life.

"I'm on my way," she states before hanging up.

When she arrives, she opens her arms. I go into them and stick like Velcro. She rubs my back, which in turn releases the tears I have been trying to keep inside for too long. Feeling my tears, my mother puts her hands on my shoulders and pushes me back.

She looks into my tear-filled eyes and says, "Honey, if you want, Robert can disappear. Forever. It happens all the time."

Shock stops the tears. "What?"

I was expecting name calling kinship of feeling, recognition of Robert's wrongness. I could have heard her wrong.

"Nothing, dear. I wanted to give you something else to think about and stop your crying. Now, tell me what happened." Mom pats my arm and goes into the front room to have a seat on the couch. She pats the space beside her for me to sit. I give her the playback of my conversation with Robert.

"Tomorrow she'll be here? Well, so will your dad and me. I'll cook for us. She can cook for him." Mom looks at me with a nod.

"Mom, you are brilliant." I hug her hard. "Robert will be furious."

She gives a mischievous smile then asks, "Did you expect less?"

"No, I knew I could count on you. Thanks. I love you dearly."

"Honey, dry your eyes and get ready for some good eating." She prepares to leave. "I'll let your father know about this latest foolishness." Sometimes you have to tell your mommy and let her make you feel better.

It's time to shower and prepare for bed. Before sleep hits me, I hear Mr. M.O.P.'s music as it fills my ears before I hear his voice caress me in a whispered, "You can do this. You can do anything." Tomorrow will prove him right or wrong.

A MIXED-PRINT BITCH

The next day catches me staying in bed to think, without coming up with any answers. With a shake of my head, my feet hit the floor to get up and face the day, which has marched forward to afternoon without me being active. Cathedral Rock would not be unnerved by anything as paltry as a bitch coming to visit, and I won't either.

Mom calls at two to let me know she is on her way over. When she gets here, she has grocery bags with Robert's favorite foods—greens, sweet potatoes, pie ingredients, potato salad fixings, and chicken legs. She goes into the kitchen to start her pots bubbling.

Robert enters with two women about ninety minutes later. I go to the entry hall as soon as I hear them to see what his new person looks like. He has a little bag of groceries that must contain what she will be cooking. Let me guess, she's cooking fish.

"Lynn, what's going on here?" Robert stands in the hall with his two women. The smells of mom's cooking waft through the hall and make them all lick their lips at various times.

"Mom came over. She is cooking for me," I gloat.

"I told you I was having my friend come over." Robert is now holding his tramp's hand and wearing his angry face.

"I didn't tell you I am having my parents." I sniff while attempting to resist the urge to stick out my tongue or throw a knife.

Robert remembers his manners and performs the introductions. "Lynn, this is Brenda, my friend, and her daughter LaTiqua. Brenda, this is Lynn." He introduces us as though we will be having any reason to communicate in the future.

Brenda has a killer shape with an unwrinkled face so perfect I want to put my fist in it to mar the perfection. She smiles at me then extends her hand. I ignore it and stand looking at her.

I notice she likes to mix her animals. Her leopard-print coat clashes with her tiger-stripe purse. The Hereford-cow black and white outfit, paired with her skunk hat is a request for a hunter to take a shot. The finale, zebra glasses make me wish target shooting had been in my repertoire. Brenda is about forty-five-years-old—old enough to know better than to come into another woman's home with that woman's husband.

"It was so nice of Robert to leave you this house," is her opening salvo.

"Well, it is not as if he were considerate enough to keep his ass out of my house or die before it came to this. He's divorcing me. But you already knew about the divorce," I toss back at her.

"He is considerate enough to continue to pay the mortgage," she says in an undertone.

She has me there. "But not considerate enough to keep the trash out of where we live," I say out loud

She smiles at Robert and heads into my kitchen with her bag swinging on her arm. She didn't falter, so I believe she has been here before.

I watch her go before turning to look at her daughter. Proper home training demands a response to the introduction. "Hello."

She rolls her eyes at me and goes into the living room to have a seat on my couch, and get on my phone. It appears she has also been here before. She doesn't attempt manners, which is not surprising since she shouldn't be here. LaTiqua ignores Robert calling her name. She is about twenty-two—young enough to be stupid. LaTiqua is also the same shade of ugly as her mother.

"You've got a real winner there, Bobby." I don't resist taunting Robert before going into my kitchen to cook with the enemy.

My mother has something on every available stove and counter space. Brenda stands there with her meager little bag. Manners dictate a cordial introduction. "Mom, this is Robert's friend Brenda."

The woman who taught me those manners doesn't look up from frying her chicken but does respond, "Honey, I don't talk to bitches."

My mother doesn't curse. A space alien must have invaded her body, or I heard wrong. Brenda and I are both looking at mom so maybe I heard right.

Brenda is outraged. She draws herself up tall and sticks out her chest to upbraid my mother. "You can't talk to me like that old lady."

"Little slut, you better be glad I don't throw this chicken in your face, grease and all," my mother says without looking at her.

"You wouldn't dare," Brenda asserts.

"At seventy-six-years-old, I sure would, and I would gladly go to jail," my mother says, turning toward my replacement. "I wouldn't do all the time they would give me anyway. At my age, I am not worried about it."

"I'm going to tell, Robert," Brenda lets us know.

"Tell him. I never liked his pretty ass anyway. He can get some too." This is a completely new side of my mother the saint, and the only side Brenda will see.

"Mom, that isn't necessary. I have a knife right here." I pick up the knife and look intently at the intruder. Brenda keeps her mouth shut. Robert must have told her of my penchant for knives. I will cut her if she says anything inappropriate to my mother.

She decides not to risk either my mother or me in full rampage. With her fish bag still in her hand, Brenda quickly leaves the kitchen before things can get worse. She leaves me in shock at my penchant for violence, and my mother frying chicken.

Robert comes in shortly thereafter. "What did you say to Brenda? She's very upset."

"I'm upset too. I didn't say anything I didn't mean," I get close enough to say loudly.

Sliding the sweet potato pie into the oven, Mom throws over her shoulder, "Robert, if your friend can't stand the heat, she did the right thing by getting out of the kitchen. Keep her out until I finish dinner for my daughter." Then she sniffs before she returns to her task.

"Mother Geraldine, you won't be here every night. Lynn will have to deal with Brenda sooner or later," Robert asserts.

"Only if you live that long. You don't come from a line of long livers. Both of your parents are gone. Pity they didn't stick around long enough to see what a gem you turned out to be." Mom delivers this without raising her voice or losing her calm. She closes the oven door and turns to look disdainfully at Robert.

The doorbell interrupts the conversation. Brenda or LaTiqua must have done the honors because my father comes in the kitchen seconds later.

"Robert, a moment of your time," Dad commands, totally void of emotion. Robert follows him from the kitchen. I start to follow them, but mom stops me.

"Let them deal with this. Robert hears in male. Your dad is all male." Mom continues to cook dinner, and I stand there bewildered. I think I should be doing something, but I don't know what.

Mom starts the conversation, "What did you do at divorce court that has Robert so angry?"

The memory puts a smile on my face. "When we went to court, Dottie asked the judge to order that Robert have a psychological exam because I think he is not in his right mind and is being taken advantage of by a scheming hussy. Then we asked for Robert to complete depositions to show he is not hiding assets."

Mom's eyes grow round. "Robert believes his word is his bond, and the world should know he always speaks the truth. No wonder he is so angry." Mom and I laugh until we are silly.

A short time later, I hear the door close and a car start. Dad comes back into the kitchen. He still shows no emotion.

"Robert and his friend regret they had to leave. They do not think it is a good idea for them to be here before the divorce is final."

We go into the dining room and have a great dinner. I don't want to know what my dad said to Robert to get him to leave, but I am thankful for the result. Dinner tastes like my childhood—comfortable. After dinner, they leave, and it's time to get ready for bed.

What happened here tonight? My mommy and daddy came to my rescue. They made me feel loved and happy I did not have to endure Robert's asinine behavior alone. However, there is the realization of the need to stand up for my own self and not abdicate my responsibilities to my mother and father. I promise myself to be more assertive, like a mountain. There's the smell of my favorite perfume and then the "yessss," and then sleep comes.

TASTING SAN ANTONIO

BUSTING OUT

Saturday morning, is a perfect time to stay in bed. Even though I did not confront Robert, the entire episode left me feeling drained physically and mentally. I lay thinking, wishing life was better.

Mr. M.O.P. makes his presence known by the scent of Caesar's Woman. "Darling, come. Let's go to San Antonio."

"I don't think so," is my token protest. "I feel useless, like I can't do anything right." I turn over and stretch both arms as far apart as possible.

"Why? Is it such a shame to need, ask for help when you feel overwhelmed?"

"I want to try to do this on my own. If it was not for my parents, especially my mother, Robert's new woman would have come in and taken over my house like she took over my husband."

"Your husband wanted to be taken over. Otherwise, he wouldn't be with her. You aren't the one who left. He was. So why are you blaming yourself? Think about your strengths. You are an exceptional woman. Come to San Antonio. There is much to experience.

"Why not?" I get up and start packing. I'll be assertive some other time. Now it's time to visit San Antonio.

"Your flight will leave at eight tomorrow, and you'll return on Tuesday night. You have to find a hotel and rent a car. See what you would like to do there. It's a fun place."

"Were you so sure you could convince me to go?" I stop packing to turn and face him.

"I choose to believe in the strength of you, even if you don't. You are as strong as mountains," he reminds me with a brief hug.

The Internet helps me to find out what the weather will be like and to book my hotel. It also has information about the Fiesta festival occurring over the week. There is a hotel close by downtown. The final step is to find a car to rent.

After getting my reservations, it is time to call the children and my parents to let them know not to look for me for the next few days.

Mom and dad understand of my need to get away. They both talk to me and encourage me to enjoy myself. My daughters are all wondering if I need to go or get another intervention. It isn't easy allaying their concerns, but this trip is going to happen whether they like it or not.

I spend the remainder of the day rearranging the furniture and hanging pictures. Robert never liked holes in the wall. He thought it devalued the property, so there were no pictures on our walls. With the judicious use of a hammer, pictures of the children now grace my front room's walls.

ON THE WATER

The next morning I keep checking the time, willing it to move faster, so I can be off again. The morning inches past, having more time than most mornings. Finally, it is time to go to the airport.

On the plane, Mr. M.O.P. has the seat next to me. We don't talk, but we do hold hands. When we take off, he kisses me and puts his hand in mine. Before I sleep, I hear the flight attendant tell me to fasten my seat belt. When I open my eyes, we are preparing to land. Mr. M.O.P. is gone but my dreams were of him, and they were sensuous.

It is a short walk over to the reserved car rental for the luxury car. I have the hotel directions from the Internet. Once in the car, I get to my hotel after spending about an hour lost. The directions I have are not fool proof.

While I'm driving over and under freeways, the time helps me focus. The curves and dips are much like my life now; it's easy to compare the ride to where I am going. I know where I was trying to arrive—, at old age with Robert. I didn't see the detours and roadblocks. This divorce is a detour to navigate in order to achieve my ultimate destination wherever that is going to be. The signs for the hotel are a beacon of better times ahead. I consider it a sign.

The festival in San Antonio occurs in various locations throughout the city. I'm most interested in the events that are occurring at the zoo and in the cultural sections of the city. They include jazz at the zoo and authentic food and music in the Spanish section of the city, as well as a stroll to visit the Riverwalk and the Alamo. My Internet research said these were good activities for tourists. I picked my hotel since it is close to those two attractions. The car can stay at the hotel parking lot. It will be easier to walk over to see what Texans are supposed to remember. With the Riverwalk and Alamo done today, the festival and mall can be my activity for tomorrow.

After getting a shower, dressing in lightweight clothing to combat the heat, and calling the children and parents, it's time to venture forth. On the way to the Alamo, I spy a Ripley's museum along with other stores and restaurants on the street around the area. Maybe Tuesday, if there is enough energy left in my body, I'll go in and wander around.

I purchase the ticket to enter this piece of Texas history. The time goes by like slow motion, and the sights are unimpressive. I would have expected a bit more. I am a little disappointed. Other people may not be able to, but I can forget the Alamo.

The attached museum has geodes, rocks you can break to find a treasure of beautiful stone. I purchase several and plan to break them myself. Bashing something with a hammer should be a great stress reliever. If the geodes represent Robert's head, it will be lots of fun, too.

The Riverwalk is a short walk from the Alamo and a few steps down the closest flight of stairs. It consists of a pathway of restaurants along a man-made river. There are various stone bridges and stairs lead back up to the street. I wander into a store that offers flavored condoms. My naiveté in the condom arena brings a smile to my face, and I decide to purchase some large and extra large, just in case. I wander around the space until the end, stopping in and out of stores and purchasing various items.

I come to a cruise office, where they offer a boat ride down the river. The purchase of a ticket and a bottle of wine to quench my thirst have me ready to cruise the river. There is a short wait for the next cruise. They start every hour from ten in the morning until ten.

The tour guide/boat captain is knowledgeable about the quirky legends of the river. He tells his boatload of people trivia about the architect who designed the area and his wife who lived overlooking the area until her death. He also recommends restaurants with the best food and most reasonable prices. When the cruise ends, I'm only halfway through my wine but have already had enough for me to be slightly buzzed.

I stroll along the river to get back to my entry area and close to my hotel. There is an alcove where people are taking pictures. One family is snapping pictures as fast as their fingers could close the shutter.

"Excuse me." The mother of the group stops me. "We're down visiting our son. He's stationed at Fort Sam Houston. Well, he's being deployed to Iraq in three days, and we came to see him for his birthday. Would you take a picture of us? We leave in the morning and don't have many pictures of us as a group."

The request pulls my heartstrings. "Sure, I'll take some good ones for you." My mistake.

They gather in a standard family pose, the mother, her brother, her two daughters, and her son. My only job is to take the picture.

I back up and for some reason think the spirit of Ansel Adams has invaded my body. I am telling them the different ways to pose and snapping pictures for about six shots. Then I instruct them on how to stand for what will be my masterpiece, backing up to get the money shot, the one that will win me a camera award if there is such a thing.

As I continue backing, people coming from both directions are stopping to help me get the shot that will proclaim me the greatest picture taker of all time. Step by step, backing further away, I make sure the picture is tight and includes everyone. One more step back and perfection will be mine.

I take that step. Unfortunately, there is no solid ground to put my feet on. I step and encounter nothing but air. Great if I were throwing a basketball at the hoop for the game winning three point play. Not good if I am on the edge of the Riverwalk with some strangers from Ohio and their camera in my hand.

As my body sinks into the river at the Riverwalk, I think, Now that I've found that life may be worth living as a divorced woman, I am going to die. In addition, I will die in some nasty ass river in San Antonio. Riverwalk my ass. It's a river swim, and I don't know how to swim.

The scream pushing its way past the terror in my throat silences birds flying overhead. I don't want to die. Water flows over my head before my flailing arms and kicking legs get me back to the top for a brief second.

"Help," I scream before starting to go under for the second time.

"Stand up, stand up," shouts the captain of yet another tour boat some few feet away.

I glimpse the solider and his family standing at the water's edge, looking and pointing in my direction as water starts to cover my head. They pick up the chant. "Stand up. Stand up."

I'm drowning, and they want me to stand up. Sons of bitches. My feet go down as my body is going down for the third, and what I *know* is the final time. They touch the bottom of the river even though my hand is in the air over my head. The temptation to try to stand is too great to resist. My knees straighten, and my head, followed by my neck and shoulder come out of the water. The water stops at the middle of my chest.

Solider boy on shore reaches out both hands to haul me from the water. I am again on terra firma, coughing and dripping while I try to recover from my ordeal.

In my hand is the now soggy camera the family has used to capture the memories of the time spent with their son. I look down at it. The rest of the family gathers around, and they all stare at the camera and then look up at me. The combined weight of the stares and my soggy clothes bend me slightly. I wordlessly stretch out my hand to them. The mother wordlessly takes the camera from my outstretched hand. The family looks at the camera now in the mother's hand and back at me. With a shuffle worthy of a ninety-five-year-old in need of hip and knee replacements, I walk away from their despair-filled looks.

Shopping is something that can wait for another day. Back at the hotel, I get a shower again because of the humidity and humiliation. In bed, I go immediately to sleep.

CIGARS? CIGARETTES?

The next morning, I set off to see the festival on the Spanish side of town. I spend the morning wandering in and out of shops. Buying a large sombrero and brightly colored scarves improve my mood. They make me feel free.

The smell of the food stalls makes my mouth water and leads me to find sustenance. The fare at a booth selling fried turkey legs looks appetizing. The turkey legs are browned with juices dripping into the waiting tray under the army of standing legs. I head closer toward the hunger killers and look over at a source of low humming.

Around a large barrel, trash receptacle is a family of six Mexicans. Each one is very round, causing them to resemble Russian nesting dolls. Each one stands with a turkey leg as big as his or her head. Each, including the youngest, which looks about five, is gripping a fried turkey leg with hand and mouth. They are gnashing and gnawing like pit bulls attacking poodles. It makes me stop to watch long enough to know I don't want anyone looking at me the way I am looking at them. A taco will have to appease my hunger instead.

After eating my authentic taco in a secluded area, it's time to head back toward the populated festival events. My next adventure takes me to an area where sweet and spicy scents are wafting. The origin is a cigar booth. I stop, even though smoking is not something that appeals to me.

Inside, glass cabinets surround the walls and sparkle a welcome. The gentleman inside is of medium height, dark, and ready to talk.

"What can I do for ya?" he wants to know in a loud, booming but friendly voice.

"Nothing. I liked the smells, so I stopped in to see what you have." Walking around there are cigars and cigarettes with a multitude of flavors including french vanilla, chocolate, and even mulberry. I may want to take up smoking since chocolate is my favorite taste.

"I'm Kevin. I own this place and a larger store in the mall. This here is my son Kevin Jr." he points to a young man about thirty busy playing in tobacco. Kevin Jr. looks up and gives a wave. Kevin Senior asks, "Do ya smoke?"

"No. I'm a looker, rather a smeller, but don't indulge," I let him know. I stop browsing and walking around to speak with big Kevin since he wants to chat.

"Ya don't sound like ya are from round here." He comes closer and smiles at me.

"I'm here visiting. I went to the Alamo and the Riverwalk yesterday and I'm visiting the festival today" is how we continue our conversation and explain my presence.

"All by yerself? That's no way to see a festival. How 'bout I take ya 'round? Show ya the best the festival has to offer. Lemme get my hat.

My brain kicks in. It reminds me to be careful because there are rapists, murderers, and mass murderers around every corner. Big Kevin looks harmless, but most murderers look innocent.

"No thank-you. I'll be fine by myself."

"Ma'am, don't be 'fraid of me. I'm harmless as a pup. I can tell ya more about San Antonio in an hour than ya could ever learn alone. If after fifteen minutes ya find ya don't want my company, I'll leave ya be. How bout it?" Kevin Sr. convinces me.

He is from the area and must know tobacco if the aromas and the variety of his offerings are any indication. We'll be in public. "Sure, you can tag along." I belatedly invite him.

He grabs his cowboy hat, and we head toward other booths and entertainment at the festival. All along the way, he tells me the history of the city and the festival. He is a wealth of information and amusing anecdotes, and the time to passes quickly.

We go to a food booth with tables. They're food being hawked is alligator on a stick, which Kevin assures me is delicious. I have never put my mouth on an alligator to my knowledge. I will not get any younger before taking a taste. Kevin gets us some, and we take a seat to continue our lively conversation.

We cover politics, the state of black entertainment, and not surprisingly relationships. We have humorous, serious, and frivolous conversation until dusk settles. He is an interesting companion, and it's not much longer before I start thinking physically.

"Won't your wife wonder where you are? It's getting late," I ask. I should have found out if he was married before now.

Kevin smiles at me, as if he knew this was a fishing expedition for his marital status. "I don't have a wife right now. I am free, single, and without a curfew."

I could take the initiative by inviting him to my hotel room or play coy and wait to see if he is into me like that. Time is short, so why waste any. "Would you like to come to my hotel, so we can continue our conversation?" I chickened out at the last minute. I was going to offer sex, but I am not that bold. Besides we are both old enough to know the only thing a man and a woman do in a hotel room this time of night is have sex. It would be redundant to say it out loud.

"I'd love to, lead the way," Kevin says as he holds out his arm to receive mine.

"What about your tobacco booth?" I forgot he was working.

"Little Kevin will take care of it. He knows the business almost as well as I do."

We go to my hotel and stop at the front desk. Not being one to overlook a minimum amount of caution. I ask the clerk, "Are there any messages for me?" I turn to Kevin to ask, "What is the name of your tobacco shop, and where did you say it is, Kevin?" I say this extra loud so the clerk overhears. You never know when you may need a witness.

"It's in the Riverwalk area."

"There are no messages." The clerk tells me. She looks at Kevin, and I know I've achieved my goal.

Once in the room, we talk a little before I ask him, "Would you like to take a shower? It was sweltering out there."

"Thanks for the offer. Don't mind if I do." Kevin goes in to get a shower while I make my evening calls home to let them know I am in my room for the night. He comes out of the bathroom with a towel riding low around his hips.

I scoot around him to get in the bathroom to clean myself. As I get out of the shower, I think about the man in the room waiting for me. Should I cover my grays? After the last encounter, I don't think so. I slip on my nightgown before heading through the bathroom door. I find him standing at the window looking out.

Kevin Sr. opens his arm and invites, "Come to daddy."

I look around the room. Did he bring a kid in here that somehow got past me? Nope. It's just him and me. He must be talking to me. That is not sexy or exciting at all. It conjures up visions of my dad seeing me close to butt ass naked and in a hotel room with a man who is not my husband. Come to daddy is a mood killer.

He decides to come to me since I am lost in thought. He stands behind me and puts his arms around me; a hand around covers each breast and still has room to hold a cantaloupe if he wants. I sure do wish I had bigger breasts. About this time, I remember the old wives' tale about hands being an indicator of penis size. If that is true, we may have a problem. I want to get laid not ripped.

Maybe the size of the feet would be a better indicator. I look down to judge his shoe size. His feet look pretty big, so I decide to ask, "What size shoe do you wear?"

"A size fifteen," he states proudly. "Why?" He probably is hoping he picked up a chick with a foot fetish. Sorry for his luck.

There may be a problem here. I head to my overnight bag to get out a condom, extra large according to his shoe size. I am not sure what condom etiquette is but I am not about to take chances at fifty-five. "You can do the honors," I tell him as I hand him the foil package.

"You think of everything," he smiles. His hands make short work of my nightgown. "Baby, put your knees on the bed. I'd like to enjoy the view."

I put my knees on the bed and allow him to bend me over and stroke around my ass. It occurs to me he may have unhealthy, unsanitary ideas about sticking his dick somewhere other than where I think it should go. He is spending an inordinate amount of time stroking and squeezing my rear.

"Um, just so we're clear here, I'm not into any kind of sticking any hole type of stuff or anything like that."

He stops rubbing to ask, "What do ya mean?"

"I just want us to be clear on where this is going. You seem to be spending quite a bit of time rubbing and squeezing my ass."

"Well, darling, ya have an impressive ass." He begins stroking it again.

"Yeah, I know, but I just want to be sure you aren't getting any ideas like... well I'm a pretty standard woman. I want some regular, basic sex. I don't want anything odd." I try to make this clear to him or we will have to fight.

"There's no such thing as standard or regular sex. It's either good or it isn't." He voices his belief.

"I don't want you to go poking the wrong hole." We had better get this straight from the start or from the middle, considering we are both naked. I prepare to get up, just in case.

He stops rubbing and squeezing. I feel him shaking. I turn around to find he is laughing. He is laughing silently but still laughing. That decreases my confidence by a hundredfold. I straighten my back.

"Darlin,' I'm sorry. I don't mean to laugh. I just got caught off guard. I'll get it in the right hole when the time comes," he promises.

I feel reassured enough to turn back around. I allow his hands to squeeze my impressive ass. Kevin puts his fingers in the important part of me. He has all of my attention and gets a damp reception. He places his hand between my shoulder blades and gently pushes my chest to meet the mattress. His fingers on the top of my hole gently tug upward, and my ass follows. He slides his fingers in going incredibly far into my essence. I start inching forward because there is not enough room.

He takes the opportunity to open his flavored condom. I hear the package ripping and he says "One minute." I pray this is not a harbinger of the sex to come.

He withdraws his fingers, replaces them with his dick and moves. One. He goes in except not as far as his fingers had gone. Two. The next stroke doesn't go in any farther. He still seems to come up short. Three. His third stroke goes no farther, so I back up to get it all. What is going on? An easy entry fourth stoke has my impressive ass at his stomach.

I have the answer to the question. There is no more. That is all. His fingers are longer than his dick. He could have put it in my nose. I would still have been able to breathe. I choke on my own spit at this revelation. He slips out. Damn, damn, damn.

I wish I were a better woman. I'm not. He could have stuck that in any hole I have, and I doubt I would notice. Of course, he has the stamina of a bull. He reenters to continue pounding until I am ready to scream from frustration. There is no need to count the strokes because I can barely tell the difference between him and the wind. I cough, and he falls out again. Great.

"So, are you finished?" I ask him.

"No. Are ya tired?"

"Of what?" It was a challenge to get my foot out of my mouth. My toenails were stuck in my teeth. I remember the yoga and wonder if this is a pose. I don't even want him to finish. I just want him to leave so I can lie sideways on the bed and think about never having sex again as long as I live or doughnuts in the morning. Men are so overrated.

I feel his stillness and feel bad. He probably gets that a lot. "Give me more. Please more." I plead in a breathless voice. He is an interesting conversationalist. What a pity. I will probably burn in hell for encouraging him, and his little cigarillo. He continues for what may be twenty-six more stokes. I quit counting because I couldn't tell when to count. Then thankfully, it is over.

I'm off the bed in a flash and put on my nightgown. "You're really something," I tell him. I do not want to say what. "If I ever get back to San Antonio, can I give you a call?" Fat chance of either of these events happening.

"I hope ya come back soon. I would love to see ya again," Kevin imparts soulfully. He is a sweetheart.

"Let me get your number. I'll let you know the next time I head back this way," I offer.

He gets up and goes to the desk to give me his number. I gather his clothes, so he will not think he is coming back to bed with me. As he turns, I am right there handing him his shirt. "Do you have far to drive?" I'm making small talk to keep him moving.

"About twenty minutes away. Don't you want me to stay the night?" He sounds serious.

I help him get his arms in his shirt by going behind him and slipping it over one hand. "No. I mean, it is hard for me to sleep with another person."

I hold his pants, so he can step into them. Thankfully, he wore sandals. He slides into them as I go to the door and hold it open for his exit.

"You are a different kind of woman. Are ya sure ya want daddy to leave?" Kevin tries for the sexy voice, but I know it's all talk and no substance.

I should tell him to cut the daddy shit with any woman over twenty-one. Maybe it works for him, and he needs all the help he can get. "No, I have to get up early in the morning to head back. It was nice meeting you." He kisses me and heads out of the door. "If you ever get to Wichita, give me a call." I can say this without fear of him taking me up on the offer. No one goes to Wichita on purpose, and he doesn't have my telephone number.

After he leaves, I climb back in bed, turn sideways under the covers, and start to drift off. I hear laughter from Mr. M.O.P. and feel his lips on my cheek before sleep overtakes me.

The next morning, I get back to the airport. On the flight, my sometimes present always insightful seatmate asks, "Was it worth the undressing?"

"You know it wasn't. I'm giving up on men. They have not lived up to their reputation." I should clarify that since he was an exceptional lover.

"Why did you choose him?" my curious seatmate wants to know.

"He was interesting to talk to, had a nice accent, and I was horny. That pretty much sums it up," I share with him.

"Maybe you should stop settling." He takes my hand in his, gives me the sexy smile, and we travel on toward Wichita.

My Travel Tips for San Antonio

Go to a festival and eat something you've never had before.

Do the cruise on the Riverwalk.

Find flavored condoms to use on someone worthy.

CONFESSION IS GOOD FOR THE SOUL

Robert's car is in the driveway when I get home. I feel ready to listen to his reasons why I should sign his divorce papers. My suitcase and I leisurely enter the house. True to form, he is in the living room on the telephone with the tramp.

"What is it, Robert?"

"Read this." He shoves a familiar piece of paper under my nose.

I take it and begin to read aloud:

Dear Mr. Westner,

Your name has been supplied to the Wichita Health Department Sexual Health Clinic by a recent sexual partner. She/he was diagnosed with a communicable disease, and we are contacting everyone who has been involved with him/her.

You are required by law to contact our office within ten days of receipt of this notice. You are required to be tested. Treatment is not an option. In the alternative, you may contact your family physician within the ten-day period. Your physician can then submit proof that you have been tested and are being treated.

We are located at 14007 Bingham Lane if you do not have a physician. Please bring proof of identification and an insurance card, if applicable. We also provide services on a sliding fee scale.

The visit may take several hours. You are not to urinate for four hours prior to your visit to our office. Additionally, we will need the names and contact information of any vaginal, anal, or oral sexual contacts you have had in the past three months.

Our efforts are solely to stop this contagion from spreading. Your quick response and cooperation are vital. They will help us in our mission to provide a safe community.

Failure to comply will result in a warrant being issued for your arrest. You will be charged with being a threat to public health, as well as being a public nuisance.

We can be reached at FOR-HELP (367-4957) if you have any questions.

Sincerely,

Sexual Health Program Staff

Wichita Health Department

I hand the letter back to Robert and turn away from him. "I think you need to leave now."

"Lynn, we need to talk about this," he has the nerve to demand.

"Do you remember what happened the last time you gave me bad news? I do. I don't think I can be held responsible for what will happen if you do not immediately leave the home you have given to me." I've warned him. I think a jury or judge would take my warning into consideration before coming to a verdict to convict or during the sentencing.

Robert is not ready to cede control of my life to me. "You have to do something about this. I will make us an appointment with our family doctor."

"Robert this letter was written over two weeks ago. Why are you showing it to me now?" I want to hear what his excuse will be. I take a seat on the sofa.

"Well, I talked with Brenda. She said I needed to tell you," he has the nerve to put into words what I already deduced. He comes to sit beside me.

"So, if she hadn't told you to tell me, you would have kept this to yourself?"

He has the decency to look ashamed. However, he does not deny it. "Believe me, I never meant for this to happen. I am sorry." He tries to take my hand. I keep it under my control. I don't want him to touch me because it is becoming very clear to me I am like gum on his shoe, something he wants to get rid of but can't.

This would be a perfect opportunity to confess. I could tell him that I am the one who wrote the letter. If I admit authorship, he will know there is no need for him to go to the sexual health clinic. He might get upset, but he would be relieved to know that he is not infectious. Of course, I would have to then spend time and energy to assuage his feelings just as I have been doing throughout our relationship.

I open my mouth for the confession. I stretch my hand to his concerned face. I tell him, "Ain't that a bitch. You probably got it from Brenda or some other tramp. But at least you're having good sex." Hey, I'm not Catholic, and this ain't a confessional. I close my mouth and stand to signal our conversation is over. He doesn't catch the hint that strangers in hotel rooms quickly understand.

"Lynn, your language." He is starting to sound like a broken record.

"Yes, it is." I take ownership of my words. "Let me know how it goes."

As he heads toward the door, I think about us. I thought Robert was my everything. He really does not give a shit about me. I've gained more perspective. I'm learning to care more about myself.

As jobs go, I might want to consider going into graphic arts. I can cut and paste with the best of them Maybe I will open a revenge center for wives who have cheating husbands. I can specialize in letters from their local health department. Yes, sometimes being a bitch feels real good. I open another bottle from the Clee Winery and savor the moment, as my soul rejoices

WHAT'S IN WASHINGTON?

Wednesday I am home, thinking work is overrated. I could learn to like doing nothing. I head to the kitchen to fix a bite to eat.

Robert comes in. "Lynn, I have tried to reason with you, but you don't want to play fair. I am not going to bring Brenda back here, but I want you to know I don't like your attitude. And you haven't been home like you always were before. I forgot to have you tell me where you've been going and why."

"A fair exchange is not robbery. I don't like you attitude cither." I channel the spirit of my youngest. "I've decided there's a great big world out there waiting to see me. I plan on taking advantage of my soon to-be-single state and see it." I mimic my mother's sniff and give a head toss.

Robert laughs. "I notice you have been traipsing across the country. I'm offering you a fair settlement in the divorce. You should take it while I am feeling generous. My mind could change if you don't stop running around."

I laugh. "Robert, I find I enjoy travel. Your offer of money will not change my enjoyment. I have worked these past few years, although it may have escaped your notice. Your offer may be fair, but I am not ready to let you go yet. I think I'll keep you until I find a replacement." I give another head toss my youngest would envy and sashay to the stove. I'm feeling strong as a mountain in Sedona and able to navigate the waters of San Antonio.

Robert follows, unable to leave without a parting shot. "Allow me to doubt you being able to find a replacement for me. I'm the best thing to ever happen to you." He beats a hasty retreat when I head to the block of wood where the knives are stored.

I alternate between hope and moping for the rest of the day. I hope Robert is wrong and there is a replacement in my future, but I can't help but mope because I'm tired of kissing frogs.

When I head to bed, Mr. M.O.P. confronts me, "Maybe you are angry because he did what you wanted to do. He made a decision to live."

I am in mid-mope, struck by the unwanted truth in his words. "Boy, you're a ray of sunshine. Are there any other words of wisdom?"

"Lynn, consider this. You have done very little in the past thirty plus years to truly satisfy yourself," he accurately observes.

"That's not true," I automatically deny.

The look he gives to accompany his words dares me to be honest. He wants full eye contact. "You told me once you had a passion. The passion you have hidden, denied, squelched. Why?"

I don't want to tell him about my efforts. "It was just a silly dream."

He doggedly continues, "But it was *your* dream. You have a responsibility to your dream. To write the words only you can write. You have a responsibility to live."

"I don't want to talk anymore," I respond because I want to avoid the forced introspection.

"Then just feel. Look into yourself and feel. Do what is right for you. Set your own self free. Go somewhere and be free."

"I am free. Why should I take another trip? "

"No, you're trapped in the artificial life you created. Come. Why not take a trip to Seattle and Vancouver?"

"At the risk of repeating myself, for what? I've never wanted to go there before, so why now"?

"To experience Washington and Canada. To find the lessons that awaits you there."

"How do I go to Vancouver? It's in another country. Besides, our borders are closed. Terrorists and stuff like that."

"You have your passport. You could get a flight to Seattle and stay a few days. Then you could rent a car and drive over to Vancouver. Seattle has interesting events to help prepare you for Vancouver. You can clear your head over a long weekend. You could take the time and leave Thursday. Go to Seattle and stay a few days. I will meet you in Vancouver. It will be good," he says with a smile.

"I guess." There is no point in arguing, I would follow him any-where because any time with him is time well spent. Following the ghost of a lover from my past makes as much sense as pining for an almost ex-husband. The next morning I get up, book a flight, reserve a car, and make my hotel reservations.

Then it's time to call my parents and each of the children to tell them I am going out of town. My dad answers on the first ring. "Hi, Dad I'll be going to Washington and Canada."

"This traveling seems to be helping you. I'll tell your mother you are leaving because she wants to know you are safe. Call and check in so she doesn't worry. Your mother loves you."

"I will, Dad, I love her. And by the way, I love you, too."

"Umm, yes. Likewise," he tells me before hanging up.

My next call is to Rene, who tries to give me a hard time once I share my news.

"Mom, I'm concerned you are traveling too much. You should probably stay home this weekend." She is unadventursome.

"Stay home and do what? I am almost single. Did you want to make plans for us to do something?" I ask knowing the answer.

"I can't. I will be busy this weekend. Lately, you are always going, going, going instead of waiting for daddy to come home. That might be why he hasn't come back yet. You are gone too much," she reasons.

"Rene, what makes you think I would want him to come back?" I shock myself by asking. On some level, it never occurred to me I would not want him back. I had never put the thought into words.

"You just need to stop," Rene is telling me.

"Gotta go, Rene. I need to pack." I don't want the negativity.

"Mom."

I can hear the intake of breath as she prepares to launch into a drama. I don't give her the opportunity to continue her comments. Taking a preemptive strike, I hang up the phone.

When I call May to tell her, she says "Off again, Mom?

"Yes. I'm going to Vancouver, and I will be back on Monday."

"Okay. Be careful."

The last call is to Lynnette. Of course, I am met with her pessimism coated with happiness. When I tell her where I am going I get the call in the morning and in the evening when you are in for the night don't talk to strangers and keep your cell phone close speech. The smile coming through in her voice is encouraging, and I promise her I will.

I decide not to bother telling Robert. It is my life after all. He is not a part of my life on any level. Maybe he will look for me and miss me. Truthfully, he will not even know I am gone, and I'm moving close to being okay with being alone.

Thursday morning I catch a cab to the airport and head to Seattle, Washington.

ႣჄ

WILD WET WASHINGTON

On the flight, my seatmate comes for the handholding during the flight.

Once in Seattle, I try to find the shuttle that will take me to my hotel. I don't plan to rent a car until I am ready to go to Vancouver. I wander around and then decide to call the hotel because I'm lost in an airport the size of a small city. They tell me exactly where the shuttle will pick me up. Once I learn it is on the other side of the airport, I make it before the shuttle driver leaves me stranded. I'll stay two nights in Seattle and take in the sights.

I check in the room early, and the clerk suggests catching the bus on the corner and going into downtown Seattle. I will try it tomorrow. For this evening, a walk around the area will complete my adventures.

I find a casino a few blocks up. I visited casinos in Vegas with Mr. M.O.P., and this place is a doghouse compared to those casinos. He has yet to put in an appearance. I stick around and put ten dollars in the nickel slots. I don't win and cut my losses early.

I head back to the hotel before dark and notice there's a restaurant next door that has a burger and fries with my name on it. Tonight is a karaoke contest, and there is a young black man up front singing one of my favorite songs by Frankie Beverly and Maze "While I'm Alone." He is about six feet, and his name should be M.D. Fine—Mighty Damn Fine. He looks built for sex, with a broad chest, mustache for tickling lower lips, and hips wide enough to spread legs. In addition, he can sing.

The thought depresses me enough to consider going back to the hotel and make my check in calls for the night. Then what would I do? Instead, I go to the DJ and see what tunes are available for me to sing if I had balls enough to actually try karaoke.

Tina Turner's "Missing You" is on the list, and I am ready to break out. I hand over my singing slip to the DJ then take a seat to wait my turn. It's not long in coming. If I had stilettos and a short skirt, people might mistake me for Tina. As it is, I am channeling her and having a ball. I give Tina my all, and she shares her energy with me. Hell, I forgot I couldn't really sing. I can move and try, which is enough. Instead of singing to Robert, I am singing to Mr. M.O.P., who is seated up front and cheering.

I am intercepted from on my journey to my phantom lover when I come off stage. A young man wants my attention. The Frankie Beverly singer. He has the smoothness of Marvin Gaye and is young enough to be my child. Mr. M.O.P. laughs and disappears.

"Can I buy you a drink?" he kindly offers. His smile will have women throwing panties onstage when he hits the big time.

I think about having coffee with him and the horrible sexual experiences I've had. He has a beautiful voice, but I'd hate to be disappointed again. "No, but thank-you very much." Maybe I'm reading too much into this.

"Well, would you like to spend some time together? Can we talk for a few minutes?"

Did he miss the wrinkles or the gray hair since it is dark in here? He is an ego booster. "Coffee, and then I have to get back to my room." I'm tired of kissing frogs.

We sit and chat for a short time, and he expresses admiration for my stage persona. I express admiration for his voice. I stand and tell him I have to leave after hearing all the other contestants and his life story.

I hear my name being called shortly after his. He won first place, which is not surprising, but I won third place, which is a surprise to me. He's headed for a career onstage. I am headed to my hotel room. I don't want to take chocolate fantasy to the hotel. I don't feel up to the disappointment. I'd probably have to teach him a thing or ten, and I'm too tired for that tonight.

THE WHEELS ON THE BUS

I get up the next morning and go out to the corner. Sure enough, a few minutes later, a bus comes. I get on and prepare for an uneventful journey to downtown Seattle. I sit directly behind the driver. The bus starts and stops every ten minutes.

At one stop, the driver gets off to help a person in a wheelchair board. The new passenger is a nice looking African American man with beautiful, almond-shaped eyes that are a warm brown and sparkle with an invitation to smile.

He speaks as he is strapped in across from me. "Hello."

I give him a bright smile and a hello. I feel great. I am in a new city, making my own way on the public transportation system. I have a twenty-five dollar gift certificate thanks to Tina Turner and drunk karaoke voters.

There is a noxious odor coming from the back of the bus. I try my best to ignore it and continue to look out of the window and at my companion across the aisle. A few stops up I see a quartet of crazy. Actually, I heard them before I saw them. There are two men and two women— a Hispanic man, a white female, an African American woman, and an African American man. They appear to be having some sort of altercation.

The bus stops and they get on. Every one of the four start towards the back of the bus, but the Hispanic man, who is holding a child's scooter, plops down beside me. The other three continue arguing, especially the two women. The bus driver says nothing. Neither does anyone else. The gentleman in the wheelchair looks over at me and smiles.

My new seat partner the Hispanic male with the kid's scooter decides to strike up a conversation. "Hi. You are beautiful." As a conversation starter, this is not doing it for me.

"Thanks." I figure if I keep conversation brief, he will follow my lead and leave me alone. What is it about me that make men using public transportation talk to me?

He is wearing a flak jacket, tennis shoes, a Rambo-style hat, purple corduroy pants, and an orange T-shirt. I do not want to talk to him, and I do not want him to talk to me. He looks suspicious, and he is carrying a child's scooter.

Rapidly approaching from the back is a bundle of unwashed humanity. I don't know what this little four–foot-two-inch person is saying, but she smells as if she should be alone. I want her to be alone. Or, at the very least, away from me.

She is gesturing and yelling. Unfortunately, she is yelling in a language unknown to me. Judging by her body language, she's upset or having a seizure. I don't know any foreign languages and certainly do not know first aid. I do my best to ignore her and am very successful in my attempt.

My seatmate who I think of as Rambo's cousin Paco champions her cause. "What happened old lady?" he asks as he springs into his superhero pose. The one where he looks fierce or as fierce as one can look while holding a child's scooter and sitting on a city bus.

Now, the lady does not speak English as a first language, but she does manage to get "nigger" out of her limited arsenal of the English language. This is said without accent, without any doubt. She then gestures with her elbow and repeats the word as though the entire bus did not hear it before. She is looking back at the three-hundred-pound black guy who got on with Paco and the two arguing women.

"Did that guy hit you old lady?" Paco questions from his pose in the middle of the aisle.

She shakes her head yes and says in perfect unaccented English, "That's why I hate black people. That's why I hate black people." She turns and plops herself down on the other side of me. On the seat behind the driver, the seat that is supposed to be set aside for the handicapped and those afraid to ride on public transportation like me.

The handicapped man across from me looks over and smiles.

Paco gets his deep voice out to let her know, "That nigger has no right to hit you." He looks at me and says "No offense."

I am feeling put out enough to tell him firmly and without wavering, "I'm going to need you to calm down." I give him my fierce look, the one where I am ready to poke my fingers in his eyes because I'm scared.

"But he hit the old lady. I am not afraid. I am a lion. I will protect you and the old lady."

The three-hundred-pound black man yells from the back of the bus, "I'll kick your ass as soon as we get off this bus." Sounds like he is not afraid either. I think I am afraid. If that big angry black man comes down front to kick this crazy guy's ass, I could get caught in the kick fire.

The gentleman in the wheelchair looks over at me and smiles even more broadly before he turns to look out of the window.

"I am not afraid of you. Just try something," Paco shouts instead of staying quiet like a sane or sober person would.

I for one do not want this extremely large, probably psycho man to try anything. I am caught between a four-foot experience in eau de garbage and superhero Paco with a scooter. I wish I had not gotten on this bus.

The two women who boarded with Paco and the big black man start to argue louder and trade insults about what will happen when they get off the bus.

The wheels on the bus keep going around. Does anyone else see there are crazy people on the bus? Could someone please call the police? The argument between Paco and the giant continues. Trading insults up and down the aisle, we continue toward downtown.

Eventually, the trio from the back head toward the front. My hope is they are getting off and not getting into a fight in front of me. Three hundred pounds of angry black man says to the superhero currently sitting next to me "Now what do you have to say. You had a lot of mouth before. Now what? Get your ass off the bus, let's see what you got."

Paco opens his mouth to say what is bound to be something stupid. I take the opportunity to elbow him in the ribs, hard, and say from the corner of my mouth "Shut the fuck up."

It would be difficult if not impossible to tell who was more surprised, him or me. It could be the shock of a fifty-five-year-old lady elbowing him or it could be that common sense kicked in, but he didn't say a word.

The two ladies continue trading insults only now they are right in front of me. The white lady ups the ante and tells the black lady what she plans to do to her as soon as they get off the bus. I believe her. The doors of the bus open. The white lady and black man get off. Ms. Limburger Cheese beside me gets off.

The black lady tells the bus driver, "If anything should happen to me, you are a witness. You heard what she said. You are all witnesses. I may need to call you all to testify." Then she gets off.

The white lady gets back on to tell Paco, "Don't forget my scooter." She heads down the few steps to the pavement. The doors shut, and we are off again.

The man in the wheelchair is ever pleasant.

Paco waves to his girlfriend. He didn't get off the bus when she did, proving he is not all the way crazy. Self-preservation if ever I saw it.

The black man starts cussing. The black lady starts running. The white lady starts cussing. And the bus continues onward.

Paco finally get off the bus three stops later. We did not converse during that time which was pleasant for me.

After Paco exits, the gentleman across the aisle says, "You just never know what is going to happen on a bus."

He is right. After few more stops, I decide the area looks enough like downtown for me to get the hell off before another experience I would rather not have gets on.

I don't have a particular destination. I do find my way to the Pike Street Market and watch them throw fish for a while before deciding some shopping is in order. I wander in and out of shops, finding some good bargains along the way. My favorite must have is a sexy royal blue dress. Thankfully, the store also has a pair of royal blue kitten-heel shoes to match.

I end my downtown excursion with lunch in a Japanese restaurant. The scallops are delicious enough to use the remainder of the bread to sop up the sauce. I feel greedy for doing so, but it was good.

The express bus takes me back to the hotel. We miss most of the stops in the city, and I get back to the hotel is in half the time. There is no plethora of crazy on the express bus, and for that, I am thankful. I've stood up for myself enough for one day. I grab a bite at the karaoke restaurant and head to my room.

The shower is warm and feels welcoming, opening my pores and mind to the events of the day. I stood up to a complete stranger, not allowing him to blast me with his nonsense. I can stand up to anything. I strike a super hero pose and expand my chest before laughing loudly at the pose and myself.

Washing quickly, I hug myself before drying off. If no one else ever does, that will be fine with me. I make my all-is-well calls to the family. When I get in bed, the kiss on my cheek puts a smile on my face just before sleep overtakes me.

MY TRAVEL TIP FOR WASHINGTON

Ride the bus by yourself, so you can see the city out the window. If you like fish, go to the fish market. Personally, I think it is over-rated, but you will be able to say you saw it. Channel Tina Turner at a karaoke joint. You might win.

FEELING VANCOUVER

OH CANADA

In the morning, my first call after checking in with the family is to the car company for confirmation of the pickup of my rental. Thankfully, the hotel offers breakfast for guests, so I get nourishment before heading out for my next bus ride this one back to the airport. There are not any incidents similar to yesterday, and I make it to the airport without any superheroes or rotten cheese/onion-smelling people.

I sign the required documents to be on my way to Canada. Armed with directions, I am looking forward to a new adventure in a new country. With any luck, I won't be required to defend myself. Although I think I can take a Canadian in a fair fight. I actually stood up for myself with the super hero. I dare a Canadian to mess with me.

I make it to the border without incident. The customs agent must think there is something suspicious about my visit, I look conspicuous, or I am on a detainee list because he doesn't wave me through as he did all of the previous cars I saw speeding past him. Instead, he wants to chat.

"Ma'am, you don't happen to have a little gun in that purse of yours, do you?"

What a stupid ass question. Why would there be a gun in my purse? "No, sir. Are you serious? What would I be doing with a gun?" If there were a gun in my purse, I would deny it.

"Well, we have to ask. We don't want any terrorists getting in here. What is the purpose of your trip to Canada?"

"To sightsee and rest for the weekend," I respond. I wonder what type of training is required in order to qualify for this job. Personally, I think all terrorists would deny they have a gun. If they admitted they had a gun, it would be confiscated. Terrorists are smart enough to know they should lie. Hell, I'm not a terrorist, and I know that much.

"Okay. Come on in and enjoy yourself," he says and finally grants me entry to the only foreign country I have ever been in except Mexico. Surely, I now qualify as a world traveler.

The ride to the hotel takes me through mountains that are green instead of the red of Sedona. They exude a different type of beauty, lush and rich instead of stark and majestic. Everything looks alive, vibrant, and new. The view holds my interest and makes the drive interesting because I make up stories about the people on the other side of the mountains.

None of them would speak English, and they would spend their days baking bread and catching snails to eat. The children would all wear red and white striped tops and be entertained by the village mime. A pleasant little village untouched by the ravages of progress. No cars would be congesting the street, no huge skyscrapers or smoke stacks spewing gray death and pollution in the air. People would walk everywhere and everyone would know their neighbor. However, I'm going to the big city of Vancouver.

Entering Vancouver I return to reality. I meander through a maze of streets to reach my hotel. I go out and walk around the hotel area. It is on the water, and the surrounding area has beautiful sights and shops. Those will have to be thoroughly explored later.

After two hours of wandering, I go to the back of the hotel and a spectacular view of the water with the sun glistening on the surface. It is soothing and takes me back to being on the river in Cleveland with Mr. M.O.P. As those memories fade, I think about where I am in my life. It is too sad, so I give in to my hunger, which has been slowly but definitely making its presence known.

I leave the hotel are in search of sustenance and find a Chinese restaurant with a shop attached right up the street. After the egg rolls and shrimp fried rice, which Robert never allowed us to eat because Chinese food is full of MSG and everyone knows it causes your heart race to speed up before it causes cancer and kills you, I wander into the shop.

The boutique has an eclectic selection of both new and ancient products. I am mesmerized by pieces of what the clerk says is ivory. They consist of eight two-by-four inch panels carved on each side with pictures and poses of an erotic nature. They are strung together to make a bracelet. Just touching it creates warmth down south, an area woefully neglected. The two frogs I've kissed left a lot to be desired.

It could be I am horny because I have not been laid properly in years, but it's probably the crude details in the carvings on the bracelet with their basic pictures of shared passion that are causing moisture in private places. The bracelet sections hold a certain beauty released when you touch the panels. I connect to the playfulness and joy in the images and smile in unity with their activities. There are women on swings with a man, obviously aroused in front pushing them with a hand between their legs. Another panel shows a man looking into a window where two women are pleasuring each other. The maybe ivory is a dark caramel color and the etching of each pose is in black. Males, females, and combinations are there for me to touch and see. I longingly stroke it. This bracelet is calling out to me to buy it and take it home with me. This bracelet may be the closest I get to sex the rest of my life.

"How much for this bracelet?" I ask the clerk-waitress.

She looks at my fingers stroking the carving, then at my purse, and then at me. "Well, it comes with the jade piece. Both the jade and the ivory are unique. It can be yours for only six hundred dollars."

The piece of jade is a green, yellow, and black two-inch circle about one inch high. The colors are interesting, swirling through and over each other, going from light to dark. But, jade is not my thing. Naked etchings on ivory are.

"Did you say six hundred dollars?" I could rent myself a large African American, a Jamaican, and two Haitians for six hundred dollars. And probably get satisfaction from each and every one, at least three times, for six hundred dollars.

She obviously saw the Bitch are you out of your mind? look on my face. "Well, today we are having a sale. You can get them separately."

"For?" I need to have a number.

"The ivory bracelet is only two hundred and ninety dollars. The jade for one fifty," she tries to convince me.

"Two hundred and ninety dollars?" She is crazy, I think to myself, as I replace the bracelet and start toward the door.

"No, no, no. my mistake. This piece, it's not a good ivory. It may be bone and not ivory at all." She is in an expansive mood and whispers this to me as if it would make me spend two hundred and ninety dollars on it.

"Who's bone?" I stop mid stride to question. I don't want an alien spore to get out and infect the state of Kansas.

Nothing throws her off a potential sale. "Bone is bone. It would be only one hundred seventy-five for the bracelet and one hundred for the jade."

She's still higher than I want to pay. "That is too bad. I would have paid two hundred and ten for the both."

"Sold. You talked me down," she says with a smile.

"What?"

"I can see that you have a connection to these pieces. Take them both for two hundred twenty-five dollars. You deserve them."

She is right. I have a definite attachment to the bracelet. I whip out my credit card and say, "I hope you take plastic."

She smiles. "Of course. We have a lot of tourists here."

She gets a smile in return from me, the proud owner of a piece of jade I don't particularly like and a bracelet I love. More importantly, it is something purchased for my own erotic pleasure. I head back to my hotel happy for getting what I consider a bargain and full from a good meal.

Once in the room Mr. M.O.P. puts in an appearance.

"How are you, sweetheart?"

"I made it here by myself. I feel really good, I feel powerful even." I do a little twirl circle to show my happiness.

"What have you been doing?"

"Eating, buying, and standing up for myself." Suddenly embarrassed by my erotic purchase, I quickly travel emotions, going from being elated about it to being militant. This is about me, with all my issues, doing what I want to do. "And I bought something for myself."

"How did it feel?" He wants to know.

"It felt guilty and kind of extravagant. I did it though." I stick my chin up and push my chest out just in case he doesn't understand. I should have known he could feel me on all of the levels that went into me making my purchase.

"I never doubted you could," he shares.

"Why?" I ask as my chin comes back so I can see him at eye level and the breath I had been taking for confrontation leaves my body.

"I have always sensed the strength in you, the strength you keep hidden. I never understood your desire to hide and not acknowledge yourself. I have known you through life and lifetimes, and know what you are capable of achieving, so I don't understand why you limit yourself."

"Because I haven't seen me as you do. I know my limitations."

"You have no limitations. You can soar if you would break your invisible ties you allow to bind you."

"Please don't do this to me. Leave me alone." I don't mean it but continue. "I can't take this. The going and coming. The not enough. The intense wanting what I cannot have. You. In the middle of the night, or in the daylight because of a smell, a word a sound that takes me back to our time together. I still want you." Forced introspection is tedious because you must face demons and desires you thought were buried. Being buried, they do not have the power to bring the tears to your eyes...

"As I want you. This time is because you must sense all there is in you. Our time for this life was short, but we will be together again." He traces my lips with a finger still rough from hard use. "Stanley Park," he says as he disappears. The scent of Caesar's Woman is all that is left.

I don't want to go to some damn park. I don't want to stop and smell the flowers. Flowers stink. I get ready for bed and wonder if he will come back. If there will be any more interaction between us in this lifetime. At every level, I miss him.

The next morning I ask the clerk if there are any interesting places in the area to go and spend time.

"That depends. Do you like flowers?"

"Yes. I guess so."

"Then you should go to Stanley Park. They have wonderful displays, and the place is huge. It will be a great sight for you to see and experience. Many Americans go there to get married. They also have music there."

This is the second recommendation for Stanley Park. I bow to the inevitable.

◉◉

I DID

Fifteen minutes later after finding a parking place, I head into Stanley Park. I don't know why someone would want to get married in Canada. It must be a hell of a beautiful park for people to come here to get married. I am walking along the asphalt trying to get in the frame of mind to enjoy the view.

I notice a large bird running toward me. I didn't see him when I first entered the park because I was minding my own business, just walking along looking to my right where there are shrubs taller than I am with topiary, sculptured foliage and color. There is a loud noise, and I turn to see a killer peacock come out of nowhere and zero in on me with laser precision. He is making strange noises and shooing me in the opposite direction from where I was headed. I don't want to go to the left. It looks lonely. There are no tall shrubs and sculptures, nothing of interest in my line of vision.

I try to stand firm. The damn thing has a sharp beak and he does not hesitate to point it toward my calf while he flaps, makes noises, and looks mean. When he stops to show me his ass, or rather his tail, spread out to emphasize the feathers and colors, I bow to the inevitable and run off in the direction he is chasing me to toward. As I am running, directly in front of me is what looks like a wedding ceremony. At this point, the killer bird finally stops chasing, so I stop running. He stands guard to prevent me from going back on the path I'd wanted to take.

I am about twenty feet from the ceremony or pre ceremony since the I do's haven't been spoken by the look of things. It appears the groom has not arrived yet. How touching in a bad sort of way, my marriage is ending, and theirs is just starting. The only thing I could want to see more is Robert lip locked with his new love.

While I'm watching, it dawns on me the marriage participants are two middle-aged white ladies. They are looking at each other through eyes that can only be described as shining with love. It's the way your eyes look on your wedding day. The time when anything seems possible — anything, except the possibility you will spend years and years with someone and they will dump you. I still stop to watch and allow my masochistic tendencies full reign. They alternately hold then release each other's hands as a third woman speaks to them.

The first bride is thick not as thick as me but not suffering from anorexia. She has khakis, topped off with a tan button-front shirt. She wears her short brown hair in a shaggy style that goes back in place as she continuously runs her fingers through it, the only sign of her nervousness.

The second bride has on a patterned black dress with colorful pink and green flowers. It provides a contrast on her pale skin. She is holding a bouquet of flowers in various shades of purple, pink, and red. She wears glasses and is smaller than the first woman by a few inches with dark, slightly longer hair. The smile on her face shows teeth and her heart as she prepares to be happy.

The marriage conductor is a thin white woman in black slacks and a white shirt. There is a man taking pictures. I don't know if he is part of the group or just a random stranger who feels like taking pictures. The ceremony is taking place in front of a huge floral arrangement composed of flowers that encompass all of the every colors of the rainbow. How appropriate. I stand and watch. They see me interested in their events and wave me closer.

"Hello," the dark-haired bride says. "Could you do us a favor?"

"Please," chimes in the short-haired bride. "We need a little help."

It doesn't seem like there is much I could do for them. Unless they want some advice on how to commit to someone so completely that when they dump you, you damn near lose your mind. I could tell them to run while they still have a chance. I could tell them, don't commit to each other because marriage will only end badly, but I doubt they'll believe me. Here comes my good deed for the year.

"What can I do for you?" Memories of San Antonio fly through my mind.

"Would you mind being a witness at our wedding? We need two witnesses, and we only have one," dark-haired bride says. Tears are forming in her eyes.

"A witness? Me? I'm sorry, but I'm straight. I mean I'm not sorry I'm straight. I'm not a lesbian is what I mean."

"You don't have to be. We came to Canada, so we could get married," says dark hair.

"Same sex couples have a hard time getting married at home," short hair informs me.

"We got a license, so we can get married, but we didn't know about the witness requirements until now," says dark-haired bride.

"What do I have to do?"

"Nothing. Just watch us get married and sign the paperwork," says short-haired bride.

Watch and sign seems easy enough. Very low maintenance, I can't break anything, and they have their own photographer.

Maybe the dark-haired bride would like a little wisdom from someone who has been there. You are trying to fix her supper of stew you don't even fucking like when she tells you she has found someone else and is leaving you. I could tell them how one will totally rip the heart out of the other. They look so happy and expectant I decide to keep my knowledge to myself. I won't give them wisdom from my experience.

Watching them, I can feel their love and my envy. At this moment, they have each other, in a state of unlimited possibilities and a future that, for now, includes each other. Is it right? I don't know. I'll leave right for God to decide. I do know what they have seems beautiful, and I wouldn't mind being loved that deeply.

"Sure, I can do that for you." I want to add, If it doesn't last don't blame me, but those words would probably put a damper on things. In time, they will learn how rough love is for themselves. They may as well enjoy the bliss while they can.

I stand beside the brunette bride. She is obviously nervous, as if she could read my mind and is ready to forget all this and get away. She starts pacing, crying, and shredding the stems of the flowers in her hands. Then short-haired bride takes the hand of brunette bride. She stops pacing, the tears stop falling, and the flowers cease to be in danger of further shredding as she smiles more broadly than before. Maybe there is hope after all.

The marriage conductor starts the show and like all wedding ceremonies, they tell each other words of forever that will probably not come true. For their sake, I hope it does. They look to be in their early fifties, so they may have twenty years together. By then, they'll be too old to think about divorcing anyway. By the time they are in their seventies, same sex marriage will still probably not be legal in the United States, so they would not have to worry about getting a divorce.

As I stand there watching and witnessing what they are experiencing, I think about Robert's request that I sign the divorce papers. What this couple is experiencing is a marriage, a joining. I am not joined to Robert. We're just married. Thinking about it brings tears to my eyes, and I know I am tired of settling for less.

Brunette bride and short-haired bride are both crying. The conductor and the picture taker have moist eyes. Nothing like a wedding to make me see I need a divorce. Through the tears, I accept the end of the wife portion of my life.

Brunette bride and short-haired bride are joined. I sign my name to witness the event. I hope they make it. I know I will make it now.

I'm going to be okay enough to begin, again, to live life, enjoy life, and sense passion. There will be some bumps, but it'll work out. It's time to move on.

There is beautiful music playing in the distance. I ask the marriage conductor what's the occasion, and she informs me that there is a concert going on in the park. Looking over at the place where the music is loudest, I see Mr. M.O.P. smiling at me from the top of a small hill.

"Come. Listen." He is holding out his hand for me to grasp.

Now I know what I am doing in this park. This must be where he made his transition. Playing in this park, right on stage with the other musicians he always called the fellows. I make it to him and place my hand in his to follow him, short-haired and brunette brides in the past. After a short walk, we get to the main stage area. The fellows are playing on stage, and they look the same as they did five years ago—except the one who's missing, the one who I miss the most.

The piano is to the left of the stage, sax and guitar on the right, and the percussions in the middle. When they start playing, the sound comes through clear as glass. It is not overwhelming, but it enters me and my insides dance.

The new guy on percussions is not as skilled. I stay to listen and re-member, caught up in the music, even though I don't know what they are singing and never have. I can feel it. Not as intensely as I did during my time with them, but the feeling of the music is again deep inside. Hand enclosed in his, still able to feel the individual muscles in his fingers developed by years of playing congas and jimbays.

I am a part of the crowd and the music, enjoying through their songs. It is not hard to remember the sounds I never understood and the emotion, of happiness, joy, and freedom to live. Again, they drift seamlessly from one set to the other. The sounds are so clear, so mellow, so moving that they ease me back to the magical two weeks that started with such daring on my part and ended all too soon. I close my eyes and feel the lure of the past.

When I no longer feel our hands joined, I look up and see Mr. M.O.P. onstage, playing percussion. He has an instrument that's played with what resembles an afro pick and produces a scraping sound like corn being cut off a cob. He looks at me and gives me the head toss and the smile I remember from years ago. I blow him a kiss and continue to remember.

While listening, my nipples are getting hard and between my legs become damp. No. I'm wet. I'm watching them again, remembering, and reliving our time together. I hold my breath on a remembered orgasm. He was squeezing my breasts and running his fingers along sensitive flesh, playing me so skillfully. I crave the feel of him, the smell of him, even now. I blink and Mr. M.O.P. is gone. The music continues to play.

An hour later, I've heard enough. It's a very poignant time, seeing them, and experiencing the music again. I am glad I came. I needed to be here at this time to know love still exists in the world, through life and lifetimes. The ladies who will be sharing their first night of many to come as a married couple are an inspiration. Seeing the fellows again, seeing where he transitioned closes a circle.

This trip has helped me become more found than lost and to know peace at last. Acceptance is here, and the anger and edge of pain are gone. I will be fine. I look around for Mr. M.O.P., but he is gone again from the stage. I cry because I am so alone in a group of thousands. I have to get over him.

I turn and walk toward what I hope is the entrance and where I parked the car. It's hard to remember without the killer peacock to guide me. Black squirrels start running toward me, and I find the car without incident.

IT'S AQUA MAN

My drive back to the hotel is calming. After parking, I watch the water and walk around for a bit before going inside. What can I do to celebrate my newfound knowledge and liberation? Maybe I'll get a tattoo.

I've wanted a rose tattoo on my left breast since I was in my twenties. Robert said tattoos would be a desecration of my body. I never got one, and it turned out to be a good thing. If I had gotten a rose tattoo in my twenties, it would now have a twelve-inch stem. There would be no petals, only thorns with larger thorns that used to be petals at the top.

At the rate my breasts are drooping, I'd have a twenty-inch stem of thorns by the time I'm sixty-five. If I ever went to a nursing home, the aides would wonder what the hell I was thinking putting a stem on my chest. That does not sound cute at all. A tattoo is not the way to go.

Standing just inside the lobby debating how to pass some time I overhear someone talking about the Gastown section of the city. People in the lobby are getting together to head over since it's within walking distance. They have a steam clock, which is considered a huge tourist attraction. I'm a tourist, and I want an attraction.

I must look lonely because I am invited to join the group of twelve who decide to go and see the clock. Various people in the group offer conversation and comments. Everyone is friendly, and we make the eight-block walk in no time.

The clock itself is standing on the street in a very eclectic district full of restaurants, galleries, and new chain stores. It is every bit of ten feet tall. As I am standing and watching, I think about my life. Seconds are steadily ticking by that can never be recaptured. Once they are gone, they are gone forever. It is past time to face the future and to be in control the way I was the one time I asserted myself and ran away. It is time to be honest with myself again.

A group of thirty-five to forty people is gathered around the clock. It is almost eight in the evening. The gas clock starts, churning out the notes to an old nursery song. With each note, the clock is emitting puffs of steam into the night air. Too soon, the show is over, and it's time to go. The next phase of my life will surely come to me when the time is right.

One of the men in my group of strangers walks over to me. He's six feet and has a twelve pack that shows through his button-down shirt, which is tucked into snug-fitting jeans. Balding, but determined to hang on to the last strands of hair by combing them over his bald spot, he also has a full beard and a mustache I'll bet would feel good on my lips, top and bottom.

"Hi, my name is James. Some of us are going to go and have a drink. Can I buy you a drink while we wait for the next chiming?"

I consider if he is worth a third attempt at good sex. Is this going to be a better experience than the previous attempts? Will it be worth the undressing or come with an oral appetizer? I try to think of other things. Nothing seems important enough to stop me from thinking about sex.

"Sure, why not? My name is Lynn"

We head to a nearby restaurant and order wine. We talk about the general nothing strangers who know they are going to end up in bed together talk about. He is a Canadian, born and raised. He speaks fluent French and believes Canada should outlaw the use of United States currency because it weakens the Canadian economy.

We have two drinks and then go out for another chiming of the clock. As we walk back to the hotel, the sex conversation starts.

"So, would you like company when we get back to the hotel?" He is standing far enough away that I don't feel intimidated or pressured to say yes.

"I wouldn't mind company," I tell him with a smile.

"Would you like to go to your room or come to mine?"

"You are welcome to come to mine." I absolutely will not go to a stranger's hotel room; it sounds too much like being a tramp.

At the hotel, I trot him over to the front desk to go through my front-desk routine before we get to the room. Even though he is staying here, he could be a killer. Unsurprisingly, I am beginning to associate sex with hotel rooms. The best and worst sex I ever had occurred in hotel rooms. I feel uncommonly nervous. Wild unbridled sexual activity is not exactly my forte, but I'm trying. Third time has to be a charm.

Once the door closes, he hugs me hard and lowers his right hand to cup my ass. He lifts the skirt and gets a cheek in each hand. He puts a finger on each side of my panties and slides them down far enough for me to step out of them. I'm still in my strappy sandals. He takes the time to bend down and unstrap them. Seeing the top of his head seems so nasty it gets me salivating.

He runs his hands up my legs as he straightens, strips, and comes toward me. Naked, smiling, and at full mast, a most impressive length of flesh greets my eyes, but it's his balls that make me choke. He has an odd color to his balls. They are purple. A deep dark purple. He isn't very dark, about the color of hot chocolate. I wonder why his balls are such a dark shade. I haven't heard of any disease able to cause discoloration of the balls, so maybe it's hereditary. Of course, they could be lacking oxygen or something. I look closely for any other clue that there may be something contagious.

I'll bet he wasn't shy about taking shower in gym class with the amount of meat he's working with. I remember Sedona and San Antonio, and acknowledge size doesn't mean a damn thing and neither does stamina. However, it would be impossible not to feel the nine by three inches he's packing.

"Would you like to get a shower?" I ask.

"A shower together would be wonderful."

I've personally never showered with anyone else except Mr. M.O.P., and I don't know dual shower protocol. In the interest of having a hopefully good sex I answer, "Sounds interesting."

Our shower involves rubbing each other, kissing each other, and getting ready for the next of the evening. We dry each other and go toward the bed, still touching. Then we stop to kiss. I hope this is going to be worth the effort.

"Can I taste your DNA?" he wants to know.

"Um. Well. Um." I start to get wet in spite of the fact I just dried off and am so glad I didn't put my mascara on below to cover the gray. It may be waterproof, but I would not want his tongue to be the same color of his balls because I was being vain. I should have checked his mouth. "Sure."

He sinks to his knees in front of me as I position myself on the wall to keep upright. A foot on the chair is the opener. He puts his hands on the back of my legs, rubs, and licks his way up. He squeezes my inner thighs. His hands are big enough for his fingers span more than half my thigh width, and I've got some substantial thighs. Those fingers turn upward and into my dampness.

His face is following his fingers. The drag of his tongue as it comes up one leg and then the other makes me whimper. He goes from side to side, left leg, right leg, in an unceasing and relentless move onward and upward. If he is not careful, he will drown in my juices. And just like his fingers touch me, his tongue follows suit. While his fingers hold me open, his tongue enters me.

He moves his lips as his mouth skates on my most sensitive skin. I make sounds of ecstasy. My orgasm can't fall to the floor or go to my feet; he sucks it right out of me. I hold my breasts because they are trying to trade places with my clitoris so they can get the same good licking.

"Baby, let's go to bed." He leads me to the king-size bed that dominates the room. We make it to the bed but not under the sheets.

He lays me down and continues to stimulate me. He is licking me like icing licks cake.

I feel pain and pleasure. The pain finally takes center stage in my brain. The pain and pleasure has me confused until I sort out the facts. The pain is emanating from my right breast. The nipple is hurting.

My titty is under my arm and my weight is smashing it, hence the pain. His tongue is under my hood moving very effectively, causing the pleasure.

I rescue my breast from under my shoulder and resist the urge to tie them both together to keep them from sliding so far under me anymore. I focus on the pleasure he is giving me. Pleasure I have missed. Pleasure I deserve. If my titties intrude on this pleasure again, I'll have no choice but to do something drastic.

He comes up between my legs, enters me, and gets a good rhythm going. Strokes one through twenty are wonderful. I can learn to like this. My eyes drift shut to eliminate distraction.

I feel a drop of water and open my eyes to see what was going on. Sweat covers his face and neck. His head looks like he just got out of a swimming pool. Worse, this deluge is disobeying the laws of gravity, at the moment, by staying on his body. It is starting to drip down on to my dry body. He is going to drown me if I do not intervene.

"Stop," I yell loud enough to make him stop moving even though he doesn't stop sweating. Profusely. "Let's change positions. I'll get on top," I say as I dodge droplets by shifting my upper body to the left and slightly out from under him.

He looks befuddled. And wet. "Well..." his voice trails off as he drips all over my chest. He would be dripping on my hair and face if I hadn't moved.

I take the opportunity to escape the oncoming flood the human faucet is making. Pulling my leg and the rest of my body away, I go into the bathroom and get a towel to dry myself. I get another two and take them to Mr. Leaky. He promptly soaks them.

"You sweat quite a bit," I inform him.

"Uh, yes. I have overactive sweat glands," he explains.

"So maybe you should be on the bottom." Him on the bottom makes perfectly good sense to me.

He looks amazed I would even suggest such a thing. "I can't be on the bottom. I'm a man. I have to be on top."

"What?" Don't tell me I have found the last remaining male chauvinist sexual idiot.

"I'm a man. I can't have you on top of me." He looks like I had asked him to turn face down.

"Look Aqua Man, if you stay on top I'll drown. Drowning doesn't seem like a good idea to me. You can either let me on top, so we can get this done or you can hold onto your macho idea of what makes a man and go to your room unsatisfied."

I am wet, horny, and glad to be out of danger. After my previous sexual experiences, I know I can take being unfulfilled. I am not going to let him drown me to satisfy his machismo.

I've been married for thirty-two years to a man who had some very rigid ideas on what a woman should and should not do. I put up with it for the security that didn't last. I have to stand up for myself this time. "So, what's it going to be?"

He looks long and hard at me as he lies down on the bed, sulking. "You can get on top," he pouts.

First, I put towels on the bed for him to lie on so none of his water will be absorbed by the sheets and mattress. I've still got to sleep here when he leaves. Then I climb on top and position my knees at his hips. This will work nicely. A lift and a twist get the puzzle pieces fitting perfectly.

This reminds me of the last time I was astride a man. I had legs on my shoulders and some serious sexing going on. It brings a smile to my lips for the memory of Mr. M.O.P.

I bring my attention back to the present, and King Neptune under me. I get a rhythm going which is all I want to think about at this point. I have to stay upright instead of putting my head on the pool of water that is his chest. From this position, I come quickly. He is quite still with his eyes closed.

Remembering how frustrated previous encounters over the past years left me, I concentrate on not leaving him in the same predicament. I am better than a doughnut. A very slow up with a very slow down followed by a squeeze of my inner walls has him start to actively participate. He comes soon after. He grabs my hips with his clammy hands and grinds his way to completion.

I look down at him, and his contented smile. As sex goes, he wasn't bad. Currently, I'm satisfied. He's satisfied. Now it's time for him to go. I wouldn't look forward to a repeat. He's too wet.

"Thank-you. It was..." I can't say great, that would be a lie. "A very pleasant evening. I'll try to look you up when I come to Vancouver again."

"What? Do you want me to leave?" Maybe it's a male thing; this thought that after sex you get to spend the night.

He's not very bright. "Yes. I have restless leg syndrome, and I snore very loudly. You would be uncomfortable trying to sleep with me."

"Oh. It was nice meeting you." He gets up and starts to dress. At least he doesn't need me to help him.

"It was nice meeting you also. I hope you are not angry I wanted to be on top."

"No. It worked out great. I wouldn't mind doing it again."

Silence may sometimes be taken for consent, and sometimes not. I remain silent while I help him out the door.

After Aqua Man leaves, Mr. M.O.P. comes. "You survived the human flood,"

"Why do you keep watching? You said I should experience each of the cities. And I am learning I like sex."

"You *loved* us. You are settling for sex," Mr. M.O.P. says from his perch on the dresser.

"There cannot be an *us.* You are dead."

"Fair enough." He concedes. "Now you have confirmation you are desirable, and your husband is an idiot, what more do you have to prove?"

"I am not proving anything. I am enjoying my life." I defend my horrible choices.

"Was it enjoyable? Were your needs satisfied?" He taunts.

"On a physical level, yes. Water is a part of life. Everyone sweats."

"You are content, happy with sex, you don't want more?"

"I want you. Wanting you makes me crazy. I dream of you. That is why I want to sleep alone. I don't want to wake up and call anyone by your name." My voice cracks and I barely get the last words out.

"We connected on every level to achieve what we had. Is it fair to hold mere pieces of meat you have met on your travels up to our connection? They will never achieve it, and you will continue to be disappointed. Have you considered what you will do differently next time you take a lover?" He is watching for my answer.

"I'm not going to get my hopes up too high. I will expect the unexpected." Then I think. "I'll be honest. These encounters have made me feel wanted, but not truly satisfied. I think I need a break from men for a while."

"Why? It's obviously not the sex you want. What you want is the companionship. Sexually, you can always satisfy yourself."

"You may be right. The sex thing isn't working for me. I think I'm over sex now. I hope I don't gain too much weight from the doughnuts I see in my future." I flop dejectedly on the bed.

His laughter fills the room, and then he is gone. I get up and continue my preparations to put Vancouver behind me. I pack and prepare for drive the next day then sleep peacefully, even though I am alone. I turn sideways on the bed to can take up more space. It feels good. The next morning I drive back to Seattle.

At the border, the customs agent barely glances at me. "Did you have a good time?"

'Yes, as a matter of fact I did." I decide not to tell him about the marriage ceremony I witnessed. He might accuse me of attempting to destroy the government. Taking everything together, I had a good time.

At the airport, after turning in the car, I am early for my flight and have the luxury of spending time journaling my travel. This time when I write about the adventures of my life, I will share the events; it will be a public diary and a testament to life.

MY TRAVEL TIPS FOR VANCOUVER

Stanley Park flowers are beautiful beyond belief and so are the black squirrels. The flora colors defy an artist's palette.

The gas clock is cheesy, but you will still want to see it blow.

Try not to get sweated on.

BREAKING THE MOLD

ALL KEYED UP

Once I get to Wichita, I take a cab from the airport home. The lights are on, so someone must have been here in my absence. Moreover, that someone is still here judging by Robert's car in the driveway behind mine. I go in and find him in the living room and on the telephone, as seems to be his habit.

"Can I help you, Robert?" I inquire of my soon to be ex-husband.

"Where have you been?" He demands.

"Well, that is not a concern of yours anymore. But since you've asked, I went to Vancouver for the weekend." I decide to inform him.

"You've just been going all over, haven't you? I don't know if I like this. I am used to you being at home. What if the kids needed you?" Trust him to try to use parental guilt.

"They would have had to make do with you, wouldn't they? I am so over your 'the kids need you shit.' They are grown. You'll have to think of something new."

"Lynn, I don't know what has gotten into you. You've changed," he remarks.

"Getting a divorce tends to change a person. I just want to move on. Speaking of which, could I please have the door key? You won't need it anymore."

"The judge hasn't ruled on anything yet. Why do you need my key? I need to get in the house if you're not here. What if I need to get in?"

"You won't. We won't be married. It's time to make a clean break," I say in my firm voice.

"What is going on, Lynn?" Robert looks perplexed. He could not come up with a reasonable argument to keep the key, but it is obvious he does not want to give it to me.

I think about Rene saying he would come home if I would just wait. I don't want to wait. I need to get on with my life, and it is much lighter without him. "Can I have that key now?"

He makes a production of removing it from his key ring and slamming it on the table. "I need the garage door opener and the back door key. I need my car key, too," I state without hesitation.

"I just hope you do not regret this, Lynn. You need me to be able to get in here. What if you have an emergency? I am just trying to look out for your best interest."

"I appreciate the offer. Maybe it is time for me to start looking out for my own best interest. If I have an emergency, I'll call 911 or someone who cares."

Robert looks as if I had stabbed him all over again. The shock may be too much. He could fall down with a heart attack from seeing his pet wife once again exert a thought other than his own. I smile because even now, it feels great to have tossed a knife at him.

He turns and leaves without another word. I pick up the keys and garage door opener. I can't help but kiss them for the power they represent. I officially live alone now. I am my own woman, and I relish the responsibilities and opportunities associated with my newly won independence.

I go to the stereo and put on some mood music. I find an old Nancy Wilson song, "I've Never Been to Me." The words, strong and beautiful, could be mine. I turn it up very loud because I can. I don't watch any television, and I am not in bed by eleven. I stay up until I fall asleep on the couch—fully dressed.

LIVES AND PAST LIVES

DOING IT FOR MYSELF

Monday morning, I go to work and walk immediately into Harold's office. "Harold, I've been thinking about it, and I guess there's no point hanging on like ivy. I am feeling better about this divorce. I must confess I won't mind being able to sleep 'til ten in the morning now I'm over the shock of being out of a job."

"Lynn, you have enough time off to cover you until this is over. I'd appreciate it if you came in once in a while and let me know how you're doing, but I'll understand if you don't," Harold says.

"I'll stop in when I can, but I think it's time for me to start living. I'll go ahead and start cleaning out my things. It's been great over the years, and I want to thank you for the opportunity."

"You are one of the best decisions I ever made."

The recognition and statement of satisfaction in his decision is a balm. I start to leave the office before remembering the important stuff. "So, how much will my severance be?"

"You will be getting about fifty grand as a lump sum. It should be finalized in about six weeks." Harold shares. "How is the divorce going?"

"I have to admit, Robert is after me to sign divorce papers." I let Harold know.

He laughs, "I remember how that goes. Make him sweat." He walks over and gives me a hug. This is the first time we have ever really touched. I feel the recognition of my importance to him in the embrace.

I leave his office and realize the curious thing is there won't be anyone I will miss. Work is a place to go to earn a living. It isn't something I particularly love; it's what I do to get by. However, it still hurts to leave it unexpectedly. But I must acknowledge, fifty thousand is a nice painkiller—much better than Percocet. What a way to live—alone with money.

At my desk, I gather my things and sort them for the packing. There are letters I received over the years, pay stubs I clean out of the middle drawer annually, food and drink items I keep in the bottom left drawer for emergency hunger and thirst times. I put everything in bags that I retrieve from the back of the bottom file drawer. Everyone knows to depend on me for a bag.

During my packing, several people stop by. All to express their sorrow at my departure. Most recall situations I have long since forgotten. Advice I had shared about children, education, or relationships that somehow made an impact on their lives but slipped my mind like roller skates on ice. It's amazing the things they remember. Finally, it is time to go, and amid tears and hugs, I leave.

The house that will shortly be mine is empty. I decide to skip dinner and go to bed early. Sleep does not come easily, and I would like some company or a doughnut at about three in the morning. I turn on the television and flip through the channels until the phrase "achieve your own orgasm" stops my fingers from moving.

The streaming words identify the speaker as a sex therapist. I stop because I never had sex and therapy in the same person. She seems to be reading my mind as she talks about the need for women to satisfy themselves. Dr. Francis insists women have become a slave to the penis. She tells me, since I'm watching, to go to an adult bookstore and find instruments for my own pleasure. What a radical thought. This must be a sign, so I intend to follow her advice. Tomorrow. At the ripe age of fifty-five, I plan to make my first visit to the adult toy store. That decision is just what I need to put me to sleep.

CꙆꙆ

HAVING A BALL

It is noon before I get up the next morning because I was up so late. I wake up with a smile of anticipation. The sign I had last night is going to come to fruition today. Dressing casually, I eat then head out to the adult toy store on the east side of town. I had passed it several times but had never gone in. I am tired of short, brief, wet, sexual interludes, and the idea of having sex with another living person leaves me underwhelmed. Doctor Francis said there would be something at the toy store to alleviate my horniness, and I believe her.

Now the time to approach is at hand, and my stomach is rebelling. It tells my brain someone, probably my parents, is going to see me going into the toy store. I park at a restaurant next door, which is closed, so I probably look more conspicuous instead of blending in. My attack of the nerves does not subside, instead, thoughts of running into friends of my daughters or friends of Robert dance on the outskirts of my mind. Determined to get my own orgasm, I open the door and get out. Shame tells me to get back in the car and drive away. Hormones tell me to keep going.

As I walk close to the store, what seems like a familiar car passes. I act as though I am crossing the street to divert attention. The only thing across the street is a car lot. I am prepared to cross the street and test-drive a car to add authenticity to my ruse. The light changes, and I start the decoy trek across the street to look at cars. The passing car gives a honk and pulls over. Why would I have to see someone who knows me when all I want is to get something for my horny times?

The woman in the car calls me. Her voice sounds familiar. I walk faster to get away. I may not have fooled her, but I tried. As her tail-lights go further down the street, the breath that had stuck in my lungs since she called me comes whooshing out. The sweat wetting my underarms starts to dry and I head back to my goal, the adult toy store.

Going in, books are in front, videos to my left, and toys to my right. The clerk greets me with, "Hello, and how are you today?" His voice is the cheery-sounding voice usually heard in grocery stores not what I imagined I would hear in a porn shop. I expected it to be dark in here. Instead, I find a well-lit shop with brightly colored walls.

"Hi," I mumble trying to act cool and be incognito at the same time. I quickly walk to the toy department and see tiny plastic penises. Harold from San Antonio must have been the model for them. Little plastic three-inch penises come in all different colors. I pick it up and read the package to see what is causing the man on the outside of the packaging to smile so broadly. What would a man want with a tiny penis or what does this guy know that I don't? Anal Appetites. The world's Favorite Anal Plug, the package tells me. Obviously, this is not for the hole I thought.

I continue my search and find there are many, many toys in the toy store. There are double penises—one small, one large. A clever picture shows the uninformed and clueless how they are to be used. The woman is smiling, but she is not fooling me. I pick up and discard more instruments of alleged pleasure than I would have ever imagined. Lubricants, vibrators, and extra-large, strap-on penises are there for the buying.

I'm not feeling stimulated, but I've been here for two hours. If I don't get something, the clerk will think I'm a pervert. On a lower shelf, a clear box holds two balls that are about two inches in diameter. I'd be willing to try them. They look harmless enough.

I get in line behind a young man who is telling the clerk how wonderful the blowup doll he purchased yesterday is working. How excited can you get? You know it's plastic. It can't talk back to you, so why bother. Maybe he had some of the same experiences I've had lately. If so, I hope his plastic can hold up under the pressure.

When it is my turn, the clerk cautions, "I hope you enjoy them. Insert them carefully."

Hmmm. They are supposed to be inserted. It helps to know. I am now in control of my own destiny, and my own orgasm. What happens is totally in my hands. I leave the store and make sure the coast is clear before entering my car. There is something more embarrassing than having someone see me leave the toy store. It would be to have them meet me inside going through the merchandise. Since I dodged one bullet, I don't want to press my luck.

With my precious purchase riding on the front seat of the car, we go home. I look all around when I am getting out of the car. I don't want anyone to know there's a toy in my bag. My guilty manner will probably have the neighbors thinking there are drugs in my brown paper bag. In the house, the noisy bag sounds like a motorcycle in an oven because the room is so quiet. I'm glad Robert is not here to ask me what I've got in the bag.

I take my bag to my room and shut the door behind me. No one is here, but I still feel like I'm being watched. I take my clothes off and get into the bed then get up to go turn off the overhead light, instead clicking on the lamp on the nightstand. It will provide all the light needed for me to get down to the business. I am in bed with my balls. I'm going to satisfy myself.

The crackling of the bag gets even louder, if possible, as I remove the small packet. Maybe I should turn on some mood music. No. I'll just do it in silence. I take out the clear plastic container that holds my silver balls. As I open the case, my hearts starts to beat faster, and I experience vaginal moistening because soon there will be an orgasm.

I am holding the balls in the palm of my hand now, the ticket to my sexual freedom, the source of my next orgasm. They're not heavy, but there is a noticeable weight to them. I look around for instructions but can't find any. Well, the clerk said to put them in gently.

I lie down on my back and put them into my waiting hole. Then I wait for the balls to perform. Nothing. I don't feel a damn thing. I try shaking my ass left and then right. Still nothing. They don't seem to be working. I turn over onto my stomach and still don't feel shit.

I turn on my back again and lift my knees to my chest. Nope that didn't do anything either. I part my knees and wiggle hoping movement and position change will get them going. It might help if I knew what they were supposed to be doing. But I don't. Was I supposed to turn them on? There weren't any buttons or switches on them now that I think about it. I get the box they came in to check again for instruction. I read the entire box. There is no place anywhere on the box that mentions where to put batteries. A thorough search fails to turn up any further instructions. I'm no closer to an orgasm than I was before the insertion.

Hell, I may as well take them out and shove them up a wild horse's ass for all the good they are doing me. The decision to remove them is quickly followed by the question. How do you take them out? They don't have a string like a tampon. Why didn't I think of this shit before I put them in?

I put my finger in the same hole that I put those damn balls in but don't feel them. I'm searching around and can't find them, so I stand up. Nothing falls out. I bend over and reach up there again. I still don't find them. I run over to turn on the overhead light. Maybe they fell out. With the light on, I continue my search. I throw the covers off the bed. Nothing. I get on my hands and knees to search the floor. Nothing. Maybe they melted. No, they're metal. Metal doesn't melt unless it gets very hot. I'm hot, but not near metal melting hot.

I get the mirror from the bathroom and try to see into the entrance they entered. All I see is pink and one hand holding the mirror and the other hand parting my lips; I still don't see any silver anywhere. Oh yes, I also see all the fucking gray hair that I missed when I was looking down. I jump up and down thinking; gravity has got to work on this. Another hand check comes up empty. The mirror still shows pink. Tears have formed and are falling from my eyes. The mirror is useless.

How am I going to make an appointment with Dr. Stone, my gynecologist, for this? Do I tell the scheduler I need to see the doctor because I put some sex balls in my pussy, and they won't come out? If I can get into the room by saying I need a pap smear, I can use the stirrups and insert the coochie opener before Dr. Stone gets there? Then what? I am not a contortionist. I still wouldn't be able to see inside of the dark hole.

I can't. I won't. They'll just have to stay in there until I die. The mortician will find them and think I'm some kind of freak. Better to keep my mouth shut and be thought a freak after I'm dead, than to tell my doctor and remove all doubt while I am alive. They're just going to have to stay in there. What if they clog up my urinary tract? I wouldn't be able to pee. I'll have to get a catheter.

Of course, I'll never make it through any airport security again. The metal would make the alarm go off. When the guards come to wand me, the beeping would start at my privates. A cavity search would be mandatory. Okay, no more plane rides.

I go sit on the toilet. To use it and hope the force of gravity will free them. There is not a satisfying clink as metal hits porcelain. When I finish, they are still stuck and now there is pee in the toilet. The cervix made weak by three children and excess belly fat does not give up the two orbs.

I could never again get an X-ray. The twin balls of shame would show up. The technician would ask, "Ma'am what are those two metal balls in your pelvic area?" No more X-rays, no airports, no buildings with X-ray security or metal detectors.

These are my thoughts as my hand is in my vagina up to my wrist. I could probably give myself a hysterectomy from here and still not find any balls. I am defeated by the desire for an orgasm. They must be working their way to my stomach where they will come out in a bowel movement that stops up my toilet. On the other hand, maybe I'll cough them up.

If I ever see that lying bitch, Dr. Francis in person, ten police with tasers wouldn't be able to pry my fingers from around her scrawny neck. I never want another orgasm again. I sink to the floor dejected, deflated, and totally devastated. I am naked, crying, rocking back and forth, as I hold myself.

ᘓᘔ

TILL WEDNESDAY

"Sweetheart, why are you crying?" asks the absolute last person, living or dead I want to see me in this position.

Not him again. And definitely not now, while I'm sitting here with metal balls stuck in my crotch. I am unable to deal with him going and coming in my life. I know that without him I probably would not have gotten myself through everything. I look over at arms that cannot hold me. Especially now I want that connection. "What are you doing here?" I release a sigh that contains the total humiliation I am feeling.

"This, what we have, it's over lives and lifetimes. Why did you think that you would be over this? Come." I get up and head toward my guide, my lover, my soul.

"I'm still in this with you. I don't know what the hell it is. As much as I resist, I am still in this with you. What am I supposed to do about that?" The tears dry up with the force of my longing for him that refuses to abate. I continue, "I can't do this. It's too hard for me. I would rather not see you than to have to face the inevitable parting." I could use a hug from those arms, but that's not possible. I feel his arms come around me. Fear has me back away from his embrace. The wall keeps me from falling.

212

I forget my metal ball crisis. I must be dead if I can feel him. The balls must have caused an allergic reaction and stopped my heart. Damn, I am dead. I look at the floor to see if my body is lying there like they say happens when you die. It's not. My body is on its way into his arms. I look up into his eyes to ask "How?"

"This is my physical time. It's an opportunity to cross lives and will last until Wednesday. Only until tomorrow. Only on this night can we physically feel each other—completely. From now until Wednesday, let me remind you of how good we are together. Let me make you feel again." He rubs my arms.

"Why are you doing this to me? I don't need to feel. It will only make me wish for what I will miss." I do feel though. I feel home in his embrace.

"Lynn, this is over lifetimes. It will never be over."

Before he kisses me, he looks at me, and he doesn't stop looking until I look back at him. I see in his eyes the strength of his desire or determination to kiss me. The he moves me closer. Then he kisses me. When he kisses me, he puts his lips on mine and takes my face into his hands. His thumbs are along my jawbone stroking. His index fingers are in front of my ears, stroking. The second fingers are behind my ear, as he gently holds me, a willing concubine.

As he kisses me, he steps even closer, between legs that have opened to accept his presence. His tongue is inside my mouth dominating my teeth, gums, and breathing, making the longing I have for him increase. He gives me his tongue, and I suck it as if it is a Popsicle on a hot August day. I touch him, inhale his scent, male, aroused, so him. My hands clutch his upper arms to keep me from falling into the pit that is him. The pit I never want to climb out of because it feels so right.

After he kisses me, he holds me close. His hands move from shoulder to hip. His breath is in my hair, and his scent is in my nose. His hand cups my breast. He holds it as though it is a Faberge egg. Gently at first, he kneads one breast and then the other. The nipples come to attention and beg him to never, ever stop.

"I love the texture of your skin. I love to touch you, feel you as you tremble in my arms." His voice has the husky timber of love, lust, and yearning.

I can no more deny him than I could deny the reciprocity of the moment. "I don't know how I can do this or if I can do this. It will leave me wanting more." There is no real choice. It's as necessary for me to touch and enjoy him as it is for the mountains in Sedona to stand and the grapes at Clee winery to grow.

"Trust. Let us take the physical. We can have this time for us." He moves his hand to put it between my legs. His fingers enter a suddenly wet passage that has been missing him for the past five years. I feel him parting me and cupping my lower lips.

He removes his hand, and I arch toward the warmth, the comfort, the orgasm. I feel his fingers move away from me. Damn, I was almost there.

"Sweetheart, were you looking for these?" I look down at his hand to see two silver balls. I didn't feel them coming out. I could say they are not mine.

"Would you believe no?" I had completely forgotten about them once he touched me.

"You won't need these tonight." He drops them on the floor and takes me in his arms. As I look into his eyes, I see anticipation for what we have ahead. Then he captures my mouth again.

I can no longer stand on my own and feel myself start to slide down the wall. He prevents the fall from happening. He bends and comes up to a standing position. His arms encircle my thighs, and he lifts me up to deposit me on his erect, pulsing package. Like a hot dog slipping into a bun, I come to rest at the base of his shaft. The orgasm is immediate. He holds me up forever and an orgasm. Damn he's good and very satisfying. Then he kisses me again.

Because he kissed me, I want more of him. I take his face in my hands and give him access to my soul in a kiss. He carries me to the bed and places me in the center. Then he climbs onto the bed and takes my breath away with his kiss. I'm lying half on him and half on the bed, as he puts my left nipple within the reach of his mouth then takes it all the way in to the back of his throat. My body feels cold and then hot. Sweat starts to drip from every pore, and the orgasm seeps from between my lips. A scoot gets him under me, and my right nipple makes its way into his mouth. I look down as I feel it being swallowed by him. The hair on his face stimulates the surrounding flesh of my breast. My titty comes out of his mouth looking like it had been sucked through a straw. I shudder from the intensity of the climax.

He puts them both together and into his mouth to suck. They feel the back of his throat as he expertly licks and sucks. His tongue plays between the breasts that are in his mouth. I watch and marvel at his ability to touch every spot I need touched in the way I need it touched.

His dick slips into me like a plug slipping into an outlet. Snug, full, right. He doesn't move. One. That is as far as I get before the first orgasm. From side to side. Up and down I move. Slowly at first, savoring, loving the feel of him. Remembering, experiencing the feel of him craving the feel of him. I move and feel what has been missing. I feel the size of him and how he fills me perfectly, completely. I feel his pubic hair as it gently scrapes my skin.

I execute a three-point turn like a gymnast. The first point of the turn has me straighten my right leg and shift my body right. The second point has my left leg cross his body over his face with me lifting on my hands for balance. The third point has my right leg cross him and I am now facing his feet. I do all this without losing a dick. Damn, I'm good, even if I do say so myself. The audible sigh of satisfaction from him lets me know the judge just gave me a ten for my perfectly executed move. He now has a perfect view of my fabulous ass riding him.

He puts his hands out and squeezes my ass with one hand while rubbing the other cheek with the other hand. He starts moving more forcefully underneath me. I lick his legs. I want to taste him. It is the taste of beauty. My titties rub on his thighs and knees. We are doing some serious loving, letting the physical say what words cannot describe.

From his knees, I feel a vibration work its way up to his dick. I know the orgasm is coming, and I can't wait to feel the eruption. It comes seconds later. I feel every ounce of cum that leaves his body as it enters mine. It is good. We still have tonight. Every nerve ending is alive, and I have not felt this satisfied in years.

I turn back to his face where the magnetism attaches and mesmerizes me. "I've missed you," I tell him.

"And I, you," he shares with a squeeze of my fabulous ass.

I climb off the best perch I have ever known to put on music. I queue up some of the best loving music that I have. First is Maxwell singing "This Woman's Work." Listening to him there aren't many breaths before another round of wanting.

We are loving. Me on top, him on top, us in a T-shape. We are seriously sexing. He is all up in me, and I am loving it. With each position change and each stroke, he is bringing me closer to an explosion. His fingers gripping my inner thighs will likely leave a bruise and the pleasure/pain adds another layer of feeling to the joy, fulfillment, and ecstasy I am feeling.

It is as though I am a balloon, and he is the water that continues to enter me. With each stroke, he fills me. With each stroke, he expands me. With each stroke, he reminds me of the rightness of being with him through life and lifetimes.

Then another explosion comes in waves so intense I freeze before tremors wrack my entire body. The force of the orgasm leaves me weak, completed and more in love with him than ever. The happiness shines as freely as the product of our loving seeps from my body. I close eyes and seconds later feel his tongue slide between my lower lips that are swollen and sensitive because they know what comes next.

He applies pressure between the tips with his tongue. He moves his tongue sideways and allows me to feel his taste buds. He captures my inner fruit with his teeth and holds it between his teeth as though it is a grape that is captured but cannot be bruised. Skin on teeth across this most tender of flesh. My knees are at the back of his head, his body between my legs. My titty is enveloped in his hand as he comes over me and enters me swiftly, forcefully.

He looks at me, and I can't look away. "Yessss." Then he kisses my lips and licks until I explode and then he does it again because we are loving for the past five years and the knowledge it cannot last. But it lasts over and over again between pauses for rest and conversation.

"I want to taste you, to touch you, and store the memories. It's not the sex. It's the feeling, the touching, and the sharing of breath, air, and time. A peak experience when I look back at my life, one of those times I know I will remember. An event set apart in time to be examined when times are unbearable and pain is the only thing you feel until even good feels bad. Then I can remember this," I tell him during one of our pauses.

"Darling, there is so much more to life. Taste me, touch me, let us do all we can with this short time we have. Know it is for always." He stretches out so I can have unlimited access to his body. I touch him everywhere. I want to memorize his features, the feel of him. Bending down to savor the taste of him. Salty, sweet, tasting like love. We continue to love late into the evening until we are exhausted and unable to do anything but sleep.

Sometime during the night, I reach out for him and meet empty space. It brings me awake and searching. He can't be gone. I still need him. I still want him. I get out of the bed to look, hoping against hope he is somewhere accessible to me. He isn't. I see a single sheet of paper on the dresser and with a sense of resignation pick it up.

'TIL WEDNESDAY
A Decision made.
Aware and accepting of consequences
So I can have you.
'Til Wednesday

Coming across miles.
Coming across lives.
So we can be together.
'Til Wednesday.

Not acknowledging the past.
Suspending the future
For the present we have.
'Til Wednesday

Right now, just now is my focus.
Through laughing, through sharing, through you
'Til Wednesday
And Wednesday came too soon.

Why did he do this? Writing is my passion not his. I am transported back to Cleveland five years earlier, when I shared my passion with him through words. I trace the words and kiss the paper as if I could internalize the words and emotion to make them a part of me forever. Yes, Wednesday really came too soon.

I am away from his face and still the magnetism attaches and mesmerizes me. I hold my gift from him against my face as I climb back into bed, alone, and content. Sleep comes easy with the thought of the next lifetime. You betcha. I smile before hearing the "yessss."

THE END

When Wednesday afternoon arrives, I'm alone and fine with that state. I hear the telephone and decide I do not feel like talking. I want to bask in the after-loving glow and plan for my future. Decision made, I get up to implement the ending of my marriage by signing the papers.

Dottie answers on the first ring. I tell her of my decision to sign the papers. She, being the top-notch attorney she is, cautions me and informs me of the legal consequences of my actions. We agree Robert's terms were essentially good. Her asking for the psychological assessment was a tactic to stretch it out at my request. She will complete the paperwork to withdraw the request.

We chew the fat and end with me agreeing to Robert's terms with one caveat. Dottie is concerned he may be entitled to some of my severance. "Lynn, I insist you don't sign unless he agrees to sign a declaration relinquishing all rights to any moneys that come to you regardless of the source."

"I don't care. Put it in there. I'm finally ready to be out of the cage. Let's have dinner soon."

"I'll have the form e-mailed to you in five minutes. Don't call Robert until you get my e-mail."

Sure enough, in fifteen minutes, her e-mail arrives. I print it out before calling Robert's cell phone and leaving a message. "Give me a call. We need to talk."

True to form, he shows up without calling. When the doorbell sounds, I can sense the frustration from his finger through the chime. He obviously does not like lacking control of entering and exiting at his leisure. I take my time reaching the door. The fact I have to open it gives me a sense of power that could corrupt me very easily.

"Hello, Robert." I open the door wide and allow him entry.

"Lynn, I think I need to have a key. What if something happened to you?" he bites out with a glare.

I cut through his bullshit. "Enough, Robert. I made a decision while I was gone. I am ready to sign the papers if you will sign one for me." I hand him the paper Dottie sent me.

He reads the form and his puzzlement is apparent. "Why you haven't been in any hurry to sign them any other time? What makes it so different now?"

"I don't know, Robert. I guess it just took that last adventure to make me see that it really is over between us and to be okay with moving on." I am not angry; the hurt is still in there, but it's muted. I am ready to end this half living.

"What do you mean moving on? You are not seeing anyone are you? We're still married." He belatedly remembers.

"Yes, we are, and that didn't put a damper on you and your relationship with Brenda. However, the answer to your question is no. I'll tell you even more since you seem to be curious about me all of a sudden. There is no one alive I want to see—right now. Here is the reality; I very much want you to live. If I can separate us, then I can live, too. I want you to live, even though it's without me. I don't want you to experience the emptiness, the sorrow that will come if you do not sense the passion. The living. There's really no substitute. To have someone who will force you to sense passion on all levels—physical, mental, and spiritual. It may not last, but it is worth the journey."

"What are you talking about?"

"I want you to go and live. If Brenda can give you that rush, that will to live, that yearning and sensing of passion, I could no more stand in your way than I could stop from envying you the journey. I wish you well, Robert."

"What will it take for that to happen, to sense passion?" Robert is clueless and curious, thinking that maybe I learned something he didn't teach me. I did.

"You have to give it your all. You start the feeling on the inside, internally, not just the physical. You have to get through the superficial to sense the passion. You have to touch it and allow it to touch you through life and lifetimes. I hope you find that."

"Why, Lynn?" Robert is wary.

"Because otherwise you settle for less and really nothing less should do. Because in my own way, I love you. Not in the way I am describing, but in my own way, I love you. Enough to wish you well. Please do not settle for less." I smile at him.

"What about you?" he questions.

"I may never find it in this lifetime again," I admit, "but I will try."

"Again?" Robert's cockiness comes to the fore. "I gave you all that?" He sticks his chest out and a smug look is on his face in spite of the fact we are divorcing.

Definitely an asshole. At one time my asshole but not anymore. I could be honest and tell him no. There is no need to tell him. I'm feeling too good. "Again, I hope maybe one day I will find someone I can talk to in the dark. Someone I yearn for and connect with through life and past lives. Someone I can sense on all levels.

I see the questions in his eyes. They are not questions that should or can be answered because on some level we do love each other. It is just not enough. It is in the tea leaves that this is over, and I now accept it. This is not a through life and lifetimes loving.

He really is the honest one who said "I want it all." I chickened out and wanted to settle for less. "Please bring the papers tomorrow, Robert. I'll sign them once you sign the one I just gave you. I stand and head to the door.

"Lynn, you have changed," he acknowledges.

"Yes, Robert. I have. Maybe it was just the me that has always been here trying to get out. Thank-you for the life we shared, Robert. I couldn't have done it without you." I open the door for him to exit. He leaves. I am alone and fine with my aloneness.

What a relief to me for this to be over at last. Instead of killing me, which at one time I thought it might, the decision made me stronger. So how do you celebrate signing divorce papers? There has to be activity to get me out of the house since I am feeling restless, free, and anxious at the same time. There isn't any reason to stay cooped up in the house. There's no city I feel a desire to go visit. Besides, without Mr. M.O.P., any place would seem a bit boring.

Maybe it's time to explore my own backyard. I search the paper for something more exciting than watching dust mites land to get me out of the house. There is a poetry reading in the events section. I plan to be committed to getting out and sensing life on all levels. I am soon to be single and ready to embrace my changed status.

THE BEGINNING

GETTING OUT

What feel-good clothes can I wear on my first single evening out? Memories of a red push-up bra with a matching thong would be appropriate. I purchased it when I was in Las Vegas five years ago with Mr. M.O.P. It makes me feel close to him, and it brings back memories of wonderful sex. The push up looks outstanding under my knit top. A push up enhances a knit top the way a shot of 1800 enhances ordinary orange juice.

Looking down at my breasts in my push up, I admire the view and then proceed to take my push up-enhanced self out to hear poetry at the local library. I don't expect to see anyone I know, but that's not a problem. It will make the evening more interesting.

At the library, I find about twenty people sitting in a semicircle. As I scan the room for perverts and psychos, my eyes stop on a familiar face. I recognize Stephanie from work, and we exchange waves.

The program starts, and everyone who wants to read has an opportunity to do so. The topics vary and cover everything from the latest news through the weather, with personal introspection emerging as a hot topic. While listening to other people read their work, I wish for the courage to write something to read, but I am not there yet. I do clap enthusiastically and even stand a time or two in order to give support and encouragement to those with the confidence to share.

Afterward, Stephanie comes over to talk to me. I never knew she had an interest in creative arts, but we aren't close.

"Lynn, I haven't seen you in a while. I hear you and Robert are divorcing after all this time."

"Yes, we are after all this time," I agree.

"I am so sorry to hear about the breakup." She is speaking directly to my chest area. The push up must be doing its job, and she is obviously envious of my great-looking rack.

"So, honey, are you ill? I mean is the sickness the reason for the divorce?" Her eyes are still looking low, right around my chest area before looking up into my face.

"Uhm, no. We are both fairly healthy." What a weird question.

"I had a friend with a breast problem, and her husband couldn't handle it," she confides to my breasts.

"Well, no. I haven't had any breast problems," I tell her while straightening my shoulders to give the full effect of my push-up bra.

She is looking at my chest intently, as it dawns on me she may very well be a down low sister. I curve my shoulders to stop her ogling before recognizing even if she is down low; she probably wants a younger woman and stick my twins back out.

She lowers her voice and whispers, "I guess it's hard to talk about something so personal with someone who's not close to you. Here's a card for a support group if you decide you'd like to speak with other women. I have a friend who's a member, and I try to pass along the information." She fumbles in her purse, pulls out a card, and slips it into my hand. Leaning in closer she tells me, "You may want to go fix your prosthesis. it seems to have slipped." She returns to her regular voice volume to say, "Good luck," and then hurries off.

I look down at the card and read.

Mastectomy Momma Support Group
For women who have undergone the loss
Meetings are the last Wednesday of the month
Location is Third Street Library at six P.M.
All are Welcome

Why would she think I have prosthesis? I may not have much, but it's enough to make an impressive bump, especially in the push up. I look down to see that my push up has failed me. My right titty looks like it's been cut in half. The bottom is seeping out from under the push-up bra, giving the illusion of putting a rubber band around a balloon. The push up is not pushing everything up.

Maybe I should catch up with her and tell her I don't have prosthesis? I can confess to some slippage and explain that my push up isn't pushing up. I'd have to catch up with her first, and I don't think she would believe me anyway. Of course, she'll spread it around that Robert left me in my time of need. I don't give a fuck. Half my boob is hanging under my bra, and I'm in public.

I cross my arms and head to the nearest bathroom to remedy the situation. Once in the bathroom behind the safety of the stall door, I grab my itty-bitty and pull it up into the cup that is obviously not running over as much as it is dropping under. Staying in the stall to collect my thoughts I wonder if anything more humiliating could happen. My husband has left me, I can't even use pleasure balls correctly, and the best sex I have had in the past five years was with a ghost.

I think the problem is my titties don't even overlap my hands. I know this because I tried it. Shit, I can put my entire left titty, a glass of cream sherry, a burger, and chocolate with walnuts in one hand, brie with ginger sauce and crackers, two chocolate-covered strawberries, a glass of chardonnay, and the right titty in the other hand. My hands are smaller than the average man's hand. I clearly have breast-size issues.

This I can actually do something about since money can fix this problem. Thanks to the generosity of my mother and father, I have money to fix this problem. Unlike other problems, throwing money at 34Bs can make a change. I'm going to be a D cup before too many more days pass. I head home determined to make a difference and go to bed after formulating my plan.

The next morning, I look up the number for Dr. Stone's office. I call and ask Rita the receptionist my question, "Can Dr. Stone refer me to a doctor who does breast enlargements? I've decided to buy myself some breasts."

There is a pause on the other end of the line. When she finally talks, she is whispering. "I can tell you who did mine. He made them look so real, no one even knows I had a boob job."

I remember seeing her in the office with her eye-catching ta-tas. I thought they were all her from the nipple back. They didn't look hard at all. They looked natural, supple, and squeezable.

"You had a breast job?" I ask in shock.

"Well, I was an A cup, and now I'm a C she tells me.

"I want who did yours. They look good. How do they feel? Do they hurt your back? I heard that could happen. Have you had any complaints from… well, you know, men?" Why am I having a conversation with a woman about her titties? 'Cause I can, and I need to know.

'My husband didn't even know I had them done until afterward. Now he loves them. He can't get over how good they feel," she says on a giggle.

"Okay, give me the information." I hang up from her and make the call that may possibly change my life but will definitely change my silhouette. My first appointment is for next week.

The time until then is spent having dinner with the parents and letting them know the marriage is over. They continue to be supportive and offer me my old room. I appreciate the offer but decline once again.

I cook dinner for my daughters and let them know that the divorce is final. Each has an opinion they are willing and eager to share. They seem to think that I need comforting. I assure them I do not. They believe I also need looking after. I don't. I experience a peace similar to the peace of Sedona that mingles with the loving and keeps me focused enough to feel strength. I promise each of them I will be in touch, and we will get together often in the time ahead.

The time crawls by until finally the day of my doctor appointment for a new me arrives. The office has pictures of breasts hanging on every available wall space. All the ladies who work here have enough going on up front that they are walking advertisements for implants. Each looks as though she was a successful patient at one time.

The doctor is a mid-sized innocuous man who gets down to business.

"How did you hear about us?"

"My regular doctor's receptionist was a patient, and I was impressed with your work." I sound like a person complimenting an artist.

"Do you mind if I touch them to see what I will be operating on?"

After I nod, he opens the front of the gown and feels me the way he would a tomato. "There is a definite lack of mass." How many cups would you like?"

"How many cups can I get? I've always wanted to be a D cup." It seems strange to talk about breasts as if they are coffee.

"I wouldn't go more than two. You are about an A now. I think it would be okay if we get rid of some of the excess skin. You'll make a great C. I suggest propping them up a bit, but nothing too drastic, just enough to notice."

"I guess you're right. I don't want drastic stripper breasts. I want them to be noticeable, but I don't want people to point at me and say 'look at the breast job' before they laugh. D would be too much of a good thing."

We talk about fees and all the specifics before I leave. Thankfully, I can be prepared for surgery the following week.

I am understandably nervous when the time comes. I do not tell anyone of my decision to get enhancements. If they ask, I will tell them. My family does such a wonderful job of overlooking me that I doubt they will notice.

Three weeks later, after the healing, I have a view of my new cleavage. I love my breasts as I haven't loved them since before giving birth or since I got my first corset in Las Vegas. They are impressive, and they are sore. However, the silhouette they cast is worth the pain. They look real. I can't find any obvious marks to show where I stop and the implants start. Even the nipple looks the same.

One of life's mysteries makes perfect sense to me now. I always wondered why men would hold themselves without conscious thought. I think they hold themselves because they are so impressed by the fact that they have something to hold, hanging between their legs. They want to make sure no one steals it. I want to hold my breasts because they look so damn good, I'm impressed.

DREAMS OF REALITY

A FALSE BURIAL

I wish Mr. M.O.P. could see my titties. I wish I could feel his mouth on them. When I go to bed, I have the most erotic dream I have had in quite some time—at least three days. Of course, it is of him, of us.

In the dream, I am at home in bed asleep. I hear a noise, someone at the bedroom door, and I wake up. It is him, coming through the door and toward the bed.

I tell him, "I was dreaming of something beautiful. I was watching the news, and the next thing I knew my head was on bare chest. Arms were surrounding me. I felt breath on my face. It was moist and warm, and I knew it was you. It felt like you. It smelled like you. When I turned my head and took your nipple into my mouth, it tasted like you. I heard your voice telling me "yessss." Then I lifted my head and saw you. You smiled at me. You drew me up into your arms and kissed me. I was immediately drenched in my essence."

"Because I have been wanting you for so long, no matter how hard I try to make it to being over you, I can't. The connection is too strong. You're still here, and I can't seem to let you go. I want to, but you are still here.

He takes my hand to comfort me. "Then come and bury me. End us for this lifetime."

"What do you mean? You have been gone for years. You are already buried. The last time you were here, you said you were leaving. Are you back now?"

"Call Alita and she will explain," he whispers before taking me in his arms for a kiss and a hug.

I continue to dream, me in his arms, content with where I am, not wanting to wake up.

The next day, I shake the fuzziness from my head. The dream is fresh and pushes through my consciousness. I ascribe the experience to my wanting him to see my new figure. I dress to impress myself and make a promise to buy some clothes that will flatter my new figure.

When collecting the mail, I see a letter in the mail written with a familiar hand. The letter reminds me of previous correspondence from her over the past three years. Always her message is the same. "Come." In her letter, she invites me to the false burial for her deceased husband. This time I decide to take the opportunity to respond by calling her.

"Hello, Alita. I got your letter."

"Bonjour, mate. How are you? You sound as though you have released a burden. Your voice rings with hope," Alita correctly identifies.

"Well, sort of." I quickly explain life's recent upheavals from my point of view, describing the interaction and influence of the man we both love. "I called because I want to know about the false burial in Liberia. What is a false burial, and how can I participate?"

"I hope you will come," Then she explains. "Lynn, the concept of death and dying is different in Liberia."

"Death is death. How could it be different?"

"When someone dies, there is much crying. We cry in the morning, at lunchtime, and in the evening when someone comes to visit. Not the refined dabbing of stray tears, but loud, hard, soul-wrenching sobs to show everyone that someone we love is gone. We will cry for a month before the body is buried. There is no laughter, only sorrow," Alita shares in her melodic voice.

"You don't have a funeral for a month? That seems excessive."

"At least a month. Possibly longer depending on the status of the individual in the community and the world. After the funeral, the family wears black for three years of mourning," Alita explains.

"Then what?" She has my full attention. My only travels to foreign countries have been to Mexico and Canada. They obviously do not compare to Liberia on a scale of cultural differences. Additionally, her voice is so captivating that she could be talking about the sand on the beach and still command listeners.

"On the third eve of the death, the family takes off their mourning clothes and puts on colors in preparation for the false burial," she tells me.

"What do you do at a false burial? He is already in the ground." I am still a little confused.

"Yet, he remains here. I'm sure you have seen him. He has been on watch for three years. The false burial is the final farewell. Then everything will be over, and he will be completely released from the physical to completely transition to his next life. Through this ceremony we release him."

"We feast beginning in the morning. The women will dance in the afternoon. They will go throughout the village dancing to the drums. We will sit and watch them honor him. There will be a war dance because of his status as a warrior. There will be much laughter and ceremony, and we will celebrate late into the night," Alita explains before repeating, "Come."

"Come where?

Alita laughs and the sound has not changed in the years since I met her. "How soon can you get here to Paris?"

"Are you sure it would not be an intrusion?" I did have an affair with her husband.

"We are mates. It is right for you to be there. Come to Paris. We will see some sights, and then we will go to Liberia to celebrate and then release him."

"I'll call you when I have made the arrangements." I hang up and think about what I would really like to do.

I pull out my computer and search for flights to Paris. Once the flights are settled, I make the required telephone calls to parents and children. Then I look in the trunk and uncover my passport. I dust it off and think about rail passes, bread and breakfast stops, and a man I met on a plane five years ago. I'm good to go.

Turn the page for a *Preview of Embracing Passion: The Adventures of a Woman* by Christy Cumberlander Walker.

Expected release in October 2010

When I first saw Alita, I thought she was a maid. When I met her, I thought she was a murderer, out to murder me. It was in a hotel room in Nashville, Tennessee. A room I was sharing with her husband, a percussion player who was out practicing for the gig he would be playing later that night.

I was taking a nap when a knock at the door woke me up. I opened it expecting to see a woman in a housekeeping uniform. Instead, there was Alita in her flowing purple-blue dress, reeking of femininity, power, and confidence. She entered the room and explained who she was. The explanation had me plotting on how to get her DNA under my nails, so the police would know who to look for after they found my body.

When she explained her presence, she only increased the aura of intrigue that surrounded her. Alita told me her husband wanted her approval for the relationship we were having. She was here to prepare me for my time with him. I was unprepared for her appearance and the time the three of us would spend together would grow even more strange.

"Mom, I asked everyone to come over, including daddy because we're worried about you," Rene my twenty-nine-year-old and the eldest daughter is speaking and interrupts my Nashville thoughts. "It doesn't seem like you're even listening. How do you expect this intervention to work if you don't pay attention?"

Rene is a fan of reality television. After years living through her need to imitate television, I am ready to cut her cable line. Maybe the lack of cable will keep her from using the latest bullshit from half-ass networks that think shows where interventions and other personal business is substituted for talent are suitable for broadcast.

It takes a minute to pull myself back from Nashville and Alita. I look around the room at my three adult daughters, ex-husband, mother, and father. They all came in response to Rene's call when she learned that I plan to travel to Europe and West Africa in three weeks. Damn this is going to be a long evening.

My father speaks. Ex-military, his voice carries the tone of command. "Lynn, I think this is ill-advised. You've been traveling too much. I, or rather your mother, is worried umph..."

My mother has sharp elbows made to stop conversation. She puts them to use on her husband of over fifty years.

"But we understand and want you to be careful." His statement cut short, dad sits down. I know those words were not what he wanted to say, and I share a smile with my mother.

My father never owns an emotion. If he can't blame caring on my mother, he goes for bravado. I have long since accepted his need to be above his feelings because I know he loves me deeply. He was concerned enough during my recent divorce to give me money and pay my legal fees for stabbing my soon to be ex-husband. Of course, he blamed the caring on my mother, even telling me my mother wanted me to move back home at fifty-five-years of age, so I would be safe. I don't know who would have been more horrified if I went back home—my mother, him, or me.

Rene starts droning on again. My mind returns to Nashville.

When she entered the hotel room, Alita made herself comfortable. She is a stunning woman able to command attention with her exotic aura. She is somewhere between forty- and sixty-years-old, with skin as black as the inside of ebony wood. Alita's face is untouched by time, not showing a wrinkle or any signs of surgery. Her hypnotic voice is a melodic mix of a French accent and her unknown native tongue. She explained her husband had called her to seek her permission for our encounter. She took the next flight from Paris to Nashville, so she could meet me and outline the parameters of my relationship with her him.

Alita taught me the concept of the elusive orgasm. She explained about people who connect on physical, spiritual, and mental levels can achieve an ultimate sexual release because they are operating on these three levels, as opposed to one or possibly two levels. She removed the hair from both of our bodies before rubbing us with oil to open our senses to the opportunity for complete and total release. Her husband and I had a fascinating two weeks together. Her only stipulation was that I not go to Paris to see him—a promise I freely gave.

Looking back, it seems unusual. I allowed a strange woman to remove the hair from my body, rub me in oil-everywhere- and then dress me, so I could experience adultery with her husband. He was my only foray into unfaithfulness. At the time, it seemed right since I was having an all but physical affair with her husband. After her ministrations, he and I did have one hell of an affair—the kind that had me dreaming of him and his touch for the next five years.

During my divorce, his ghost came to me and helped me move forward. He shared places with me and helped me see that I had the strength and ability to be single after practically thirty years of marriage. My last dream of him had me waking in tears. In it, he told me to call Alita.

Now, after he has been dead two years, I'm going to Paris to connect with her. Then we will both travel to Africa for his false burial, an event I don't completely understand. However, I have to go, so I can end what is between her husband and me for this lifetime.

May, the twenty-seven-year-old middle child remains quiet. She obviously has not made up her mind since she has not made a pronouncement. May likes to take the time to carefully weigh her thoughts before sharing them. Once she makes a proclamation, she does not change her mind. She has a finely honed sense of right and wrong, and does not waver once she decides to take a stance. "Now, young lady," my father starts before being caught in the ribs again by my mother. He starts coughing, and I see a brief reprise for me.

"Let me get you something to drink, Dad." I make my escape. Unfortunately, Robert follows me into the kitchen.

"Lynn what are you thinking? This is obviously a midlife crisis you're going through."

"A midlife crisis is what I would have called your decision to leave me for the mixed-animal-print-wearing tramp you're with now. But I'm so over you, I'd call this getting on with my life. It happens to include a trip overseas." I turn to look in the refrigerator for juice for my father.

Robert grabs my arm and turns me to face him. The shock and surprise I feel shows on his face. Never during our marriage had he put a hand on me. Verbal and emotional abuse, sure. But the bastard never crossed the physical line. I look down at his hand, which he immediately drops under my gaze. My eyes travel up to his face.

"Lynn, I'm sorry. I don't know what that was about. I guess it's my nerves. You've really changed, and I don't like it one bit. You've been wearing different bras, and they make your breasts look too breasty. I think I can see the outline of your nipples."

Poor Robert. I could tell him the bra isn't what's making my breasts look too breasty. It's the skill of a wonderful breast-enhancement doctor. The nipples added a bit to the cost because I wanted them to be noticeable, and they make me smile.

But he left me for a slut who doesn't know better than to wear leopard spots with tiger stripes with zebra print. As if she has to wear all her animals at one time. I don't owe him any explanation about anything.

"Robert, I think it's time for you to leave. I'm sorry the children thought you could have any effect on my decision. You don't. I intend to be on a plane in about three weeks, and if I'm extremely lucky, I'll have some adventures. Please stop trying to influence my decision on this or anything else."

"Well," Robert hems and haws.

I fold my arms and look at the door.

"I hope you won't live to regret this plan of yours."

"Allow me to doubt your sincerity. You hope I'll come running home after two days."

"You had better listen to me," Robert warns. "You can't go running all over everywhere by yourself."

My head tilts to the side, and I smile at him. He is so transparent. His attempts to continue his rule of me and the house, even after getting the, divorce are almost comedic.

ABOUT THE AUTHOR

Christy Cumberlander Walker is the proud mother of seven and then some. Writing has always been her passion, but it was put on hold until she became an empty nester. She enjoys traveling and has presented in the area of dispute resolution across the country, Canada, and Scotland. Her favorite place is Liberia, to which she has made many humanitarian visits.

Christy is available to visit book clubs and welcomes feedback from her readers. You can contact her at:

Christy@christycumberlanderwalker.com

Please visit her Web site:

www.Christycumberlanderwalker.com

Made in the USA
Charleston, SC
04 June 2010